ALL GIRL 4

LESBIAN EROTICA BUNDLE

VICTORIA RUSH

COPYRIGHT

For the uninhibited...

TURN UP THE HEAT IN YOUR LIFE!

To receive more free books and other steamy stuff, sign up for my newsletter.

Victoria Rush Erotica

VOLUME ONE

PERSONAL TRAINER

1

PUMPED UP

Over the past few months I'd noticed some unsettling changes in my body appearance. It was nothing drastic— just little things that had been creeping up on me. A slight loosening of the tone on the underside of my arms, softening of my stomach muscles, and tightening of my jeans. I still felt I was in better shape than most women my age, with firm breasts, a tight ass, and shapely legs. But my three-times-a-week yoga sessions focused mostly on stretching and relaxation. It was time to get serious about reconditioning my aging body.

One Saturday morning, I went down to my local health club to talk about my fitness goals. When I stepped through the front door, I was surprised with the level of intensity permeating the gym. Near the front window, a group of scantily clad trainers huffed away on a long bank of treadmills and elliptical machines. On the side wall, a collection of young women in tight leotards stretched quietly on a padded mat. Near the back of the facility, burly guys in tank tops and loose sweats grunted noisily as they lifted weights.

Virtually everybody was in excellent shape, and as they moved through their paces, their sinewy muscles rippled under their dewy skin. Feeling a bit intimidated, I was just about to turn around and head out for a coffee to contemplate what I'd gotten myself into, when a cheerful woman's voice addressed me from behind.

"Can I help you with something?" she said.

I turned around and saw a young staff member in tight leotards.

"I was just—looking around," I said. "I'm not sure I'm ready to get started with a weight-training program."

"We've got a lot more than just weights at our club," the girl said. "There's a full complement of cardio devices, Pilates machines, and an aerobics studio if you want something different. Were you looking for a self-paced program, or something with instructional support?"

"I'm kind of new to this sort of thing," I said. "So far, I've mostly just participated in yoga classes..."

"We have those too, if that's what you're most comfortable with. Perhaps you'd like to start with an introductory session with a personal trainer who can assess your fitness goals and design a custom workout program for your individual needs?"

"I suppose that makes the most sense. What are your fees?"

"A complimentary personal training session is included with a three-month trial membership. The basic monthly fee is forty-nine dollars per month, and you can cancel anytime. Additional training sessions are available at negotiated rates, depending on your trainer."

"That seems pretty reasonable," I said. "When are your trainers available?"

"Normally, we need at least forty-eight hours advance notice for scheduling, but we happen to have one available right now if you'd like to get started today."

I glanced around the gym at all the buff bodies and nodded.

"I think I've stalled long enough already," I said, removing my wallet from my purse. "Let's get the ball rolling."

After I signed the personal waiver and provided my credit card details, the receptionist gave me a combination lock and told me to store my personal effects in the women's locker room. I changed into my yoga tights and when I returned to the reception area, someone else was standing behind the desk. An attractive, athletic woman about my age was scribbling something on a clipboard and looked up.

"You must be Jade," she said, lowering her clipboard.

When she revealed what she was wearing, I gasped. She had on a one-piece black leotard with a large opening in the front of her chest, revealing the muscular cleavage between her large breasts supported by a crisscrossed elastic strap wrapping around her neck. Her breasts were perfectly round and firm, flexing gently as she moved her arms. It was obvious that she wasn't wearing a bra, with her spandex outfit cradling her bosom in a sensuous X-shaped pattern, with the faint protrusion of her bare nipples pressing against the stretchy fabric. Not that she needed one. I was quite sure that her breasts would have sat just as firm and high on her chest without any support whatsoever. Her bare arms and shoulders rippled as she held the clipboard in front of her, and I ran my eyes shamelessly over her body, taking in her exquisite form.

If this is what a little weight-training will do for my body, I thought, *count me in.*

"Um, yes," I stammered, returning my gaze to eye level. Even her *face* looked sculpted, with sharply-defined cheekbones, an angular jaw, and full, sensuous lips.

"I'm Kate," she said, extending her hand. "I'll be your personal trainer today."

I clasped her hand and Kate squeezed mine firmly as she smiled at me.

"Why don't we take a few minutes to clarify your fitness goals before we get started?"

She pointed to a tall round table with high stools in the corner behind the reception desk.

"Let's have a seat and get to know each other first."

When she emerged from behind the reception desk and began walking toward the table, my eyes almost bugged out of their sockets. Kate's ass and legs were even more firm and shapely than her arms and tits. Her tight leotard hugged every curve of her round, athletic butt, and her calf muscles flexed sensuously as she walked. When we both took our seats at the table, I exhaled audibly, trying to control my excitement.

"So then," she said, looking at me with her pretty hazel eyes. "What were you hoping to achieve from your training program?"

I had a hard time concentrating with her sharply defined cleavage staring me in the face.

"Just improve my tone, I suppose. Basically, I'd like to look like you. I'm guessing you're pretty close to my same age, but I don't look anything like—*that*."

Kate smiled as she quickly ran her gaze over my arms and chest.

"You've got some good raw material to work with. May I ask your age?"

"Thirty-five," I said.

"You're in great shape for someone—" Kate hesitated, as she scribbled some notes on my chart. "...our age."

I smiled, feeling more comfortable knowing I'd have a contemporary guiding me through my paces.

"Did you want to focus on any parts in particular?" Kate asked. "Because from my vantage point, everything looks to be pretty nicely balanced."

"It might be balanced, but I'm not honed like you. I'd just like to tighten everything up a little. Reduce my body fat, add a bit more shape to my arms and legs, maybe firm up my ass a little."

"I can work with that," Kate said. "How much time can you afford to invest?"

I chuckled at Kate's implication that this was going to be a long haul.

"Do you think it's going to take that long?"

"I meant per week—per session."

"Oh. I dunno. Will an hour per session, three times a week get me there?"

"It's a good start. As long as you keep at it. I'm sure you've heard the expression *use it or lose it*. Once you begin to make some gains, you can lose them just as quickly if you stop. Personal health and fitness is a journey, not a destination."

I peered up at Kate and smiled.

"That's what I've got *you* for, right? To keep me honest and straight."

"I don't know about the *straight* part, but I might be able to guide you in the right direction."

I paused for a moment, trying to glean Kate's meaning. Was she trying to tell me that she was attracted to women also? Suddenly, my pussy began tingling in excitement.

"It's a deal," I said. "Let's do this."

"Alright then. Let's get started with a short warm up. It's always best to start with some gentle stretching to elongate your muscles and get the blood circulating before you do anything too strenuous. I'm going to suggest you do ten minutes of stretching, followed by a half an hour of lifting, then twenty minutes of cardio as a start."

"Yes ma'am," I said, beginning to feel my blood rushing to other parts of my body already. "Your wish is my command. For the next sixty minutes at least, I'm all yours."

Kate led me to the stretching mat then stood beside me facing the bank of mirrors.

"First, let's loosen up your shoulders with some gentle windmills."

As she began swinging her arms in circles over her shoulders, I watched her tits shaking on her chest while her pectoralis and deltoid muscles flexed. As I mimicked her motion, I pretended to watch myself in the mirror, but the whole time I was fixated on her cleavage jiggling in the center of her chest. As I swung my arms with increasing frenzy, I fantasized about burying my face in her glistening valley.

"Now the other way," Kate said, swinging her arms in the other direction.

After another minute or so, she stopped and turned her body away from the mirrors.

"Now let's loosen up your lower body. Spread your legs about four feet apart then bend at the waist and try to place your palms on the floor between your legs."

Kate lowered her torso in a perfect V-shape and rested her forearms on the mat in front of her. I tried to match her pose, but I could barely get my fingertips to touch the floor.

"Don't worry if you can't get all the way down," she said, noticing my struggle to bend myself as far as she had. "Grip your ankles and gently pull yourself down toward the mat one inch at a time, pausing every fifteen seconds to let your muscles relax. Look between your legs in the mirror to find a setpoint to push yourself a little further."

When I looked between my legs, the only setpoint I could focus on was Kate's exquisite upturned ass staring me in my face. I glanced at the junction of her thighs near the bottom of her ass and detected a slight darkening in the fabric.

Was that sweat, or was she getting as turned on as I was watching her in the mirror?

"Yes," I said, feeling my own juices beginning to accumulate in my pussy. "I can feel things loosening up. My muscles are already relaxing."

"Good," Kate said. "When you get your palms flat on the floor, begin to wiggle your feet closer together, pausing and relaxing every fifteen seconds. You should begin to feel the pressure moving from the inside to the back of your thighs."

"I feel it in—*both* places," I said. But what I really meant to say was that my pussy was burning for an entirely different reason.

Kate led me through another ten minutes of stretching on the mat, with each pose giving me another opportunity to gawk at her magnificent figure. By the time we'd finished the split-knee hip stretch, I didn't want to get up off the mat while I fantasized about comingling our bodies in a more direct manner. Plus I was forming a large wet spot in the crotch of my tights that I was afraid would show if I stood up.

"Okay," she said, suddenly getting up. "I think we've got you plenty warmed up. Let's see if we can start working on that muscle tone you talked about."

She led me to the bench press station where a bar with two forty-five-pound plates rested on the rod. She lay down and lifted the bar off the rests and demonstrated five effortless reps.

"This will help tighten up your chest muscles and provide better support for your breasts," she said as she pumped the bar up and down. "Just remember to lower and raise the bar slowly, always keeping the weights under control. I'll watch you from behind to guide you."

She got up from the bench and motioned for me to lie down. Then she removed the two big plates on opposite ends of the bar and returned them to the stack.

"No weights?" I said, looking up at her inquisitively. "I know you're a lot stronger than me, but I didn't think I was *this* pathetic—"

"The bar alone weighs forty-five pounds," Kate said. "This is typically one of the weaker exercises for women. Let's start low and work our way up. We don't want you hurting yourself on the first day."

I lifted the bar off the rests, surprised at how heavy it felt. As I slowly lowered and raised the bar, Kate stood behind me at the head of the bench, leaning over with her palms just under the bar to catch it if I faltered. Every now and then, she glanced further down my body toward the wet patch between my legs.

"You're doing great, Jade," she said.

But all I could concentrate on was her firm breasts hanging over my head, mere inches away from my face. From this posterior angle, I could appreciate the full weight and shape of her bosom, and my mouth watered whenever she leaned closer, while I fantasized about sucking her protruding nipples. After the sixth rep, I began to grunt, struggling to lift the bar.

"Two more, Jade," Kate said. "Feel the burn. That's the good kind of pain. It means your muscles are growing stronger."

My pecs weren't the only part of me that was burning watching Kate's tight body hover over me. My sex drive was also growing stronger by the minute.

"Uhnnn!" I grunted, trying to pump out the last rep.

"Good girl. Whenever you can break through your limits, that's when you know you're making gains."

I looked up at Kate, breathing heavily.

"You're not going to make me look like Arnold Schwarzenegger, are you?"

"Don't worry," Kate laughed. "We're just going to push it far enough to improve your muscle tone a little. When you start to see your body fat diminish and your muscles become more prominent, we'll know when to back off."

"I hope so," I said, sitting up on the bench and resting my hands on my thighs, still huffing. "What's next?"

"Let's do something for your butt and thighs now. This one's a little tougher, but it does wonders for your derriere."

Kate walked me over to a vertical weight station where another bar with two large plates on each side rested about shoulder height on the support bars extending from the rack.

"This is the squat station," she said. "This one's a bit more strenuous, so it's super-important you do it slowly and with proper form. Let me show you first."

Kate bent her knees and dipped her head under the bar then lifted herself up with the bar resting on the back of her shoulders.

"Jesus," I said, watching the bar flex from the heavy plates. "Do you ever lower the weight, or do you just lift whatever the guys leave on the bar?"

Kate smiled as she looked at me in the mirror.

"I've been doing this for a while, and this is one of my stronger exercises. But believe me, I still feel it."

Kate proceeded to lower her body with a straight back until her legs were at a ninety-degree angle, then she slowly lifted herself back up to a standing position. As she lowered and raised herself in repeated repetitions, she talked to me as if it were a walk in the park. All the while, I stared at her bubble butt as it stretched and flexed from the strain of the weights.

"Remember to breathe in at the top of the movement, then exhale slowly as you raise yourself back up. Try to keep your back straight and don't go lower than ninety-degrees, so as not to strain your knees too much."

After four or five repetitions, Kate placed the bar back on the supports then stepped back and removed the plates, adding a twenty-five-pound weight on each end.

"That doesn't look like much," I said, disappointed in her lack of confidence in me. "I used to run track at school. I think I can do more than that."

"You probably can," she said. "But let's focus on your form to begin with and work our way up to your max. Remember, you said your goal is to tighten your tone, not add strength or bulk. We'll leave the heavy lifting to the guys."

Kate moved a bench into the center of the station and instructed me to straddle it with my legs.

"This will help give you a little support and let you know how far to go down. Let's do a couple of sets of eight reps to start, trying to touch but not rest your hips on the bench on the way down."

As I spread my legs and straddled the bench, I looked in the mirror, seeing the expanding wet spot in my tights.

"Sorry," I said, glancing between my legs. "I guess all this pumping and burning is getting more than just my muscles worked up."

"Not to worry," Kate smiled. "It does the same thing for me. That's another side benefit to strenuous exercise. It also boosts your sex drive."

I placed my head under the bar as Kate had, and when I lifted the bar off the supports, I immediately regretted asking her to add more weight. I hobbled backwards and slowly began to lower myself to the bench.

"Argh," I groaned, as I flexed my knees and tensed my thighs to support the weight. "You're right. That is pretty heavy. Do I have to go all the way down?"

"Go as far as you feel comfortable," Kate said. "Ease into it at first, lowering yourself more with each rep. You just need to get used to the movement. It won't take long for you to improve your form."

As I moved through each repetition, I watched myself in the mirror. The top of my thighs were burning, but I wanted to show Kate that I wasn't a quitter. When my ass touched the bench on my fourth rep, I was tempted to sit down and rest, but I forced my legs to push myself back up.

"That's it, Jade," Kate said. "That's a good rep. See if you can do four more, touching but not resting on the way down."

Each time my ass touched the bench, I could feel my pussy spreading apart. By the seventh rep, my thighs weren't the only part of me tingling from the heavy exertion.

"One more, Jade," Kate said. "Feel the burn."

"Oh, I'm feeling it alright," I panted.

"Try to push through your limits," she said. "That's what ultimately will help you reach your goals."

"You're pushing me to places I haven't been in quite a while, Kate," I said, exhaling deeply as I finished the eighth rep.

"Okay, now take a thirty-second rest, then we'll do one more set."

"Are you kidding me?" I protested. "This is my first workout! Didn't you say I'm supposed to *ease* into this?"

"No pain, no gain, girl," Kate said. "I'm trying to instill a good work ethic so that when I'm not around to push you, you'll remember to push yourself."

I looked up at Kate, realizing how dependent I'd already become on her guidance and supervision.

"How much pain am I going to be feeling tomorrow?" I said, massaging my throbbing thighs.

"You'll probably feel a few aches tomorrow morning. But remember, that just means your muscles are rebuilding and growing stronger. This is the first step to improving your shape, tone, and firmness. You'll thank me later."

She glanced back at the bar resting on the rack.

"Now, one more set."

"Right," I groaned.

I stepped back under the bar and lifted it off the supports then lowered myself toward the bench. I was glad Kate had placed it there to catch me, since my thighs were definitely nearing the point of exhaustion. But I was also glad she'd put it there for another reason. Each time I dipped down and touched the bench between my thighs,

I felt a charge run through my body as I rubbed my clit softly against the padded surface. By the time I finished my last rep, a small puddle had formed in the middle of the seat.

"Good job," Kate said. "Don't you feel like you're pushing through your limits already?"

"Definitely getting *close*," I panted, feeling my pussy tingling between my legs.

"Just one more exercise for today," Kate said. "Time to work on your core muscles. This next one is one of my favorites. Not only will it strengthen your midsection, it gives you great definition in your stomach."

Kate led me over to a strange contraption that looked like a cross between an airplane cockpit and a torture rack.

"This is the ab crunch machine," she said, positioning herself in the seat then reaching over her shoulders to grab the support handles.

"Try to pull your upper body down with your arms and lift your lower body up with your legs at the same time, so you work both parts of your abs. If you do it right, you should feel a gentle burning feeling in your stomach muscles."

Kate demonstrated eight perfect abdominal crunches, then she hopped off the machine and motioned for me to get on it. There was a hump in the pad directly in front of my crotch, and as I sat down on the seat, the pad rubbed against my still-tingling clit.

"Focus on pulling your chest down to your hips, curving your spine forward, instead of bending at the hips," she said. "I'm going to stand behind you so I can make sure you're keeping your back in the proper position."

Kate stepped behind the machine, then placed her hand between the two separated pads and touched my lower back.

"Try to keep your back pressed against my fingers as you pull down. Now, lift the weight slowly as far as you can go down."

I tensed my abdominal muscles and pulled my hands down, and the two halves of the back rest parted as my head lowered to my knees. The further I pulled forward and down, the harder my crotch pushed forward against the raised hump in the pad. With each rep, my clit got more and more stimulated, until I began to feel an orgasm welling up inside me.

"That's it, Jade," Kate said, caressing my lower back from behind the machine. "You're doing great. Keep your back pressed against my hand and go as low as you can, bringing your elbows and knees together. Can you feel the burn?"

"Yes," I panted. "It feels good."

"Good. Just four more reps."

As I felt the pleasure continue building up between my legs, I had no intention of stopping at four reps. I pulled forward faster and lower, pressing my pussy harder against the pad each time.

"Uhnn," I groaned, nearing climax.

"Keep going, Jade," Kate encouraged me. "Press through the limit."

"Yes," I panted. "I can feel myself reaching the limit. Ohhh!" I moaned, feeling my orgasm pouring over me. On the last rep, I held the machine in the crunched position, pressing my cunt against the pad until my contractions ended, then I pulled back on the machine as the plates loudly fell together.

Kate smiled at me as she came back around to the front of the machine.

"Did you feel that in your core?" she said. "You did particularly well on this machine."

"Yes," I said. "I felt that *deep* in my core. Do you mind if I do another set?"

2

———

FEELING THE BURN

fter my hot workout session with Kate, I immediately booked another personal training appointment. Even though she'd set me up with a full regimen of exercises, I liked having her push me to my limits. With her sexy body standing beside me, it definitely made me work harder. Not only did she boost my energy level, but she also represented the perfect figure that I could aspire to.

I wanted to go back for another session the next day, but Kate suggested I wait forty-eight hours to let my body rest and recover. She warned me that I'd likely experience some muscle aches in the areas we'd targeted, and the next morning I could barely pull myself out of bed. Which wasn't so much of a problem, since I languored for the first hour or two fantasizing about having her fuck me in every conceivable position.

By the second day, the aches were beginning to subside, and I was charged up for another intense training session. But if it was going to be anything like the last session, I figured I'd better wear something a little less revealing. Although Kate didn't seem to mind, I definitely felt self-conscious about the wet spot showing in the crotch of my tights. I threw on some terrycloth sweats and a loose T-shirt, but dispensed with the bra and panties. Looking at myself in my dressing mirror, I nodded approvingly. I showed just enough curves to keep myself—and hopefully also Kate—turned on while I worked out.

When I got to the gym, Kate was waiting for me with my training chart on her clipboard. This time, she wore a form-fitting two-piece outfit that revealed most of her midsection. Below her truncated top, her toned stomach flexed with muscles and striations. I could see the faint outline of a six-pack, with a sexy indentation running down the center of her abdomen. Her tight leotards rested low on her hips, revealing a tantalizing patch of smooth, tanned skin below her navel, and the crest of her hip bones on either side.

The separated garments accentuated her hourglass figure, with her large, firm breasts swelling above her flared hips. Even with her legs straight together, I could see a small diamond-shaped patch of light emanating from the cleft at the top of her thighs. She couldn't have had more than five percent body fat anywhere on her body.

"How are you feeling today?" she said, stepping forward to greet me. "Any aches and pains after your first workout?"

"Oh yes," I said. "You weren't kidding about the next day training effect. I could barely walk yesterday."

"That's actually a good sign," she nodded. "There's two kinds of workout pain, and that's definitely the right kind. It means your muscles are breaking down and rebuilding stronger. Just like a broken bone, they heal back stronger and sturdier."

"That's good to know, because I think you almost broke me last time." I said, smiled coyly. "But I kind of liked it."

"Workouts produce an odd mixture of pleasure and pain. It's a lot of hard work, but the endorphins you produce from stressing your body give you a natural high."

"Well I definitely experienced a few highs," I said, remembering the intense orgasm I'd experienced on the ab crunch machine. "What have you got in store for me today?"

"I think you should stick to a balanced routine of stretching, weights, and cardio, but I'd like to mix up the exercises a little bit today. Besides keeping your body guessing what to expect next, it will give you more time to rest each set of muscles between sessions. Today, I want to work on your extremities, to boost your strength and stamina in some of the smaller muscles."

"Yes," I said, glancing again at the cleft at the top of Kate's thighs. "Let's definitely work on the extremities."

"Alright. Let's get you warmed up first with a little stretching."

Kate led me back to the stretching mat where she sat down in front of me and spread her legs.

"Spread your feet apart, then touch mine. We're going to hold each other's hands and pull each other to stretch our inner thighs."

"I like the sound of that," I said, smiling at Kate.

I reached out my hands and Kate clasped them firmly, then gently pulled me toward her. As she tensed her stomach muscles, the striations rippled across her abs.

"Uhnn," I grunted, feeling the pull in my hamstrings and adductors.

"Can you feel that?" Kate asked. "I'm going to hold you here for a moment, while you breathe slowly and try to relax your muscles."

After a few seconds, I could feel the tension begin to ebb in my legs, and Kate pulled me forward another few inches. Each time she pulled me closer, she pushed my feet slightly further apart as my face got closer to her toned stomach and the bare skin below her navel. Just as I was getting tantalizingly close to her crotch, she eased up and suddenly sat forward.

"Now it's your turn to pull me toward you. This will stretch the top of your thighs and also strengthen your lower back and buttock muscles. Do the same thing I did—pulling me slowly forward until you feel the tension in my body.

I leaned back, pulling Kate's arms with me, and she flexed her body in a perfect V-shape, bobbing her head forward until her ponytail flopped down just in front of my crotch.

"Can you feel the stretch in your thighs?" Kate asked with her nose touching the mat.

"Among other places," I said.

We continued pushing and pulling each other for the next few minutes, pressing our legs further and further apart. Each time I pulled her forward, Kate's soft hair caressed the top of my mound as I unconsciously pushed my hips up in a fucking motion. By the time we finished the routine, my pussy was soaking wet, and I was glad I'd worn the heavy sweats.

"Okay," Kate said, standing up. "Let's work on loosening up your shoulders now. Extend your arm straight in front of you, then grab your elbow with your other hand and pull your arm slowly across your chest like this."

Kate demonstrated the movement as I watched her breasts mash together and press upward. I did the same, pretending to stretch my arm up and down as I rubbed the cotton fabric of my shirt against my bare nipples.

"Now the other side."

As I mirrored her technique, I couldn't take my eyes off her beautiful melons, wishing it were my face mashed up against them instead of her arm.

"Okay," she said. "This next stretch is a little more challenging. It's called the cow-face pose, and you should feel it under your arms and in your shoulder blades."

Kate lifted her arm over her head then reached behind her back with her other arm and joined her hands between her shoulder blades. I tried to copy her technique but grunted trying to touch my fingers.

"Don't worry if you can't join your hands together right away. As with our other stretches, just go as far as you can, then pause and breathe and try to push it a little further."

After a few more seconds of grunting and straining, I was finally able to touch my hands.

"Good," Kate said. "Now try to curl your fingers and pull your hands closer together. You should feel the stretch in your lats and deltoids."

"Oomph," I grimaced, feeling the strain in my back. "Now I see why they call this the cow-face pose."

"Well for the record," Kate said, "you don't look anything like a cow."

"Um—thank you," I said, running my eyes up and down Kate's taut figure. "I don't think you look remotely like any barn animal either."

"All right then," Kate chuckled. "Let's go find some new pastures to graze in. I think we need some fresh material to get charged up on."

She led me to the back wall where a bunch of jocks were lifting free weights in front of a long mirror. Kate positioned a bench in front of the mirror then lifted two twenty-pound dumbbells off the rack and sat down on the end of the bench. She lowered the weights behind her head until her arms were in a ninety-degree angle, then she raised them straight up.

"This exercise will tighten up the underside of your upper arms. Try to keep your elbows stationary beside your ears as you lift the weights straight up and down. I'll stand behind you to watch your form."

She motioned for me to sit as she had on the bench, then she removed two five-pound dumbbells and placed them in my outstretched hands.

"That's only a *quarter* of what you were doing," I said. "When can I expect to reach your level?"

"I've been training pretty intensely my entire adult life. If you get there much quicker than me, I'm going to be a little envious."

"You mean I have to wait *fifteen years* to start looking like you?"

"It won't take that long," Kate chuckled. "Remember, fitness is a journey, not a destination. It should only take a few months for you to start noticing some significant changes."

Kate stepped behind me and placed her hands around my elbows.

"Now, lower the weights slowly until your arms are in a ninety-degree angle."

Feeling Kate's bare hands close to my chest sent a chill down my spine, and I began pumping the weights up and down quickly.

"Slow down, girl," Kate admonished. "This isn't a race. Slower is always better. There's less chance of getting a muscle strain, and it places more even force throughout the entire range of motion."

"Right," I said, staring at her rack sitting just above my head. "Slower is better."

By the time I finished ten reps, my tricep muscles were burning, and I rested the dumbbells on my thighs.

"Good job," Kate said. "Just two more sets."

I looked at her like she was crazy, and she simply nodded.

"No pain, no gain," she smiled.

"You're a cruel woman," I said, pushing the weights back over my head.

As I began lowering and lifting the dumbbells, I noticed Kate's gaze drifting to my chest as my loose breasts swayed under the thin cotton fabric of my T-shirt. Within a few seconds, my nipples had hardened, producing two noticeable bumps in my shirt. I was happy to see I wasn't the only one attracted by nice tits, and I proudly lifted my chest, pressing my breasts further forward and higher.

"All right," Kate said after I finished the third set. "Let's get a pump going to your antagonist muscles. It's always good to keep your strength balanced on both sides of your body to avoid injury and to build a symmetrical shape. Now we're going to work on your biceps."

"Biceps?" I said. "Aren't those just for *guys*? I thought you said you weren't going to make me look like Arnold Schwarzenegger."

"Not to worry. We're going to use light weights. I promise you won't bulk up. Do you think *I* look like Arnold Schwarzenegger?"

"God, no," I said, admiring her slender but strong arms. "You look more like an Amazon. A very *sexy* Amazon. If this will make me look like you, I'm all in."

"Follow me then. Let's *pump you up!*" she said, feigning a German accent.

I was beginning to enjoy my playful banter with Kate. The more time I spent with her, the more infatuated I became.

She walked up to the weight rack and picked up two five-pound dumbbells. Then she stepped back a couple of feet and began swinging her hands up and down in alternating arcs. As she lifted the weights, I stared at her arm muscles flexing with sinewy firmness. I wanted to jump up on her shoulders and clamp my legs around her head while she held me up with her strong arms as I ground my pussy into her face.

"Jade?" Kate said, running her hand in front of my glazed eyes. "Are you still with me? It's your turn now."

"Yes," I murmured, snapping out of my daydream. "I was just concentrating on your—*technique.*"

Kate passed me the five-pound weights and as I began to pump the dumbbells up and down, she moved behind me and gripped my shoulders to keep my body from swaying. Every time she placed her hands on me, I fantasized about her touching my more private parts.

Looking out the corner of my eyes, I noticed a few muscle jocks leering at us from the other side of the gym.

"Do you ever provide *private* lessons?" I asked.

"You mean outside the gym?"

"Yes. It can be a bit disconcerting doing all this intimate lifting with so many eyes on you."

"I can do outcalls," Kate nodded. "But it's a little tougher to achieve the same intensity without access to all this specialized equipment. Do you have a suitable area of your home in which you can work out?"

I paused for a moment, contemplating my options.

"I could probably clear a space. But I don't have any equipment. What about *your* place? I'm guessing you have a more complete setup."

"I have a small studio with a few free weights and cardio machines," Kate said. "We could create a workable routine just using your own body weight."

"That sounds very liberating. Can we try that next time?"

"Of course. Let's finish up here though today. Don't mind those muscleheads. They're harmless."

As I continued my bicep set, Kate's grip on my shoulders tightened, until her fingertips pressed into the side of my breasts. Whether she was just trying to steady my swaying body or she was turned on by my invitation for a private get together, was unclear. Either way, her firm grip got me even more worked up, and I hammered out three sets before realizing how much my arms were burning.

"Doesn't that feel good?" Kate said, motioning to my pumped-up biceps.

I looked in the mirror and flexed my arms, admiring the new curves produced by the opposing arms exercises.

"Yes," I nodded. "I like where this is going."

"Okay," she said. "Just two more exercises. Let's see if we can finish up on another high today."

"Are you taking me back to the ab crunch machine?" I asked, feeling my pussy pulsing between my legs. "Cause that thing has a *special* effect on me."

"Not today. But I have something you might like just as much."

She led me over to a weight machine shaped like a gynecologist's chair. Leg rests extended out from the machine in a V-shape, with hand rests beside the padded seat. Kate sat in the machine and adjusted a handle beside the seat to spread her legs wide apart. As she pulled her legs together, the weight stack on the front of the machine began to rise.

"This will tighten and strengthen your groin muscles," she said. "It's another good one for enhancing your sex life. Keeps everything nice and tight down there. You never know when you might need to wrap your legs around something—"

"Indeed," I said, recognizing another dark patch forming in the crotch of her tights. There was only one place I wanted to wrap my legs around at this moment.

When she finished demonstrating the machine, Kate lowered the weight and asked me to do a few sets. I pulled my legs together and grunted from the tightness in my groin muscles. But within four or five reps, I was getting the hang of the exercise as I began to feel a more pleasurable sensation between my legs.

"That's it, Jade," Kate said. "Spread your legs nice and slow. This is one muscle you definitely don't want to pull."

"Not *this* way at least," I said, smiling at Kate.

As I continued fanning my legs in and out, I fantasized about having her face buried in my pussy as I wrapped my legs around her head.

"I can see what you mean, though. This exercise is definitely very —*invigorating.*"

After two more sets, we moved to the adjacent machine which focused on our outer thighs and hips. By the time I finished the requisite three sets, the terrycloth lining of my sweats was already soaked through again. But this time, Kate rarely took her gaze away from the wet patch between my legs.

"I knew you'd like these ones," she smiled. "It looks like you're just about ready for the big finish."

"Yes," I said. "I need to finish soon. All this flexing and straining in my groin area is getting me pretty worked up."

"Let's see if we can take you to another new peak," Kate said, smiling.

She led me to a tall weight rack with padded shoulder rests and an elevated foot rest.

"This one works on your lower legs. It will give you a nice pleasing shape to your calves."

"*Lower* legs?" I said. "I was kind of hoping we'd finish with another core exercise."

"I think you might find this one just as satisfying," she said. "It's a bit more interactive. But this time, I want *you* to go first. I'm going to stand behind you to guide your movement. Then we'll switch and you can return the favor."

I pinched my eyebrows, intrigued by Kate's cryptic description.

"Okay, but how does it work?"

"Place the balls of your feet on the edge of the elevated foot rest, then rest your shoulders under the padded supports and lift your heels as high as you can with a straight body."

As I began to raise my heels and lift the weight stack, Kate pressed her body against mine to keep my body straight. When I lowered my heels, she pushed her hips against my ass. I smiled as I looked around the gym, glad that this machine was nestled in the corner behind a tall rack of barbells. For the next few minutes, Kate and I would have almost complete privacy.

"That's it," Kate said, pressing her mound against my ass. Her hands gripped the sides of my hips as she pulled herself against me. "Keep doing what you're doing. Up and down—nice and slow."

A flush began to form on Kate's cheeks with each lowering of my hips, and I began to push my ass into her as she tilted her crotch up to meet me. Even though she'd intentionally set the weight on the stack low so I wouldn't exhaust too quickly, by the twentieth rep or so I began to feel my calves burning.

"That's good, Jade," Kate said, exhaling heavily against the back of my loose shirt. "Try to push out five or ten more reps. We're almost there."

I noticed her breathing had picked up in intensity and her face now had a full flush.

"Two more, Jade," she panted. "Push it."

Suddenly, Kate pressed her face against my back and I felt her body shudder against my ass. I held my heels up in an extended position, pressing my butt against her pussy, until I felt her grip loosen against my hips.

"That was very good," she panted. "You really pushed through your limits that time. Now let's switch positions and see if you can stimulate some *other* parts of your body while I do all the work."

I looked into Kate's eyes and smiled.

"Do you need a moment to recover?"

"I'll be fine," she said, glancing at the wet patch in the front of my sweat pants. "*You're* the one who needs attention right now. Stand behind me and guide me as I guided you. Let's see if we can finish with an extra-big pump."

"I like the sound of that," I said, caressing Kate's hips as she stepped in front of me. "Just don't put too much weight on the stack. I don't want you to get exhausted before I do."

Kate stepped on the foot rest and playfully pressed her ass against me as she dipped her shoulders under the supports. I moved in close behind her and looked around the room to make sure nobody else was watching. When she straightened her body and lifted her heels, I felt her ass tighten and flex against my stomach. I placed my hands around her waist, pressing my thumbs into her rock-hard butt. When she lowered her heels, she paused at the bottom and shimmied her glutes across my mound.

"Yes," I purred. "You have such great form, Kate. Don't stop. Show me how to perform this exercise properly. Nice and slow..."

I smiled at Kate in the mirror in front of us as she lifted herself up and lowered herself slowly, sensuously sliding her ass down the front of my sweats. The coarse lining of my pants rubbed against my clit, like a French tickler.

"Uhnnn," I moaned. "That feels good. Pump that weight. Fuck me with your tight ass."

There was no point withholding any further pretense. We both knew what we were doing, and I had no intention of disguising the effect she had on me. As she continued sliding up and down the front of my body, my hands migrated further and further toward the front of Kate's leotard, until my fingertips probed the cleft between her legs.

"Yes, Jade," she panted. "I'm beginning to feel the burn. Let's push through our limits together this time."

We pressed our bodies tighter together, and as Kate rubbed her body over my pussy, I diddled her clit with my two hands.

"Yes, Jade," Kate grunted. "It's coming. I'm reaching my peak. Oh, fuck!"

Kate's buttocks suddenly began vibrating against my mound, and I pressed my clit into her hard ass as I gushed into my terrycloth sweat pants.

"Oh God," I panted. "Fuck me, Kate! Fuck me with your sweet ass!"

I gripped her pelvis tightly as I thrashed against her butt, hissing against her back, trying to suppress my exploding pleasure. For the next twenty seconds, we spasmed against one another, savoring a quiet and intense simultaneous orgasm.

3

PUSHING THE LIMITS

After my second exciting workout with Kate, she gave me her personal contact information and we scheduled a private session for later in the week. Normally, she preferred to visit her clients at their residence for outcalls, but in my case she was willing to make an exception and meet me at her home.

As with my first training session, I was sore in the new muscles we'd targeted, but especially so in my abs, which had gotten a particularly intense workout while grinding my hips against her ass during the calf raise exercise. If it was her intent to use sexual gratification as an incentive to make me work harder, I could only imagine what she had in store for me during our third session.

On Saturday morning, I followed the directions to her home and at eleven o'clock I tapped on the front door of her house. When she opened the door, I was disappointed to see her wearing a full-body sweatsuit. Knowing nobody would be watching us today, I'd worn my skimpiest two-piece yoga outfit. I no longer had any reservations about Kate seeing first-hand the sexual effects her workouts were having on my body.

"Good morning, Jade," she said, inviting me inside.

"You have a beautiful home," I said, looking around her tastefully appointed house. "Thanks for inviting me. I was beginning to feel a bit self-conscious with all those mirrors and prying eyes surrounding us at the gym."

"That's the problem when you have two attractive, toned women working out around all those muscleheads," Kate nodded. "It's like they'd never seen a fit woman before. Today, I just want you to relax and let yourself go. I've got a special routine worked up for you."

Kate motioned to her kitchen at the opposite end of the hall.

"Can I get you something to drink? How about a nice healthy smoothie?"

"That would be lovely."

Kate led me to her kitchen and suggested I sit on a stool beside the island while she prepared the refreshment. As she loaded an assortment of fruits and vegetables into her blending machine, I watched her round ass bend and flex in her sweats. When the machine finished its cycle, she poured the mixture into two tall glasses then sat beside me at the island. I took a sip of the dark green concoction and puckered my lips from the bitter taste.

"Do you drink this stuff *every* day?" I asked.

"Pretty much," she said, "especially before or after a training session. There's lots of good vitamins and protein in there. Helps to rebuild your muscles after a workout. I'm guessing from your cowface that you're not digging it?"

"Sorry to make light of your culinary skills," I chuckled. "I'm sure it's very good for me. No pain, no gain—right?"

"Unfortunately, that's the way it is with most good things if life," Kate nodded. "You need to make certain sacrifices in order to achieve your goals."

"Speaking of sacrifices," I said, peering at her heavy sweatsuit. "I have to admit I'm a little disappointed that you're covering up your pretty body today. Seeing your magnificent figure really gave me the motivation to push harder."

Kate smiled as she glanced at my firm breasts in my tight yoga top.

"Don't worry," she said. "I have some interesting ideas for pushing your limits today. I think we'll get plenty of opportunities to see our muscles pumping up close today. Finish your smoothie, and I'll show you what I mean."

Kate's suggestion that I'd see more of her body once we started working out was all the encouragement that I needed. I gulped down the rest of my smoothie then followed her downstairs to her finished walkout basement. When we got to the bottom of the stairs, I looked around the expansive room and nodded in appreciation. The entire lower level was filled with an assortment of free weights, training mats, and cardio machines. Three sides of the room were lined with floor-to-ceiling mirrors, while the side facing her fenced-in yard had tall windows streaming in the morning sunlight.

"Wow," I said, widening my eyes in wonder. "This is quite the exercise studio. No wonder you're in such great shape. I'd want to workout out here *every day* I had this setup. It's almost as big as the gym!"

"Not quite," Kate said, "but thank you. It's taken a while to equip, but I have to admit, I've got no excuse to miss a workout with just about everything I need so readily available."

"Where shall we begin?" I asked, looking at all the gleaming equipment.

"Let's start on the stretching mat. I've designed most of the exercises using only your own body weight. Besides enabling you to do them away from the gym, they're also a little more *interactive*."

"Interactive sounds good," I said, smiling at Kate.

She led me to a large padded mat near the back wall then paused, looking at me in the mirror.

"The first thing I think we should do is disrobe," she said. "Besides giving you a little extra incentive to push out that extra rep, it will give me a chance to see first-hand the effect each exercise is having on your body."

My eyes flung open as my pussy twitched between my legs.

"Completely?" I said.

"You said seeing more of my body made you work harder, didn't you? By extension, the more we reveal, I'm guessing the harder you'll work."

As much as I wanted to see Kate naked, the thought of working out in the buff felt strange.

"Maybe," I said. "But it could also be a little distracting—"

"Let me worry about keeping you focused on the exercises. You just concentrate on following my instructions. Are you comfortable with this idea?"

"Are you kidding me?" I said. "I've been undressing you with my eyes from the moment we first met."

"Alright then," Kate said, unzipping the front of her sweat top. "Let's do this."

She lowered her zipper all the way, then pulled her jacket off her back and threw it in the corner of the mat. She wasn't wearing anything underneath, and I gasped when I saw her large breasts resting on her chest. They had to be D-cup sized at least, yet they sat firm and high on her chest. They were perfectly round, with a sharp crease from her defined pec muscles separating them in the middle. Her large pink, medallion-sized areolas were punctuated with thick nipples extending almost a full inch from the surface of her skin . My pussy throbbed as I felt my tights moistening in excitement.

"Holy shit, girl," I said. "Are those things *real*? They look like something straight out of a Playboy centerfold."

"One hundred percent natural," Kate smiled. "I was blessed with large breasts from a young age. They were even bigger than this before I started working out. That was one of my primary motivations for getting in shape and reducing my body fat. I was always self-conscious about the size of my breasts."

"Well you shouldn't be," I said, shaking my head as the wet patch widened in my crotch. "They're absolutely magnificent. Most women would give their right arm to have a rack like yours."

"Maybe," Kate said. "But not everybody likes big boobs. They can be a little annoying when I'm exercising, particularly when I'm on the treadmill."

"I bet. You could take an *eye* out with those things if you aren't careful."

"I'm sure you know what I'm talking about," Kate smiled. "You've got a pretty healthy set yourself, Jade. Speaking of which, isn't it time for you to do a little show and tell yourself?"

"Oh—sorry," I said, hooking my fingers under the hem of my yoga top. "I just wanted to soak up your body for a few seconds."

I pulled my shirt over my head then threw it on top of Kate's sweatshirt. As I stood facing Kate with my naked breasts, my body trembled in excitement.

"Perfect C's," Kate said, nodding appreciatively. "I suspect that's more like what most women aspire to. I don't think you need any help there."

"Maybe not," I said, running my eyes down the length of Kate's body. "It's the *rest* of my body that needs work."

"Let's see what we have to work with the rest of the way then," she said, suddenly pulling her sweat pants down to the floor and throwing them in the pile.

Once again, she was completely naked under her pants, and my mouth gaped open when I saw her exposed lower body. Her mound was shaved completely bald, and her hips swelled in a sexy hourglass shape with exposed hipbones framed by abdominal ligaments angling toward her pussy. Her thighs flared in a gentle muscular arc over diamond-shaped calves and narrow ankles. Her entire body looked like it had been carved from a slab of marble.

"You've got to be kidding me," I panted. "You look like a Greek Goddess. I just want to eat you up."

"We might be able to arrange that a little later," Kate said, staring at the giant wet patch that had formed in the crotch of my leggings. "First let's get you out of the rest of your clothes. You look a little uncomfortable in those wet leggings."

"What if I leak all over your beautiful workout studio? Won't it bother you if I soil your clean stretching mat?"

"Not at all," Kate said. "It will just add some helpful lubrication to some of the exercises I've got planned. Let's get started by celebrating our mutual figures. I want you to start by turning around and spreading your legs about two feet apart. I'll stand behind you, then we'll bend at the waist and view ourselves between our legs."

"I like the sound of that," I said, quickly turning around and bending over.

But when I peered through my legs, I saw that Kate had moved closer to me, and I struggled to tilt my head far enough down to see her full back side. As she started to bend forward, the muscles in her calves and the back of her thighs rippled in sexy striations. She smiled at me when me made eye contact, but she was too close for me to see her upturned ass and exposed pussy.

"No fair!" I protested, straining to look further up her legs.

"I *told* you I was going to make this a little more interesting today," she said. "If you want to see more of my naked body, you're going to have to work for it."

I groaned, feeling my hamstring muscles straining as I struggled to push myself further down to give me a better viewing angle.

"Don't push it too fast," Kate said. "We've still got a long workout ahead of us. I don't want you to hurt yourself before you have a chance to do some closer contact activities."

She wiggled her feet away from me a few inches, allowing me to see a few inches higher up her thighs, but her honeypot was still just barely out of view. I placed my hands around my ankles and pulled my body a few inches lower, until I could see the bottom of her slit. Kate quickly scurried closer to me, reducing my field of vision.

"You little tease," I growled, frustrated by my inability to get a clear look at her cunny.

"I never said this was going to be *easy*," Kate said. "The main purpose of a personal trainer is to push you further than you would by yourself."

As I gawked at Kate's shapely legs, I could feel my juices running down the insides of my thighs.

"Yeah, well if you keep teasing me like this, I may need to take matters into my own hands pretty soon."

"There'll be plenty of time for that later. You're not allowed to touch *anything* until I give my permission. Take a deep breath and exhale slowly. Feel the pressure in your muscles relax, then you'll be able to stretch a little lower."

I did as Kate instructed, and as I felt my breasts press against the front of my thighs, my field of vision rose another two inches up the back of Kate's legs.

"Almost there, Jade," Kate said, wiggling a couple of inches closer to me. "Pause and relax. Just a couple more inches..."

I closed my eyes and concentrated on my breathing as the pressure in my hamstrings slowly abated. When I opened them again, Kate's tight box sat directly in front of me between her splayed legs. The cheeks of her muscular buttocks cupped her bare vulva like a catcher's mitt, her puffy lips spreading apart sensuously to reveal her dark glistening slit.

"Fuck yes," I purred, when I saw her exposed snatch. "Even your pussy is perfectly tight and ripped. Why am I not surprised? Come a little closer and let me feel your ass press against mine. I want to fuck that sweet, sexy pussy."

Kate smiled at me as she licked her lips.

"You've got a sexy kitty too, Jade. We'll have plenty of opportunity to join our bodies soon enough. For now, I want you to hold that position while you stretch your hamstrings just a little longer."

"God damn, girl" I hissed. "You weren't kidding when you said you had a special plan for pushing me past my limits today."

"You haven't seen anything yet," Kate said. "We're just getting started."

Kate suddenly stood up and turned around as I lifted myself back up slowly.

"Now we're going to work on another part of your body," she said. "This will give us a chance to admire a different piece of our anatomy. I want you to lie face up on the mat, with your body in a straight position and your legs together."

I pinched my eyebrows and looked at Kate quizzically as I lowered myself to the mat as she instructed. Then she straddled my legs and began to walk on her hands and knees up my body.

"Yes please," I said. "While you're down there, would you mind—"

"Shush, little girl," she said. "I have something *else* in mind."

She crawled two more feet up my body, then stretched her legs out behind her and lifted her body up on her palms and the balls of her feet. As she stared directly down onto my face, she smiled at me slyly, then lowered her body until her breasts almost touched mine. Then she raised herself back up until her arms were straight and repeated the sequence two more times.

"This is what I call a reverse bench press," she said. "It works the same muscles on the back of your arms and the front of your chest, but in a more fun and interesting way. We're going to switch positions in a moment, and I want you to mimic my movement, lowering your body with a straight back as far as you can without touching me. Do as many reps as you can until you reach exhaustion."

"Without *touching*?" I said. "Where's the fun in that? I thought you were going to use your sexy body as an incentive to push me further. If I can't touch you, where's my motivation?"

"That's the whole point of the exercise," Kate smiled. "I'm withholding the touching part until the last to encourage you to work harder. If you're a good girl and you do everything the way I tell you, there'll be a nice little reward at the end."

"There better be," I said. "Because if my muscles don't give out first, surely my willpower will."

"Get on top of me and fantasize about what you want to do to me later. That should give you plenty of motivation to finish your exercises."

Kate rolled over on the mat beside me and straightened her body out as I had. Then I straddled her hips and looked into her eyes mischievously.

"Now that I've got you where I want you, what makes you think I won't just take advantage of you right here?"

"Do you really think you can take me that easily?" Kate taunted. "Keep your dick in your pants, girl. Don't make me teach you a different kind of lesson today. Now straighten out your body and pump out some push-ups."

"Yes master," I said, winking at Kate.

As I lowered my body, I struggled to keep my body straight, with my arms shaking from the force of my weight levitating over Kate. As our bodies came closer and closer together, I peered down to see my nipples mere inches away from Kate's inflamed nubs. Momentarily overcome with passion, my arms suddenly became weak, and our nipples touched.

"No contact!" Kate admonished. "If you can't hold yourself in the lower position, straighten out your arms and rest for longer at the top. Use our nipples as a guide. I want you to get as close to me as possible without actually touching. Now—straighten back up!"

I did as Kate instructed and paused with my arms in a locked position above her. My heavy breathing blew loose strands of hair at the sides of her head.

"Okay," Kate said. "Try it again. This time, get as close as you dare —but no touching."

"You're *killing* me!" I protested, half from exhaustion and half from sexual frustration.

I lowered myself again, peering between my tits to get as close to Kate's nipples without actually making contact.

"That's it, babe," Kate encouraged. "Lower those tender melons. Let me see your hard nipples lining up with mine. Feel the electricity between us, like a spark between two terminals. Feel the burn in your arms and your stomach while you hold the position."

"I feel it," I panted, dripping from my soaking pussy onto her upper thighs. "Not only there. But I can't hold it much longer—"

"Lift yourself back up into the extended position," she said. "Just two more reps."

I looked at Kate and shook my head.

"I don't think I can do it. Not without collapsing onto you. And if that means ruining my chances with you later, I don't want to risk it."

"Alright," Kate said, peering up at me. "I'm going to give you a little break. Rest your knees on the floor while you do the last few reps. That will lower the load on your arms and make it easier for you to do the push-ups. Continue."

I lowered my knees to the mat beside Kate's hips and immediately felt half the weight release from my arms.

"That's better," I puffed.

"Good. You should be able to do *four* more reps now with the lower weight. Now bring those titties back down to Momma."

I lowered my body, concentrating on the narrowing distance between our breasts, but I hadn't calculated on the effect my kneeling position would have nearer our midsection. Just as I was inches away from touching Kate's nipples, my sopping pussy rubbed against Kate's mound.

"Oh *Gawd*," I moaned, as another surge of wetness seeped out of my pussy onto Kate's abdomen.

"Keep your body straight!" Kate ordered. "Lift your hips. No touching is allowed."

"I'm *trying* to keep my body straight," I protested, furrowing my brow. "It's just that our hips are closer together this way..."

"Fair enough," Kate nodded. "Next rep, lift your hips just high enough to keep from touching me down below too. That will help tighten up your stomach at the same time. Now—three more reps."

"At this rate, I'm not going to have any energy left for the fun part at the end," I panted, lifting myself back up.

"Don't worry," Kate said, smiling into my eyes. "We'll rotate the exercises so you don't exhaust any one part before you run out of steam. Now finish up. I've got something even more exciting lined up for you next."

I managed to eke out three more reps with my hips in an elevated position, then I rolled over and collapsed onto the mat, massaging my aching arm muscles.

"C'mon, girl," Kate said, extending a hand and pulling me back up onto my feet. "Let's give those arms a rest and begin to work on your lower body. I've got something very special in store for you with our next exercise."

She led me over to the corner where a long, padded bench rested in front of another panel of mirrors. She straddled the bench facing the mirror and demonstrated a deep squat, lowering herself up and down just far enough to not touch the bench with her ass and pussy.

"Your turn," she said, stepping away from the bench.

"That doesn't look like all that much fun," I said. "We already did this one in our first workout together."

"You'll see," Kate said, smiling at my coyly. "We're going to mix it up soon enough."

"No weight?" I said, touching my hand to my shoulders.

Kate shook her head.

"We're going for more reps this time. You'll feel the burn as intensely as before, if not more so. Just remember as with the pushups, to go down as far as you can without touching the pad."

"You're a cruel woman, Kate," I said, straddling the bench.

"Hopefully you won't think so by the time we finish. Now let's pump those legs."

As I began to lower myself over the bench, I watched myself in the mirror directly in front of me. Each time I lowered my pussy to within an inch of the bench, I could see my tingling clit poking out between my legs, begging to be caressed by the soft vinyl padding.

"Are you sure I can't touch the bench, even just lightly?" I pleaded. "I promise not to rest my weight. I just want a little stimulation down there. All this near-contact is killing me."

"Not yet," Kate said. "Do ten more reps, then we'll see if we can find a way to make it more stimulating for you."

I hammered out the ten reps faster than I'd ever done before. By the time I finished, another pool of clear liquid had pooled on the bench directly under my hips.

"You were right," I said, massaging the front of my thighs. "I feel that in my quads just as much as last time. But I don't know how many more of these I can do."

Kate looked at me with a sinister grin.

"Oh, I think you've got a few more left in you," she said. "You just need a little extra motivation."

She turned around and reached into a dresser drawer beside the bench and pulled out a long, fat, realistic dildo. It had a suction cup on the bottom, and Kate rubbed the cup against my juices on the bench, then pressed it firmly down against the fabric.

I looked up at her with wide eyes.

"You're not actually expecting me to do more of these without touching *that* thing also?"

"This time I'm going to allow you to touch it," she said. "In fact, *more* than just touch it. I want you to lower yourself fully down and fuck the dildo by pumping up and down on it. The only catch is you can't sit all the way down to rest your legs. I think you'll find the cock gives you plenty of motivation to do a few extra reps and get an extra long pump."

"Holy fuck," I said, shaking my head at Kate. "You really *have* been dreaming up all the ways you can torture me today, haven't you?"

"You said you wanted to take it to the next level. You must have known that by coming to my place, we were going to get a lot more interactive with our exercises than before."

"Yes," I said. "But I hoped it would be more interactive with *you*, not some fake plastic dick."

"We'll get there soon enough," Kate said. "This is just a warmup for the final act. Now get down on that cock and see if you can reach a new peak."

Looking at Kate's beautiful naked body standing before me in the mirror, I didn't need any further encouragement. At this point, I would have fucked just about any object she placed in front of me. I slowly lowered my ass over the bench until I hovered a mere inch over the tip of the erect cock, then I looked at Kate in the mirror and she nodded. I lowered myself another couple of inches and moaned as the thick dildo spread my pussy apart. I sat down a little lower, feeling the cock fill me up until my ass almost touched the bench.

"Do I have come all the way back up?" I asked, looking at Kate in the mirror.

"Only if you want to. But I think you'll enjoy it more if you do a bunch of mini-reps with the cock embedded inside you. Just remember not to rest your weight at any time on the bench."

As I began to fuck the dildo up and down with my pussy, I could feel my thighs beginning to burn. I was just about to stand back up to take the pressure off my legs when I saw Kate place her hand between her legs and begin to finger herself. That encouraged me to keep myself squatted over the dildo, and we began to moan together as we watched each other in the mirror. As we both watched the giant cock emerging and disappearing into my snatch, I began to feel my climax stirring inside me.

"Fuck, Kate," I said. "This feels good, but I don't know how much longer I can continue. My legs are burning so bad."

"Just a few more reps, Jade," she said. "I can see you're so close. I'm going to try to come with you. Fuck that cock with everything you've got."

Seeing Kate moaning as she watched me suddenly gave me a second wind, and I began humping the dildo harder and faster. Within a few moments, my orgasm poured over me.

"Yes, Kate!" I screamed. "I'm cumming!"

As Kate watched me gushing all over the cock and the bench from my powerful orgasm, she suddenly hunched over in a series of jerking spasms.

"Fuck, yes," she groaned. "That's so hot. Fuck that big cock, Jade."

Thankfully, my orgasm was over within a few seconds, and I quickly raised myself up over my quaking legs. Kate moved forward to hold me, and we melded into each other's arms as we came down from our highs.

"Thank you for letting me touch it this time," I panted in her ear. "I really needed that. It's a good thing you saved this one for last, because I'm really spend now. But I was really hoping to feel you—"

"We're not done yet," Kate said. "Lie down on the stretching mat and relax for a moment. I have one last little exercise that I think you might find a last boost the energy to perform."

As we lay down on the mat beside each other, Kate rolled onto her side and kissed me gently. I pushed my body toward her and pressed our breasts and hips together, thankful we finally had a moment to revel in each other's bodies.

"Whoa, girl," she said, pulling away a few inches. "You've got to *earn* the final reward, remember? Working out was never meant to be easy."

"What the fuck?" I said. "But I thought—"

"I'm going to let you touch me soon enough," she smiled. "I just want you to get a bit more of a workout while you do it."

I looked at Kate and shook my head.

"Are you *always* all work and no play? Can't I ever just have a little fun with you?"

"We can do that when I'm off the clock," she said. "You've still got ten more minutes left in your workout."

"I can't imagine what else you could possibly want me to do," I said, exhaling heavily. "Haven't I pretty much exhausted every muscle in my body?"

Kate lifted herself up on one elbow and ran her fingers through my hair.

"Remember when I said it's important to work your muscles in pairs? We're going to finish up by working the agonist muscle to your quads, which is your hamstrings. But this time, I promise we'll have more fun doing it."

"As long as I can *touch* you," I said, "I don't care what kind of position you put me in."

"Good. Then lie down on the mat and lift your right leg into a ninety-degree angle. I'm going to lie facing you and do the same while we hold hands. You might need to crunch your stomach a little to pull far enough down to reach me."

Kate shimmied her body on the mat toward me until the right sides of our asses were touching each other, then she hooked the back of her right thigh behind mine. She reached out her hands, and I pulled forward to clasp them. Then she gripped me tightly and began pushing her leg toward me.

"Try to resist my movement and push back against me," she said. "See if you can oppose my force with an equal force. This exercise not only helps to strengthen your hamstrings, but it makes for a great tummy workout too."

I grunted as I pushed my thigh back toward her while gripping her hands to maintain pressure. Kate resisted my force, then pushed my knee back all the way up onto my breast.

"I'm not as strong as you," I protested. "I can't push as hard as you can."

"Don't worry about that," she said, peering over her shoulder at my splayed pussy. "Just push as hard as you can, feeling the pressure in your hamstrings and glutes."

I peered up at Kate and saw her glancing at my exposed snatch.

"You *like* that, don't you?" I said, feeling my juices running down the crack of my ass. "This is just another excuse to look at my wet pussy again, isn't it?"

"Yes," she said. "Not to mention your pretty little rosebud. Now push. Try to resist me!"

I grunted as I pushed my leg back toward her, and we see-sawed back and forth until the moisture emanating from both of our slits made us slide closer together. Suddenly, our pussies were directly touching, and I could feel Kate's ass rubbing up against mine. I spread my legs further apart and pulled myself up a few inches to peer at her between my legs. As Kate did the same, our hips tilted down until our clits touched.

"Oh God, Kate," I moaned. "Fuck me with your pussy. I want to cum all over your beautiful ass."

"Uhnnn," Kate grunted. "Lift yourself up higher, Jade. I want to see your pretty tits while I fuck you."

I pulled harder on Kate's hands, lifting myself into an elevated crunch position, and began pumping myself harder against her vulva. Within a few minutes, I began to feel an equally intense burn in my abdominal muscles and my pussy.

"I feel the burn, Kate," I panted. "Come with me. I don't know how much longer I can last. I'm getting close."

"Yes, Jade," Kate said. "Just a few more reps. Pump my pussy with your wet cunt. I want to feel you cum all over me."

Her words soon pushed me over the top, and as we thrashed against each another's pussies, we screamed out loud, climaxing in blissful union. As I pulled myself forward to watch our cunts gnashing together, suddenly Kate squirted her juices through her tight slit, spraying her cum all over my tits and face.

"Fuckkkk, Jade!" she grunted, spraying her juices in a wide arc all over my torso. "You're an excellent trainee," she hissed. "We're going to have to make this a regular part of our routine."

"Yes, Kate," I panted. "You really know how to push me past my limits."

Ready for more erotic chills and thrills? Enjoy the next volume in Jade's Erotic Adventures:

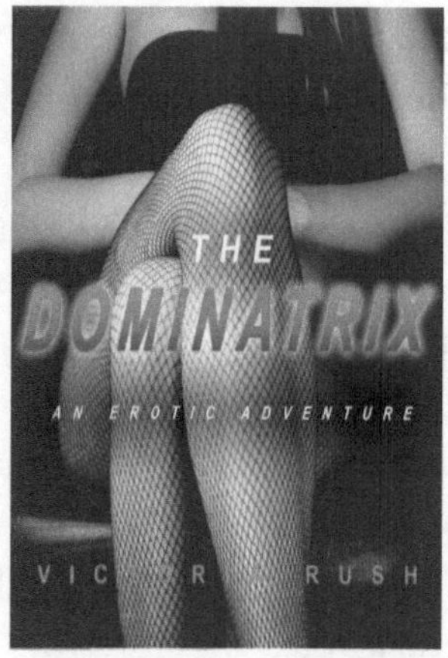

Every good relationship involves a certain degree of trust...

Sneak peek:

I did as I was told, lying back against the cold perforated leather. The harness looked like a small hammock, with large holes to permit maximum access to the recliner's skin. Velvet kneeled down and straddled my waist, and my pussy throbbed as I envisioned her rubbing herself against me. But instead, she reached over my head and grabbed the ropes splayed out on the floor beneath me, wrapping them tightly around my tits. She encircled each breast with the nylon cord, then ran a figure eight across the front of my chest and tied the two ends securely around the back of my neck...

READ MORE..

VOLUME TWO

THE HAREM

1

As I walked through the open-air market in Marrakesh, I could feel my heart pounding in my chest. I'd never been to Morocco before, and the hustle and bustle of the *Souk Semmarine* was a feast for the senses. With so many tourists and locals crammed into the narrow laneways, my eyes darted from one distraction to another. While I strolled past their stalls, shopkeepers noisily hawked their wares, begging me to make an offer on everything from cheap jewelry to handbags. The pungent aroma of grilled kebabs, fresh hummus, and fried snails permeated my nose. Everywhere I looked, women in long, full-body burkas or face-concealing niqabs passed calmly by, seemingly unperturbed by the chaos of the teeming bazaar. With my long blonde hair and tight jeans, I definitely stood out like a sore thumb in this conservative muslim metropolis.

After a half hour or so, I grew tired of the peddlers confronting me, and I ducked into one of the shops to try on some head scarves, hoping to distract attention from my obvious Western appearance. When I tried a pretty pink and teal colored one on and looked at myself in the tiny mirror on the wall, the owner came up behind me, smiling at my reflection.

"Very pretty," he said. "You like?"

"Maybe," I said, mindful of the hard-sell personality of local merchants that I'd been forewarned about. "How much is it?"

"For you, pretty lady, only five hundred dirham!"

Knowing the local exchange rate was roughly ten dirham for one U.S. dollar, fifty bucks for a scarf didn't seem out of line. But I also knew that shop owners in North African bazaars were notorious for fleecing unaware tourists and that haggling was an expected and necessary condition of purchase.

"That's more than I can afford," I said, placing the garment back on the rack.

"Perhaps we can make an accommodation," he said, lifting the scarf off the shelf and placing it back on my head. "Since the colors match your eyes so perfectly."

"Um-hmm," I smiled, knowing full well he was just buttering me up for a sale.

"How about two-fifty?" I said, placing my hands on my hips defiantly.

"Ps-shaw!" the merchant scoffed. "That is well below my cost. This is an authentic Moroccan hijab. Other merchants sell this style for much more."

"Well, I guess I'll just have to go check *them* out then," I said, placing the scarf in his hands and turning to exit the stall.

"Ok, ok!" he backpedaled, catching up with me and blocking my exit. "New price, only for you. Four-fifty. But that's as low as I can go."

"That's not much of a discount," I huffed. "Other vendors have offered far better. Three hundred is the best I can do."

The man threw up his hands, wrinkling his brow with a sad puppy dog face.

"My lady, I wish I could help you, but I'm just a poor merchant with high overhead. Don't you expect me to make a profit?"

"Of course," I said. "But I know most of these items have a high markup. I think you've still got plenty of profit to work with here. Perhaps I'll come back after comparing prices with some of the other sellers."

"Wait, wait," the man said, stepping in front of me again. "I can't have you leave without purchasing something. Four hundred is my best offer. But at that price, you're practically *stealing* it from me."

I picked up the scarf again, turning it over to look for some kind of label.

"How do I know this is even made here? There's no tag."

"Oh please," the man said, crossing his arms. "Now you *insult* me. We only sell authentic textiles manufactured in this country. Look at the intricate stitching. This is hand-embroidered right here in Morocco."

"And the fabric?" I said, rolling the cloth between my fingers. "Is it genuine silk?"

The man placed the garment under an overhead ceiling light, slowly tilting it from side to side.

"Can't you see how the patina changes color when you bend the fabric? I would never sell cheap polyester at my store. This is where all the local muslim women come to purchase authentic Arab clothing."

"Okay," I said, shaking my head in surrender. "I'll offer a little more since I can tell it's a quality product. "I will pay three hundred and fifty dirham, cash. That is all I have on my person."

The merchant paused for a moment, scanning my face with a stern expression as if trying to divine my thoughts. Then he burst into a broad smile, nodding enthusiastically.

"Only for you, my pretty American," he said. "And only because I don't want to see you walking around the bazaar in a cheap knock-off sold by the other vendors."

"Good," I said, turning back toward the mirror. "Do you mind showing me the proper way to wear it? The way the local women do?"

"Of course," he said, draping the scarf over the top of my head and pulling the ends softly under my chin, tying them in a gentle knot. "The idea is to cover your hair and tie it so it covers as much of your face as possible. Our culture requires women to express their modesty by covering their bodies when they are out in public."

"Thank you," I said, pulling some bills out of my pocket and handing him the agreed-upon amount.

"Please, come again," the man said, bowing with his palms centered over his chest. "I have many more items of clothing that you would look beautiful in."

"I'll try to come back before I leave your beautiful country," I nodded. "Thank you for your time."

"Safe travels," he said, waving goodbye to me as I exited the stall.

While I continued down the main thoroughfare jostled by distracted tourists, aggressive shopkeepers, and beguiling snake charmers, I realized the thin head covering provided limited camouflage from my fair skin and Western clothing. By the time I exited the packed marketplace, I was visibly sweating and exhausted. I found a nearby cafe and ordered a strong coffee, then found a vacant table in the corner and sat down, nursing my drink.

Most of the patrons appeared to be Westerners, but on the far side of the room sat a lone man in long white robes wearing a traditional headdress, sipping a beverage. I'd always been fascinated by the clothing and customs of native Arabs, and as he appraised the boisterous tourists gathering in the cafe, he peered at them bemused. The man had dark, weathered skin and a closely cropped beard with soft brown eyes and a square jawline. Appearing to be in his late thirties or early forties, he was quite handsome, with the juxtaposition of his flowing cream-colored kaftan and his golden-brown skin making him look like a young Omar Sharif.

As he casually glanced around the cafe, he caught me staring at him, and I quickly looked away. Moments later, my gaze was drawn back to him and this time he smiled when our eyes met. When I looked away again, he stood up from his table and went to the front counter where he placed an order for something. A few minutes later, the clerk handed him two steaming cups and the man began walking in my direction.

"Excuse me," he said, approaching my table. "I noticed you were sitting alone and wondered if you'd like some company. I brought you a cup of mint tea if you'd like to sample some of our local fare."

"Um..." I hesitated, looking around the room to make sure it was safe to be seen in the company of a stranger.

Normally, I'd quickly rebuff someone who made such a bold and unsolicited advance, but there was something about his quiet demeanor and warm eyes that put me at ease.

"Thank you," I said, shifting my chair back a few inches. "That would be lovely."

"My name's Amir," he said, handing me the cup of steaming tea.

"Jade," I said, nodding politely toward him.

"That's a lovely name. It sounds Asian or Moorish, but you look much *fairer* than that."

"Yes," I laughed. "I suppose my light skin gives me away. I'm from Chicago actually, in the United States."

"I know it well," he nodded. "The Sears Tower, Navy Pier, Millennium Park..."

"You've *been* to the United States?" I said, surprised by his fluent English and knowledge of my local landmarks.

"I spent four years studying law at Columbia University and traveled throughout the country during my summers off."

"I *wondered* where your perfect English came from," I said, smiling at his handsome face. "I never would have guessed–"

"That a sheep-herder like me might be so worldly?" he joked.

"No," I stammered. "I meant–"

"It's okay," he laughed. "It's a common reaction I get from Westerners. They either expect me to be some kind of sultan or a terrorist wearing these clothes."

"I'd never judge a person simply on the basis of what they're wearing," I said, furrowing my brow in sympathy.

"That's very wise," he said, peering up at my scarf. "What about you? You seem to be a little more...*restrained* compared to your fellow countrymen."

I lifted my hand self-consciously to my scarf and chuckled.

"I felt a little exposed walking around the markets with my long blonde hair. I think I was too easy a mark for your local merchants."

The man took a sip of his tea and chuckled.

"They can be a little overbearing at times when it comes to

approaching tourists. There's something to be said for exercising a little decorum and good manners."

"I couldn't agree more," I said, lifting my cup in agreement.

"So, what brings you so far from home?"

"Just looking for a change of pace, I guess. I've never been to this part of the world and I wanted to experience the unique culture of North Africa."

"Where have you been so far?"

"Just the medina and a few of the museums. But I'd love to see more of the countryside."

"You mean the *desert*? There's really only two climate zones in the Mediterranean crescent–the fertile orchards near the sea and the barren plains of the Sahara."

"I guess I'm more drawn to the desert. Maybe it's from watching all those romantic films like Lawrence of Arabia and The Wind and the Lion. There's something about the natural beauty of the red sand and the windswept dunes that seems so peaceful and alluring. It seems to be about as far away from the hustle and bustle of the urban jungle as you could possibly get."

"Have you ever ridden a camel?"

"It's on my bucket list."

"Would you like to join my caravan for a little excursion?"

"Caravan?" I said, widening my eyes. "You're traveling in a *caravan*?"

"Yes," he nodded. "It's a modest group. A few camels, some livestock, and my small coterie."

"Is that how you get around?" I asked, suddenly intrigued by this mysterious stranger. "Where are you from originally?"

"I was born in Jordan, but I come from a Bedouin family. We're nomads, moving from country to country, buying and selling livestock and living off the land."

"So you really are a–"

"Goat herder?" he laughed. "In a manner of speaking. But as the leader of my tribe, I'm officially considered a *sheikh*."

"But what about Columbia...?"

"My wealthy parents sent me there hoping for bigger things for me. But I prefer this simple life. There's something to be said for the freedom and stress-free life of a traveling vagabond. I get to meet interesting people in all the countries along the North African peninsula."

"Just like Sean Connery in the movie The Wind and the Lion," I smiled.

"I suppose, insofar as being the king of my domain and living a nomadic lifestyle. So what do you say? Do you feel as brave as Candice Bergen?"

"As I recall, she didn't exactly go *willingly* into the Sahara wilderness with her would-be captor. And I don't have any romantic intentions..."

"No worries," the man said. "You can stay as long or as short as you prefer, or even just for a day trip through the edge of the desert on one of my camels. I assure you that I have plenty of *other* distractions at my disposal."

I pinched my eyebrows, appraising the mysterious man in luxurious robes. I had no doubt that he had little trouble attracting beautiful women wherever he traveled.

"How would this work exactly?" I said, crossing my arms. "I've never run off with a strange man into the desert before."

"I understand your hesitation," he said. "My camp is just outside the city limits. You can join my troupe for an authentic Bedouin dinner while you stay with my other wives in a separate tent. If you feel so-inclined, you're free to join us on the next leg of our journey toward Algiers. I'll be happy to pay for your safe passage back to Morocco if that's where you've made return travel arrangements."

I paused for a moment, scanning his face for any sign of ill intent. I'd heard about the legal practice of polygamy in certain Arab countries, and far from turning me off, the idea of being surrounded by other women who could satisfy his sexual needs gave me a certain degree of comfort.

"That won't be necessary," I said. "It shouldn't be too difficult to change my airfare if necessary. But how can I be sure you don't intend to steal me away like Sean Connery and add me to your stable of harem girls?"

"That's not the way we operate," he laughed. "As you probably learned from watching that movie. Honor is the most important character trait among we Bedouin. But of course, I would encourage you to leave a message with your friends and family before you leave."

The man took a menu scrap from the table and scribbled something on the paper.

"This is my full name. I'm well known in most towns along the coast. The last thing I need is the American cavalry hunting me down like in the movie. I assure you, this is an honorable offer between friends. You have my word on that."

"Can you give me a day to think it over?" I asked, still not convinced this was a good idea. But the lure of joining a real caravan through the Sahara Desert was awfully tempting.

"Absolutely," Amir said. "If you decide to join me, let's meet in this cafe at the same time tomorrow. If you're not here, I'll understand and there will be no hard feelings. But if you do decide to come, we can take a taxi to the outskirts of the city where my aide will meet us and escort us by camel to my camp at the edge of the desert."

"How will I keep from falling off?" I smiled.

"It's not as scary as it looks to ride a camel," he said. "There are comfortable and secure saddles, and they walk quite slowly. But if you're still worried, you can always ride tandem with me."

"I'm sure I'll be fine," I smiled, turning my wrist to check the time. "Thank you for your kind offer, Amir. I look forward to meeting you again tomorrow at five p.m. And thank you for the tea."

As I rose to leave, he stood along with me, extending his hand.

"I hope to see you again, lovely Jade," he said, clasping my hand softly. "And keep an eye out for those carnival barkers. Best to keep your hijab on while you're walking about town."

"Will do," I said, heading toward the exit door.

After I left the cafe, I closed my eyes, inhaling the warm arid air of the Moroccan town square. Something told me that my North African adventure was about to take an interesting new turn.

2

———————

For the next twenty-four hours, I vacillated back and forth on whether to entertain the handsome sheikh's offer. On the one hand, I'd always dreamed about trekking through the Sahara Desert on a camel. But I knew that traveling into the wilderness with a total stranger was not without its risks. He could easily abduct or molest me, with no guarantee that the local police would make any effort to find me or hold him to account. I knew that muslim law was highly skewed in favor of the man's rights and that women were often ostracized or worse for any kind of perceived sexual indiscretion.

The following morning after enjoying a light breakfast, I approached the front desk of my riad to enquire about the mysterious man. If he was as important and well-traveled as he claimed to be, I figured the staff of one of the best hotels in Marrakesh would have heard of him. But if he was an unknown or persona non grata, I'd simply ignore his invitation and remain in the relative safety of the downtown tourist areas.

"Excuse me," I said, slipping Amir's handwritten note across the counter towards the attending clerk. "Can you tell me if you've heard of this man?"

The clerk squinted at the writing then looked up at me and smiled.

"Of course," he said. "Mr. Haddad is one of our frequent guests. Would you like me to see if he's staying at the hotel?"

"Um, no, thank you," I said. "It's just that he invited me to take a tour with his caravan and I wondered if this was, you know–*safe* or irregular."

"I can't vouch for how often he entertains Westerners in his cavalcade, but he is often seen in the company of attractive young women such as yourself, and I've never heard of any complaints or misconduct. The Sheikh is widely respected as a man of honor and prestige in these parts. I'm quite sure that you would not only be safe, but indeed well-protected while under his guardianship."

"Thank you," I said, placing the note back in my pocket.

As the hour approached for our planned reconnection, I packed a light duffel bag of overnight clothes and sent an email to my best friend Hannah from back home.

> *Han,*
>
> *Enjoying my trip to Morocco so far. Will send more pics soon. I've accepted an invitation to go on a private caravan tour of the local desert with a prominent bedouin leader. His name is Amir Haddad. Apparently his family is quite prominent in Jordan.*
>
> *If you don't hear back from me in a few days, contact the local embassy to see if they can track my whereabouts. I know this sounds crazy, but I've always dreamed of traveling the Sahara on camelback, and you only live once!*
>
> *Talk soon,*
>
> *Jade*

I knotted my silk scarf under my chin, then placed a wide-brimmed straw hat on my head and headed back towards the cafe where I'd met the sheikh the previous day. With my heart beating a million miles an hour, I strolled past the bustling souks wondering what I'd gotten myself into.

When I entered the cafe and saw Amir sitting in the corner with his legs crossed sipping a cup of tea, he smiled and stood as I approached his table.

"I'm glad you decided to join me again, Jade," he said, holding out his hand as he supported me while I lowered myself onto the adjoining chair. "I was afraid that I might have scared you away with my rather direct proposition."

"I went back and forth considering it, to be honest," I said. "But I asked around, and you were truthful about your reputation. Apparently, I'm not the *first* tourist you've entertained in this manner. But I left your credentials with the U.S. Embassy just in case."

"I would expect no less from such a wise and pretty lady," he smiled. "May I order you a cup of tea?"

I looked at my watch and glanced outside at the lengthening afternoon shadows.

"I'm already pretty charged up about this adventure," I said, concerned about traveling at night deep into the outback. "Shouldn't we head out to your camp while there's still good light?"

"As you wish," he said, standing up and extending his hand as he surveyed my wardrobe. "I see you've come well prepared for the elements. Though I'm not sure about that hat. You look more like *Audrey Hepburn* in Breakfast at Tiffany's than Candice Bergen in The Wind and the Lion."

I smiled at his genteel manners while he opened the cafe exit door for me then hailed a passing taxi. After we got in the cab and he gave the driver directions in arabic, he glanced down at my overnight bag.

"It looks like you're intending to stay for a while," he smiled. "I must not have scared you *too* much with my abrupt proposition."

"I've heard it's a pretty big desert," I said, pulling my handbag closer toward me. Unbeknownst to my host, I'd included a can of pepper spray under my belongings in case he got the wrong idea. "A girl can never be too prepared on these kinds of expeditions."

"Indeed it is," he smiled. "Did you know that the entirety of the Sahara Desert is even bigger than the continental United States? But never fear–my caravan has enough provisions to keep us comfortable for as long as you choose to stay."

As the taxi sped towards the outskirts of the city, I watched the passing scenery as it became progressively less populated and more barren. Within twenty minutes, the dusty streets soon gave way to grassy hillsides. When we crested the final ridge and I saw the open expanse of the desert stretching out in every direction, I gasped. The late afternoon sun cast long shadows over the undulating red sand dunes, making it look like a different *planet*.

"Is this your first time seeing the desert?" Amir asked, noticing my wide eyes surveying the eerie landscape.

"First time up close and for *real*," I nodded in a daze. "It's even more magnificent than I imagined."

"It has a way of transporting you," he nodded. "There's something about the open vistas and the way the sun reflects over the shifting sands that's quite captivating. Perhaps now you can begin to appreciate how I'm are attracted by its allure."

"It *is* mesmerizing, I grant you," I said. "But how do you navigate your way across this moonscape? There are no roads or landmarks to know which way you're headed?"

"We navigate by the shadows of the sun during the day and the stars in the evening. Plus, the desert isn't all sand. There are bluffs and oases and mountain ridges that point our way. We bedouin have traveled the deserts of North Africa for thousands of years. We know it as well as the back of our hands, as you Americans say."

"I'll have to take your word for it," I said, suddenly feeling the dryness in my mouth. "But something tells me I should have packed more bottles of water in my overnight case. How far away is your camp?"

"It's only twenty or thirty minutes by camel ride," Amir said as the taxi skidded to a stop at the end of the road. Nestled in a shaded dale of the hillside, I noticed a dark-skinned Arab man in a long tunic tending to three camels. "My aide brought an extra ride for you. Don't worry about the water. We've long-since learned how to manage our scarce resources in the parched desert."

Amir paid the taxi driver then escorted me to the dale where he introduced me to his servant.

"This is Ali," Amir said, motioning toward the other man. "He'll look after all of your needs during your stay with us."

The man bowed slightly at the waist, acknowledging me as Amir's guest. I found it a bit strange that Amir didn't introduce me by name, but I assumed it had something to do with the customs of his tribe and his status as leader of the clan.

I glanced at the three oddly shaped animals nibbling on grass besides us. With their long knobby legs, U-shaped neck, and large hump in the middle of their back, they looked like a cross between a llama and an oversized donkey. Towering at least two feet over the top of my head, I was already starting to get vertigo imagining myself trying to balance on top of their precarious mounds.

"These are a lot *taller* than I imagined," I said, noticing an absence of stirrups hanging from their woven cloth saddles. "How will I ever get on top of it?"

"You don't climb up on a camel like you would a horse," Amir said. "They kneel down for you to get on top of them."

He mentioned something to his aide in arabic and Ali pulled on the long hair on the side of one of the camels, then the animal knelt down on the ground with its front knees and lowered its back end until its belly was lying flat on the ground.

"Wow," I said. "That's certainly convenient. Have you trained them this way only for your guests, or is this the way *everybody* mounts a camel?"

"They're very domesticated," Amir said. "It's easy enough to climb atop a standing camel if you know how, but this certainly makes it a lot easier."

"I'll say," I nodded, seeing the top of the cloth saddle now resting at hip height.

"But you still need to be careful to hold on to the pommel at the front of the camel's saddle to make sure you don't get bucked off when it stands. It jerks forward and back as it rises, and if you're not used to it, you can easily be thrown."

Amir said something to Ali and he held out his hand, motioning for me to climb atop the saddle of the resting camel, and I swung my leg up over his hump and sat down on the surprisingly comfortable seat. Although the frame appeared to be made entirely of wood, I noticed a padding of straw and palm leaves under the thick woven blankets draped over its flanks.

"Okay," Amir said. "Now grasp the knob on the front of the saddle tightly and clamp your legs against the side of the camel as he rises."

I did as Amir instructed, then Ali tapped the side of the animal and it lurched forward lifting its back end, then it stepped forward with both front legs until it was fully erect. My body swung wildly as it see-sawed up to a standing position, and I could feel my heart beating as I stared down at the ground ten feet below me.

"Are you good?" Amir called up to me, seeing the fright in my eyes.

"Yes, as long as I don't fall off," I grunted. "But how do I *steer* this thing?"

"Don't worry about that," he laughed. "Ali will lead your camel with a tether behind his animal. But watch out as he begins to walk. They have a bit of a jerky gait. Try to relax your body and let it sway with the animal's movements. Are you ready to head out to our camp?"

I nodded my head then Amir and Ali mounted their camels, heading out in a straight line toward the open desert with Amir in the lead. It didn't take long for me to get used to my camel's rhythmic up-and-down gait, and as I began to relax, I looked out over the vast expanse of russet-colored dunes at the exquisite beauty of the desert. Looking like a giant Rothko painting, all I could see was an endless sea of golden waves juxtaposed against the brilliant blue sky.

The air was hot and dry, and I blinked as sprinkles of sand dusted up into my eyes from the strong wind sweeping across the dunes. More than once I had to grab my hat from falling off my head from the gusts shooting overtop the crescent-shaped hillocks. As I watched the long shadows of our three camels traipse across the soft turf, I smiled at the serene beauty and solitude of the glittering landscape. I wasn't sure what awaited me at Amir's camp, but for the time being, the gentle loping of my camel and the whisper of the warm Saharan breeze lulled me into a blissful, trancelike state.

3

———————

Thirty minutes later, I noticed a clump of trees on the horizon, and I squinted through the shimmering haze wondering if it was a mirage. But as we got closer, I saw a small collection of tents nestled among the palms and a flock of livestock grazing on the grass surrounding the perimeter of the encampment. Hardly believing my eyes, I called ahead to Amir, wondering how anything could grow in this barren wasteland.

"Is this your camp?" I shouted over the howling wind.

"Yes," he said, pulling his camel up beside mine so I could hear him better.

"I thought my eyes were playing tricks on me at first," I said, shaking my head in astonishment. "How does any vegetation survive out here without any water?"

"The desert is riddled with a labyrinth of underground aquifers," he said. "In certain places, natural springs bring the water to the surface, feeding the surrounding vegetation. At other oases, manmade wells tap the aquifers, supplying much needed water to traveling caravans such as my own."

"I thought oases were just a figment of Western movies. I had no idea they actually existed in the middle of the desert."

"There are actually quite a few scattered across the Sahara," he nodded. "But because of the vast size of the desert, it can take many days on camel to travel between them. They've been the lifeblood of we bedouin for centuries."

As we got closer to the camp, I noticed a large herd of camels and scores of sheep and goats grazing quietly in the grass.

"And there's enough water to feed all those *animals* too?"

"Yes," Amir said. "The aquifers are practically endless. There's a veritable ocean of water underneath this arid surface. Did you know that the Sahara was once an enormous sea before the Earth's shifting plates separated the large continents of Eurasia and Africa?"

"I had no idea," I said, growing increasingly impressed with Amir's knowledge of world history and geology. "But why do you have so many camels and livestock? You must have quite a large entourage."

"Actually, it's mostly just me and Ali and my stable of wives. The animals are primarily used to transport our gear and provide food for our band."

"Wow, you really *are* a self-contained entity out here in the middle of the wilderness, aren't you?"

"Everything we need is supplied by the animals and the desert," he nodded.

"And your *wives*," I smiled, peering ahead toward Ali plodding along in front of us, wondering how he satisfied some of *his* more primal needs.

"Yes," Amir smiled. "And my wives."

When we reached the edge of the trees, I noticed a group of women kneeling in the sand preparing food. They all wore loose-fitting tunics and cotton headdresses that wrapped tightly around their heads and faces, providing protection from the overhead sun and the dusty wind. As our retinue approached the center of the camp, the women looked up and stared at me like I was from another planet. They all seemed young and strikingly beautiful.

Maybe Amir doesn't need to entertain Western women after all, I thought.

The two men dismounted their camels, then Amir tapped my

animal and he knelt onto the ground, where Amir offered his hand to help me dismount. Then he led me into one of the two large tents in the campground where an attractive dark-haired woman roughly my age was folding clothes in the corner of the enclosure.

"This is my wife, Laila," he said, introducing me to the woman. "Laila, Jade will be joining us for dinner this evening, so please make sure she has everything she needs."

She turned around and smiled at me with her piercing eyes. I was surprised how beautiful she looked bereft of any makeup or other embellishments. Her wraparound headdress framed her pretty face, highlighting her high cheekbones and golden-brown skin.

"Pleased to meet you," Laila said, bowing slightly at the waist.

It was hard to discern her figure under her layered cloak, but my pussy fluttered when I saw her face flush slightly in modesty.

"You speak *English*?" I said, surprised by her absence of any discernible accent.

"Yes," she said. "My family is from Cairo and we learned English in elementary school. I'm a bit rusty, so it will be nice to have a native speaker to help me brush up on my skills."

"We'll be having dinner when the sun goes down," Amir interrupted. "Then I'll be providing some special entertainment in my tent later on. You may wish to put on some warmer clothes, as it can get quite chilly outside after dark. I'll see you in another hour or so."

After Amir exited the tent, I peered at Laila with a quizzical look. "*Entertainment?*"

"Never fear," she chuckled. "He often entertains visitors with a traditional arab dance. Though it's usually for the benefit of other men. This is the first time he's brought a Western *woman* into his camp."

"I guess I should be honored then," I shrugged, wondering exactly what kind of dance he had in mind.

Laila peered at my cut-off capri pants and light linen blouse and smiled.

"Would you like to change into something more comfortable? As

Amir said, it gets quite cold at night and you'll want a bit more protection against the blowing wind."

"Sure," I said, happy to adopt the local customs during my brief visit with the group.

"If you'd like to remove your clothing, I can store them in a safe location while you stay with us."

"*Everything*?" I said, wondering what arab men and women wore underneath their long garments.

"It's more comfortable that way," she said. "Unless you need to wear something because it's that time of the month...?"

"No, thankfully," I chuckled, curious how they also managed *that* aspect of their personal hygiene.

As I began to remove my clothing, Laila peered at me, noticing the strange tan lines around my bra and upper arms. I paused for a moment before pulling off my panties, and her eyes widened when she saw my shaved pubis. I felt like a bit of a freak, realizing that she and the rest of the women rarely went outside with any exposed skin and almost certainly abstained from any kind of intimate grooming.

Laila fetched a neatly folded garment from the corner of the tent then opened it up to reveal an ankle-length tunic with long sleeves and an opening at the top. I held up my arms and she draped it over my body, stepping in close to me as she peered into my eyes. She smelled of jasmine and lemongrass, and my heart fluttered as her full lips neared my mouth when the garment fell over my shoulders. Then she wrapped a long cotton scarf over my head and under my chin, fastening it with a bobby pin at the ends to hold it in place.

I guess they're not completely bereft of Western conveniences, I smiled.

When she finished, she stepped back and nodded approvingly, smiling at the unusual appearance of a Western woman dressed in traditional arabian garb.

"Do you have a mirror or something to view myself in?" I asked, intrigued to see what I looked like.

"I'm afraid we don't," she said. "It is not part of our culture for women to primp over their external appearance. But I assure you that you look quite beautiful."

"Thank you," I said, reaching into my bag to retrieve my phone. I tapped the screen a few times then handed the device to Laila. "I know this must sound terribly touristy of me, but would you mind taking a picture of me? My friends back home will never believe that I got myself into this arrangement, and I'd love to have a keepsake of my visit to your camp."

"Okay," Laila said, squinting her eyes at the phone. "But this is a little different from the phones I remember using in my youth. How does it work?"

"Just step back and angle the phone until you see my entire body on the screen, then tap the red button at the bottom to capture the image."

Laila did as I requested and I heard the familiar shutter sound when the phone took the picture. She handed it back to me and I tapped the thumbnail image in the lower corner of the screen to view the full-size image. I laughed when I saw myself encased in the flowing robes, with only my pale face peering through the wrap-around fabric.

"That's certainly a different look for me," I said, feeling the soft fabric brushing against my hardening nipples and bare mound. "But I have to admit, it's a lot more comfortable than my usual attire. Is it comfortable to wear in the heat of the day?"

Laila pulled the fabric up over my shoulders and I felt a puff of air press up from the floor toward my exposed pussy.

"The cotton fabric breathes nicely, and the loose fit permits the wind to flow over our bare bodies underneath," Laila smiled.

"Yes, I can see that," I said. "I'm *already* beginning to appreciate the extra freedom of movement in this dress. Although I don't imagine you call it that in your native language."

"We women refer to it as a *thawb*, but when men wear similar robes, they call it a kaftan."

I nodded, beginning to understand the various ways arab culture subjugated women under the control of men. I crossed my arms, beginning to feel the chill as the sun began to set over the horizon.

"Do you think this will this be warm enough in the evening?"

Laila pulled a wool blanket off the pile of clothes in the corner and placed it over my shoulders.

"This shawl will help keep you warm," she smiled. "And it can also be used as a bed covering later on at night."

"Speaking of," I said. "I see you don't have any traditional beds in the tent..."

"We bedouin can't afford such luxuries," Laila laughed. "Everything has to be light enough to pack onto the backs of our camels when we move from one location to the next. We sleep on woven blankets on the soft sand. I think you'll find it's quite comfortable, actually."

"Does everyone sleep in this one tent?" I said, peering at the limited amount of floor space in the twenty-by-twenty-foot enclosure.

"All of the *women*, yes," Laila nodded. "The men have separate tents, of course. Everything is tightly controlled in our caravan. Nothing goes to waste."

"So I'm beginning to learn," I smiled, imagining myself lying on the soft desert sand next to the covey of beautiful women at night.

"Are you hungry?" she asked.

The mention of food made my stomach grumble. I suddenly realized that I hadn't eaten since early in the morning.

"Oh yes, very."

"Come, let's show you how we prepare our traditional bedouin meals."

Laila led me outside, where a large open fire cackled in a sand pit with a wooden frame erected overtop of its perimeter. The women sat in a large circle around the flame, hunched over in their long robes, kneading their hands into large porcelain bowls.

"It smells heavenly," I said, breathing in the fresh scent of milk and spices. "May I ask what the women are preparing?"

"It's a rice dish infused with fresh goat milk, lentils, and chopped onions, seasoned with saffron and turmeric."

"So you're all *vegetarians*?"

"Oh no," Laila said. "We also eat goat meat and lamb. But that's usually reserved for special occasions, like when we have a guest such as yourself."

"I see," I said, noticing Amir flipping open the canvas door of his tent and walking in our direction.

"I see that Laila has gotten you into some more comfortable clothes," he nodded approvingly. "Are you ready to enjoy our traditional bedouin dinner?"

"Absolutely," I said. "I don't know if it's this desert heat or the long camel ride, but I'm famished!"

"Well, we won't delay any longer then," he said, brandishing a curved knife from under his kaftan. He walked up to one of the younger sheep grazing quietly at the edge of the pasture and he grabbed the animal by the back of its head, calmly slicing its throat. The lamb staggered for a moment in shock, then fell to the ground twitching its legs for a few seconds, then lay still as the blood from its neck coated the desert sand. Seconds later, Ali approached the dead animal, and using a longer knife proceeded to slice open its belly, pulling out its entrails.

"Oh my God," I dry-heaved, turning away from the scene of the gory slaughter.

"You've never seen a live animal killed before?" Amir said, seeing my discomfort.

"Never up close and in person like this," I coughed, trying to keep myself from retching.

"But you eat meat?"

"Yes, it's just that–"

"You Westerners are insulated by your supermarkets and hidden slaughterhouses from the act of killing and preparing the animal."

"Yes," I said, realizing how hypocritical it was of me to be offended by the practice of killing live animals for consumption.

"A halal slaughter is considered the most humane way of killing an animal in our culture," he said. "The animal hardly feels a thing before it loses consciousness and quickly bleeds out."

"I'll take your word for it," I said, watching Ali skin the animal and thread a stake through its mouth as he placed it over the fire pit.

"I hope this won't diminish your appetite for the meal. Everything should be ready in another half hour or so."

"I'm sure I'll be fine," I said, smelling the scent of the fresh meat cooking over the pit. "I just need a moment to collect myself."

"Come join me then by the fire while the women make the final preparations."

Amir motioned to a blanket spread out on the sand about ten feet away from the fire, and he held my hand while I sat down on the mat.

"So, what do you think of our little caravan so far?" he said, sitting down cross-legged beside me.

"It's certainly *authentic*," I said, peering at the group of young women preparing the dishes in the circle around the fire. "But I'm wondering about the ratio of men to women in your troupe. Are all of these women your wives?"

"Not in the *legal* sense," he said. "I prefer to think of them as my courtesans."

"They're all so young and pretty. How did they come to join your caravan?"

"I bought them," Amir said nonchalantly.

"You *what*?"

"I know this is a custom frowned upon in the West. But it is quite common in conservative muslim cultures, especially among we bedouin. Families consider it an honor for their daughters to be indentured to a prominent sheikh such as myself."

"And when they get *older*? Do you simply dispose of them when they no longer suit your fancy?"

"They're sold off to other prominent men as maids, nannies, and cooks. The women are always treated well, generally enjoying lives far more comfortable and secure than in their own impoverished families."

"And in the meantime, they travel in your caravan for your own amusement?"

"Well, as you can see, they perform many *other* useful functions. Nobody goes for want in my troupe. Everyone's needs are fully satisfied."

"What about *Ali's* needs?" I said, noticing his servant dutifully turning the roast lamb on the fire spit. "Does he also enjoy the company of these attractive ladies?"

"He would never dare *touch* one of my women for fear of instant execution," Amir said, suddenly clenching his jaw. "But he's well compensated for his service to the caravan. He satisfies his more primal needs in the many small towns along our route."

"I see," I said, watching him remove the charred carcass from the spit then carving it up into smaller chunks and passing them around the circle. Each of the women took a piece and sliced it up into bite-sized portions, mixing them in with their bowls of rice.

"Come," Amir said, taking two bowls and placing them in front of us. "Let's not be concerned about such indelicate matters over dinner. Let's enjoy our feast under the stars of this magnificent canopy."

He picked up his bowl and dipped his hand into the dish, pinching skewers of meat and rice between his fingers and bringing it to his mouth. Looking around the circle, I saw the rest of the entourage doing the same, and I picked up my bowl not wanting to be rude, following their lead. The food was surprisingly moist and tender, with the milk-infused rice keeping all the ingredients bound together, making it easier to take bite-sized chunks in my fingers. I hummed appreciatively at the piquant taste of the freshly prepared ingredients, soon forgetting about the unsettling scene that I'd witnessed with the young lamb moments before.

As we all ate quietly around the circle, my eyes scanned the faces of the pretty young women peering at me curiously across the dancing flames of the bonfire. It didn't take long for my mind to wander to what *other* forms of entertainment they used to keep themselves amused when Amir was otherwise occupied. Surely, he couldn't keep *all* of them satisfied at one time, I thought. As my pussy twitched from the cool desert breeze wafting up under my fluttering robe, I began to look forward to sleeping on the soft desert sand later in the evening.

4

A fter dinner, Amir invited Laila and me to his tent to enjoy the planned entertainment. He motioned for two of the girls to prepare for the event, and they left the circle while the rest of the women cleaned up the dishes. When I entered his enclosure, I was surprised at how large it was for one person. More than twice the size of the women's shelter, it was bedecked with persian rugs, beautiful tapestries, and a large wood-frame bed with luxury linens.

Wow, I thought, shaking my head in dismay. *Arab men really do enjoy all the advantages in this culture.*

Amir invited the two of us to sit on the plush carpet in the center of the tent, then he fetched a heart-shaped guitar from the corner and sat down between us with the instrument cradled between his legs. A few moments later, I heard two women's voices outside the front door of his tent and Amir replied to them in arabic. When they pulled back the flap and entered the room, my eyes flew open in shock. Instead of their usual long robes and wraparound headdresses, they wore a skimpy ornamental bikini costume.

Their long black hair was held in place by a beaded headband with long tassels hanging down over their eyes, festooned with little silver bells. Dangling from their tasseled bikini bottom hung a knee-length black cloth that provided a modicum of modesty to cover their crotch area. But the rest of the costume left little to the imagination, showing the deep cleavage between their tightly compressed breasts and their exposed bellies and thighs glistening in the soft candlelight of Amir's tent.

Shifting from the ultra-conservative full-body covering of their traditional frocks to this bawdy costume was a shock to my system, and I soaked up the women's taut, sexy figures like I hadn't seen a near-naked body in weeks. Which I damn near *hadn't*. Suddenly realizing that I hadn't felt the touch of another woman's body since I left home, my pussy throbbed while I ogled the sexy girls standing only a few feet in front of me.

"Are you ready to watch a real arabian belly dance?" Amir said, noticing my pupils dilated in excitement.

"Definitely," I smiled, eager to see the two women gyrate their bodies next to me.

He nodded toward the two girls and they stepped back a few feet, then he picked up the guitar and began strumming a rhythmic folk tune. As the melody filled the cabin, the two women began to undulate their hips in unison, matching the beat of the song. My eyes flickered over their bodies, absorbing the sensuous spectacle while their stomach muscles flexed and their navels swayed from side to side like two winking eyes. As they stepped forward and back in perfect harmony, they snapped the castanets on the tips of their fingers together, providing a rhythmic accompaniment to Amir's lilting melody.

Just when I thought this guy couldn't get any more suave and sophisticated, I thought. *He even plays the guitar perfectly.*

In another place and time, I might have fallen for his seductive demeanor, but for the time being I was utterly hypnotized by the sensual moves of the two beautiful women dancing before me. As I watched their eyes gazing at us behind their swinging ringlets, I tried to place how old they were. Their bodies hardly had an ounce of fat, and their skin was as soft and supple as a teenager's. Knowing many arab countries had few restrictions against marrying much younger women, I wondered if they were even of legal age. As if that actually mattered out here in the middle of the desert.

Amir softened the strumming of his guitar and the girls eventually slowed their movement to a stop, then he turned toward me and smiled.

"What do you think of our traditional arab music and dance?" he said to me.

"It's beautiful," I said, shifting my position on the warm carpet, suddenly realizing how wet I'd become watching the two girls. "And very sensuous."

"Yes, it is," he said. "Do you have a particular request?"

I shook my head, unsure what he meant at first, then I cleared my throat when I realized he was talking about the music and not what I wanted to do with the girls.

"You mean like a Western *song*?"

"Yes," he nodded. "I always like to satisfy my guests' preferences."

I thought for a moment about a song that resonated with me that was also slow enough to fit with the girls' style of performance.

"Do you know the Bob Marley song Waiting in Vain, but played in the style of Annie Lennox?"

"Of course," he said. "It's one of my favorites."

He began strumming his guitar again, and the familiar melody of the song filled the tent while the two girls swayed their hips in harmony with the rhythm, clapping their castanets softly to provide gentle background accompaniment. A few moments later, Laila began humming the tune and Amir turned toward her, encouraging her to join him.

From the very first time I laid my eyes on you, girl, she sang with an angelic voice. *My heart said follow through. But I know, now, that I'm way down on your line...*

I turned to face her, amazed that she knew the lyrics to the song and enthralled by her gorgeous tone.

But the waiting feeling's fine, she cooed, meeting my gaze. *So don't treat me like a puppet on a string. 'Cause I know how to do my thing...*

Suddenly my thoughts echoed back to earlier in the day when she slipped my robe over my naked body, and the way she peered at me as she leaned in toward me.

Had she felt the same sexual attraction I'd had for her when we first met?

As she sang the words, she looked into my eyes and smiled while I tapped my feet rhythmically against the soft carpet.

I don't want to wait in vain for your love, she sang, gazing at me directly as my mouth parted in a spellbinding stupor. Suddenly, I couldn't wait to get out of Amir's tent and back into the women's enclosure where I could lie next to her on the warm desert sand under my soft wool cape.

As the song wound down and the girls' movement slowed to a stop, Amir placed his guitar to one side and reached around behind him, placing two odd-looking drums on the mat in front of him. Made of different-sized hollowed-out ceramic bowls with dried animal skins stretched over top, they looked like homemade bongo drums. As if on cue, Laila reached beside her and picked up a wooden reed instrument fashioned in the manner of a flared flute.

"That was beautiful," I said, peering at the two of them. "I don't think I've enjoyed that song as much as I did just now. This whole experience has been a feast for the senses."

Amir smiled as he pulled the drums in closer toward his knees.

"I'd like to finish with song I wrote myself for this kind of occasion," he said. "Unfortunately, I can't sing as well as Laila and her mouth will be otherwise occupied during this tune, so you'll just have to enjoy the *other* elements of the performance," he said, nodding toward the two belly dancers.

As he began beating on the drums with two hands, Laila picked up the flute-shaped instrument and began humming another arabic tune, tapping her fingers rhythmically over the holes on top of the shaft. The girls began swinging their hips slowly at first, but as Amir began increasing the pace of his tapping, they gyrated their hips faster and faster, turning their bodies around as I watched their buttock muscles flexing and shaking under the silk tassels hanging down from their tight bikini bottoms. As Laila matched Amir's escalating backbeat in pace and volume, the girls grew increasingly animated with the shaking of their bodies, looking like they were building up to some kind of climax.

While they shook their bodies with increasing passion and fervor in the form of a simulated sex act, I found myself shifting my weight again on the warm carpet underneath me, growing progressively wetter from their suggestive body movements and facial expressions. Amir became increasingly energetic pounding his drums with his two hands, and I noticed that he was staring at the girls with a lustful look in his eyes. The sexual tension in the room was now at a fever pitch, and as he banged out the last part of the performance, I saw a light sweat dripping over his brow. When he finished the song with two loud bangs on the drums, for a few moments everything in the tent became still as I listened to the sound of everyone's heavy breathing.

"Did you enjoy our little performance this evening?" he said, turning to face me after a long pause.

"Yes, very much," I panted, suddenly realizing how much the performance had raised my *own* heartbeat.

"If you'll excuse me now," he said, looking at the two scantily clad girls in front of him and motioning for them to stay behind. "I think it's time for me to turn in now. Laila will look after your sleeping arrangements. I'll see you again in the morning."

"Thank you," I said, as Laila and I stood to leave. "I'm sure I'll sleep very soundly this evening."

When I followed Laila out the front flap of Amir's tent, I noticed a dark shadow moving away from the perimeter and I recognized Ali's shape in the flickering moonlight. I shook my head realizing that he'd been spying on the erotic performance through a hole in the tent and picked up my pace to catch up with Laila.

"It's as simple as *that*, is it?" I said, referring to Amir's unbridled control over the girls. "He only has to nod, and the women submit to whatever his request?"

"Unfortunately, yes," she said, peering at me with sad eyes. "He's bought and paid for us, and we have to do whatever he says."

"Even if that means sleeping with him whenever he demands?"

"*Especially* that," she said.

"You seem somewhat less eager than the other girls," I said.

"He's had his way plenty enough times with me," she shrugged. "Thankfully, he now prefers the younger girls. Did you at least enjoy the performance?"

"Yes," I said. "It was very–*stimulating*. But honestly, I enjoyed your singing more than anything else. You have a gorgeous voice. Even when you played the wind instrument, I couldn't take my eyes off of you."

"Thank you," she said, noticing me pull my wool shawl over my shoulders to protect against the biting desert wind. "You have a very intoxicating manner about you as well. Come, let's get out of this cold desert air and bundled underneath something warmer."

When we entered the women's tent, all the other girls were already lying fast asleep on their blankets on the sand, with only one small open spot left in the corner of the enclosure. Laila laid a large blanket down over the space, then nonchalantly pulled her dress up over her shoulders, folding the robe and headdress on the ground next to the blanket. I couldn't help staring at her voluptuous body, highlighted by the lone flickering candle next to the makeshift bed. Her breasts were full and firm, resting high on her chest with dark medallions encircling her thick, pointed nipples. Her bare hips curved sensuously around the dark patch of pubic hair on her mound, tapering to long but muscular legs. In the dark shadows of the enclosed pavilion, she looked to me like some kind of sexy Amazon.

Then she picked up a large woolen blanket and threw it over her shoulders, lying down on the carpet peering up at me.

"Are you just going to stand there, or are you going to get under the covers and help keep me warm?"

"In the *buff*?" I said, unsure what the proper protocol was for women sleeping together in the tight confines of the communal tent.

"It's more comfortable that way," she said. "The less washing of our clothes that we have to do, the better. We prefer to air them out overnight. Besides, the sheepskin feels so much better against your bare skin. Come join me if you feel brave enough."

I pulled off my shawl and lifted my thawb over my shoulders, placing them gently on the sand on the other side of the blanket, then lifted the fluffy duvet and nestled in next to her.

"Oh, I'm feeling brave enough," I said, turning to face her.

"Good," she said. "Because those dancing girls weren't the *only* thing distracting my attention this evening."

5

______

Laila turned her body toward me, then shifted her weight closer, wrapping her legs around my hips. I could feel her soft bush caressing my bare mound as she pressed her breasts firmly against my chest. I placed my hand against the side of her head and leaned in to kiss her, and our tongues melded together in a different kind of erotic dance.

"Laila," I whispered. "I'm so happy we have a chance to sleep together. I've wanted you from the moment I laid eyes on you."

"Why do you think I joined the two of you in Amir's tent?" she said, smiling into my eyes. "I wanted you all to myself."

"Weren't you worried that I might have stayed with *him* instead?"

"Possibly," she cooed. "He certainly knows how to put on the charm when he wants something."

"I already made it clear to him that I didn't come here for *romantic* reasons," I said. "Besides, men don't really do it for me any longer."

"Oh?" she said. "You prefer the company of women?"

"Only *certain* ones," I purred, grinding my pussy against hers.

"Do you mind if I examine you more closely?" she said. "I've never seen a Western woman up close and naked before. You're very–*different*."

"Absolutely," I said. "I've been fantasizing about you strumming your fingers over something other than that *flute* for the last half hour."

"Mmm," she groaned, moving further under the blanket.

As she nibbled her way down my body, I felt her hard nipples etching a line over my trembling stomach. When her mouth reached my breasts, she circled my teats with her warm tongue then sucked them hard into her mouth as she squeezed my mounds with both hands. Unlike the tender manner of most new lovers, I reveled in her rough and dominant style of lovemaking. If this was the way arab women made love to one another, I was ready to be taken.

I placed my hands on the back of her head and pulled her harder against my chest, burying her face between my cleavage. Then I lifted my right knee and pressed it between her splayed legs until it stopped against her wet vulva. She sighed as I began to rock my hips forward and back, stretching the skin of my thigh over her burning pussy.

"Lick me down below," I panted, rolling my hips frantically against her belly. "I need to feel your hot lips on my pussy before I explode."

"Soon enough," she said, blowing softly on my belly as she inched her way down toward my aching snatch.

But when her face reached my shaved mound she paused, feeling my bare skin while she rolled the sides of her cheeks against my soft flesh, kissing me softly at the apex of my slit where my labia merged together at the top of my clit.

"Oh *God* yes," I panted, feeling her warm lips touching my sensitive organ for the first time. "Lick my slit and taste my juices. See how wet you've made me."

She pressed her head a few inches lower, then ran her flat tongue over the length of my folds, lapping up my dripping juices.

"Yes, I can see that," she purred. "You taste much better than goat's milk over rice."

"Yes," I gasped. "Suck on me like a tender lamb. I want to feel your tongue probing every part of me."

Laila curled her tongue as she mashed her face between my legs, pressing it deep into my hole. I grabbed her head, pulling her harder against my cunt, rubbing her face up and down my dripping crease. There was something about the raw act of fucking her naked on the desert sand that I found incredibly arousing. Seeing her wrapped up in her full body covering and suddenly feeling her naked body writhing next to mine took me to new heights of pleasure.

"Mmm," I groaned. "I need you to suck my button now. I want to feel your tongue on my clit. Suck me, Laila."

"Hmm," she purred, moving her head higher up on my slit.

When she surrounded my jewel with her lips I almost came right away, but she seemed to sense my heightened state of arousal and for a long moment she held her head still between my legs while she felt my clit pulsing in her mouth. But when she began rolling her tongue over my nub in slow sensuous arcs, bathing me with her warm saliva, I couldn't help moaning out loud.

"God, yes," I panted. "That feels so good. I needed this so badly."

"Mmm-hmm," Laila nodded, feeling my juices running down her chin and neck.

I could feel my passion beginning to rise and I could have come quite easily from the action of her tongue alone on my raging clit, but what she did next took me to an entirely new level of ecstasy. She slipped two fingers of her right hand into my hole and buried them knuckle deep while stretching her little finger further down my perineum and circling it over my tender anus.

Fuck me, I thought. *This girl really knows how to make love to a woman.* I wondered just how much extra-curricular activity went on at night in the privacy of the women's tent while the other men were sleeping. I had no idea, but I was certainly interested in finding out.

When she began curling the two fingers inside me toward my G-spot, I arched my back and began grunting like a wild animal. I couldn't hold back the floodgate of pleasure any longer as my orgasm suddenly overtook me like a freight train.

"Yes, Laila!" I wailed. "I'm going to come, baby. I'm going to come all over your pretty face."

Part of me wanted to warn Laila about my tendency to squirt when I was this wet and worked up, but there wasn't any time. I suddenly felt the muscles of my pussy begin to clench uncontrollably, gushing my pent-up juices all over her slippery face and the soft blanket below us.

"Uhnn," she groaned, seeming to enjoy my orgasm almost as much as I was while she felt the walls of my pussy contracting powerfully on her fingers still deeply embedded inside me.

It must have taken over a full minute for me to stop coming in her arms with the most powerful orgasm I'd had in months. When I finally began to calm down, I collapsed onto the moist blanket and turned to kiss her softly on her lips.

"Thank you," I said, running my fingers through her hair. "I really needed that."

"You seemed to be already pretty worked up. Did you get that excited watching the two girls performing their special dance?"

"I have to admit that I did," I nodded. "I don't know if it was because I was so surprised to see their almost naked figures or because of the way they were moving their bodies, but it didn't just put *Amir* in the mood for some extra nighttime fun."

"So you're attracted to women also?"

"Definitely," I said. "I find women are more adept at satisfying my sexual needs, just as you were a few moments ago. In fact, your special expertise suggests this wasn't the first time you've made love to a woman either."

"Of course not," she smiled. "What do you think we girls do with ourselves in this tent when we're left to our own devices?"

"*All* of you?" I asked, feeling my juices dripping out of my slit once again at the thought of the pretty girls having a group orgy in their little pleasure dome.

"Um-hm," Laila nodded. "There are twenty women but only one penis in our traveling caravan. How *else* do you think we satisfy our needs?"

"What about poor Ali?" I said. "Isn't he ever allowed to get in on the action?"

"Amir would never share the women he's bought and paid for with another man. It would be considered a violation punishable by death if he so much as *looked* at one of us the wrong way. Besides, with his hooked nose and foul-smelling breath, none of us would ever be interested in him that way."

"Well I'm certainly interested in *you* that way," I smiled, threading my thigh again between her legs toward her steaming pussy. "It's my turn to give you the kind of pleasure you just administered to me."

As I began to move my body lower under the blanket, Laila suddenly stopped me, flipping me over onto my back.

"Why don't we *both* share the pleasure this time?" she said, rolling her body on top of me and lifting my left leg while she pressed her wet vulva against my pussy.

"If you insist," I said, smiling up at her.

"I want to watch you this time while I make love to you," she said. "I've never made love to a white girl before."

I smiled at her reference to me as a white girl, even though we were both technically caucasian. But there was no denying that she was considerably darker than me, and I felt a similar sexual attraction to her exotic appearance.

"I'm sure it's not so different from the *other* girls you've fucked," I said, feeling her thick bush pressing against my bald pubis. "Other than being *bare* down there."

"Like a little girl," she grunted, beginning to grind her twat against mine.

"Does that turn you on?" I said, reaching up to pinch her thick nipples as her large breasts swayed overtop my chest.

"Maybe," she said. "I've never felt a woman's bare *kus* before."

"Not even when you experimented when you were younger?"

"Never like *this*," she panted, rocking her hips more rapidly against mine as the sound of our wet pussies slapping together filled the cabin.

"Fuck my girly pussy, Laila," I teased her, recognizing that she was getting turned on by the naughty imagery. "I want to gush all over your furry snatch when we come this time."

"Yes," she huffed, throwing her head back in pleasure as we squeezed each other's breasts tightly with both hands. "You're so wet and slippery down there. I like the feeling of your bare sex against me."

"Would you like to try it yourself sometime?" I said, lifting my hand to her face as she sucked my thumb into her mouth. "Perhaps I can groom you myself while I'm here."

"I'm not sure Amir would appreciate me defiling my body in a way that's not in accordance with muslim custom."

"But you already said he rarely shows interest in you that way. This can just be between the two of us. It will grow back within a few weeks after I leave."

"I'm not sure I'm going to *want* you to leave after this," she said, pulling my leg up higher as she wrapped her arms around it, pulling it tightly between her sweating breasts. "Come with me, Jade. I want to feel your juices mingling with mine when you climax this time."

"*Fuck* yes," I panted, just waiting for her signal. "Grind your pussy against mine. I'm going to cum all over your hairy bush. Here it comes, baby."

"Uhnnn!" Laila suddenly grunted, throwing her head back in rapture, and for the second time that evening, I felt my body pushing over the precipice as another powerful orgasm washed over me and I began squirting jets of liquid all over Laila's twitching pussy.

As we watched each other's bodies convulsing atop one another in the dim light of the tent, I suddenly heard the soft squealing sounds of the other women around us while they pleasured themselves listening to the two of us. Something told me my little caravan excursion was about to stretch out into a longer adventure than I'd planned.

6

———————

The following morning, Laila and I rose at the break of dawn and got dressed, heading outside for breakfast. Amir was already sitting around the fire pit with a scattering of women preparing the meal. He smiled when he recognized me wearing my thawb and invited the two of us to sit beside him.

"Did you sleep well last night?" he asked me.

"Yes, thank you," I said. "I found it surprisingly comfortable sleeping on the desert sand."

"It's fine as long as you have a thick blanket underneath you. The grains have a way of finding their way into every nook and cranny of your body if you're not careful out here. I prefer to sleep a few inches off the surface myself."

I peered around the circle and recognized the two girls from last night's belly dance performance back in their long robes and head-dresses, baking flatbread atop a curved metal hotplate.

"That smells wonderful, whatever it is you're making," I said, choosing to ignore his none-too-subtle intimation about our sleeping arrangements.

"Fresh flatbread and yogurt," he said, motioning to the tall trees surrounding the encampment. "With a side portion of dates, harvested directly from these palm trees."

I shook my head in awe at the simplicity of their nomadic lifestyle.

"I'm amazed how self-sufficient you can be simply from what you carry with you across the desert."

"Yes," he nodded. "Our goats provide milk, cheese, and yogurt, and the sheep provide all the meat we need. Everything else is supplied by the markets we visit along the fringe of the desert on our caravan route."

"If you don't mind my asking," I said, watching the women flipping the sizzling flatbread over the metal hotplate. "How do you pay for the extra materials? I mean, how do you earn hard *currency* while traveling across the desert?"

"Primarily from our livestock," Amir said. "Our animals are quite prolific, and there's a strong demand for these animals wherever we go. The camels in particular are very valuable commodities since they live for so long and can travel long distances without any water."

I glanced at the herd of camels grazing on the sparse grass and drinking from a wooden trough next to the well.

"And they're able to carry your entire entourage with all of its regalia across the open desert?"

"Yes, they're very strong and hardy animals. We'd never be able to survive out here in the middle of the desert without them."

The girls placed some of the fresh flatbread on individual plates along with bowls of yoghurt and chopped dates, then passed them around the circle to the now fully assembled group.

"Please—eat up," Amir said. "You'll need your strength if you plan to stay with us a little longer. The desert provides, but it also takes away. Your body burns a lot more calories in this sweltering heat."

I watched him dip his flatbread into the bowl of yogurt and pick up the dates with his fingers, and I followed his lead. Everything tasted incredibly fresh and delicious and when I finished my plate, I licked my fingers clean like the rest of the group.

"Oh my God," I sighed. "I could get used to this way of life. Everything is so simple and easy out here. Even the food tastes better than what I'm used to at many five-star restaurants. Talk about farm to table!"

"Are you enjoying it enough to *join* us on the next leg of trip to Algiers?" Amir smiled.

I paused for a moment, remembering what I'd told Hannah before I left my hotel in Marrakesh.

"How far away is it? I told my friends they should expect to hear back from me in a few days."

"It six or seven days by camel ride. But we'll be sleeping out in the open most nights under the stars. We only set up camp when we stop near towns or at the few oases along our route."

"I think I can manage that," I nodded, smiling at Laila remembering how much I enjoyed sleeping next to her on the warm sand last night. "But only if you let me help clean and pack up like everyone else. If I'm going to join your troupe for a few days, I want to feel like a productive member of the tribe."

"If that's what you wish," Amir nodded. "Laila and Ali can look after whatever you need. Will you have any trouble making return travel arrangements from Algiers?"

"It shouldn't be a problem," I said. "As long as it has an international airport."

"Indeed it does," he said, standing to leave. "I'm going to collect my things while Ali begins dismantling the tents. We'll be setting out within the next hour."

I was surprised how quickly the group broke down the camp, neatly arranging all the tent poles, coverings, and contents atop the backs of the camels. When we were ready to leave, we filled our saddlebags with enough water to last us for a few days, then we headed east two-abreast atop the remaining camels. It was quite a sight watching the long train of animals traipsing through the pretty sand ripples lining the undulating desert with nothing to keep us occupied but the shifting shadows of the sun and the howling desert wind.

At nighttime, we circled the camels and livestock around us to provide a modicum of cover from the blowing breeze, then laid down on our individual blankets and woolen duvets to keep ourselves warm. I missed sleeping with Laila and more than once thought about sneaking under the covers to join her, but I dared not risk disturbing Amir and Ali who were sleeping nearby.

After three days, we came upon another small oasis and set up the tents once again to provide a respite against the searing overhead sun. I was thrilled to have another chance to make love to Laila in the relative privacy of our own tent, and after the girls fell asleep, she let me shave her mound with the travel razor I'd packed in my bag, using goat's milk and yogurt as an improvised shaving cream. Afterwards, I licked her clean as she knelt over my face writhing in pleasure while I sucked her bare vulva and clit into my mouth.

But the following morning, something happened that forever changed the course of my dreamlike desert adventure. As I flipped open the flap of our tent to fetch some water from the well, I noticed Fatima, one of the girls who'd performed the belly dance a few nights earlier, lifting a pail out of the well while Ali snuck up behind her, trying to lift her robe while he pulled his erect penis out from under his kaftan. When she ducked aside to evade his unwanted advance, he suddenly lost his balance and tumbled head over heels into the well, screaming all the way down until I heard a loud splash when he fell unconscious at the bottom of the pit. Fatima looked around her with frightened eyes and we she saw me watching, she rushed toward me crying, throwing her arms around me wailing in arabic.

Not wanting her to be discovered, I ushered her quickly into our tent and explained to Laila what had happened. A few seconds later, Amir emerged from his tent alarmed by the commotion, calling out Ali's name. Suspicious when he didn't immediately hear his reply, Amir went back into his tent and came out carrying a flashlight, pointing it down into the well. When he saw Ali's body floating face-down in the pool of water, he turned toward our tent and stormed toward it, angrily flipping open the door covering.

He glared at Laila with steely eyes and a red face, speaking loudly to her in arabic. She said something back to him and shrugged her shoulders, feigning ignorance at what had just transpired. He then approached each of the girls separately, asking them if they knew what had happened. But we got to Fatima, he noticed that she was shaking and he placed his hand under her chin, raising her face to meet his angry gaze. She shook her head, afraid to admit any involvement in the incident, but when he saw her dried tear tracks, he grabbed her hair, dragging her outside.

I looked at Laila bewildered and asked what was going on.

"It's not good," she said, following Amir outside. "Just stay close to me and don't say anything."

"Why don't we just tell him the *truth*?" I said. "That it was an innocent mistake, and that she was just trying to protect herself from Ali's unwanted advance?"

"It doesn't work that way," Laila said, shaking her head. "The scales of justice are tipped greatly in favor of the men in our culture. If she were discovered to have been involved in his death, even incidentally, it wouldn't end well for her."

"So what happens if nobody's willing to talk?"

Laila gritted her teeth as she watched Amir remove his long curved knife from under his belt and place it over the fire. I watched the steel grow red-hot in the flame, then he pulled Fatima's head back and placed the hot blade next to her face. He said something angrily to her and she shook her head frighteningly. Then he forced her mouth open as she slowly extended her tongue. He placed the flat side of the knife on it and she screamed as the blade made a horrible sizzling sound against her flesh.

"What the *fuck*..." I said, stepping toward her trying to intercede.

"Don't," Laila said, grabbing my arm.

"But what he's doing to her in *inhuman*," I protested. "She's just an innocent bystander–"

"This is the way justice is administered in the bedouin culture. When there's a dispute involving a serious crime and no one comes forward to admit guilt, the men administer what is called a *bisha'a*, which is a type of trial by ordeal. The accused person is forced to lick a hot piece of metal and if the tongue shows any sign of a burn or a scar, this is considered a sign of guilt."

"Of *course* her tongue will burn!" I exclaimed. "He just placed a red-hot *knife* against her flesh!"

Amir removed the knife from Fatima's mouth, then doused her tongue with a ladle of fresh water. Then he peered closely at it and threw her down on the sand, cursing at her in their native tongue.

"So what happens now?" I said to Laila.

"If a woman is convicted of this type of crime, she's usually sentenced to death, often by public stoning. But Amir won't do it himself. He'll have to take her to a local tribal court where judgement will be formally handed down and administered by the muslim council."

"You've got to be kidding me," I said, hardly believing what I'd just seen and heard.

Amir turned around noticing that Laila and I had witnessed the entire scene, and walked toward us with flaring nostrils.

"I'm sorry you had to see that," he said to me. "But what Fatima did was a serious crime that cannot be ignored. She will have to face the consequences of her actions. Laila, I want you to coordinate with the other women so we can pack up the camp immediately. We'll be heading out to Algiers as soon as possible to have Fatima's fate decided."

"Wait!" I said, stepping toward Amir in desperation. "I saw the whole thing. She didn't do anything wrong. Ali assaulted her and she was simply trying to defend herself. It was just an accident when he tripped and fell into the well."

Amir paused for a moment as his eyes flashed over my beseeching face, then he shook his head dismissively.

"She must have done something to provoke him," he said. "He couldn't have fallen so easily into the well. We will see what the tribal council decides in Algiers."

"And if she's found guilty?" I said.

"She'll be put to death immediately," Amir said, turning to head back to his tent.

I tried to follow after him, but Laila grabbed my robe, holding me back.

"He can't get away with that!" I said, turning toward her. "It's barbaric!"

"Unfortunately, this is the way of our culture. If a muslim woman is even *suspected* of fraternizing inappropriately with a man other than her husband, Sharia law dictates that she be summarily executed."

"By public *stoning*? What about the guilt of the *man*? What if it's simply one person's word over another?"

"In our culture, the man is always presumed innocent since they have free rein over the women and females are instructed to refrain from fraternizing with anyone other than their husbands."

"I'd hardly refer to what they were doing at the well as *fraternizing*. There's only one place for everybody to collect water out here. It's inevitable that there'll be some form of close contact among such a small group in close quarters. Surely something can be done–"

"I'm afraid we have no control over the situation," Laila said, looking at me sadly. "It's out of our hands now."

Later that evening, we stopped in the middle of the desert to rest for the night and grab a bite to eat, and everybody sat around the campfire looking sadly at each other. Nobody dared say a thing, knowing full well what Amir's intentions were. I peered at Fatima, shivering next to the fire as Laila wrapped her arms around her, trying to provide a modicum of comfort. When we dispersed after the meal to make our individual beds in the sand, I took Laila aside and peered into her eyes.

"We can't just let this poor girl be unjustly punished for a crime she didn't commit," I pleaded.

"What would you have us do?" she said. "*He's* the one with all the power and the control. We can't just overpower him and run away."

I crossed my arms and shook my head at the absurdity of the situation.

Laila paused for a long moment, then looked up at me through narrowed eyelids.

"There might be *another* way we can extricate ourselves from this unfortunate situation," she said. "What if we steal away in the middle of the night and take all the camels with us? He won't be able to follow us, and he'll run out of water long before he gets to Algiers."

"But he'd *die* out here in the middle of the desert without any food or water!" I said.

"It's either him or Fatima," she said. "Who do you think is more deserving to live? The innocent girl who did nothing other than try to protect herself from a violent rape, or the man who summarily judges her based on his ludicrous code of honor?"

"But he seemed to be so–"

"Sophisticated, and a man of the world?" Laila said. "There are two sides to every man, and this one is no different. He may have been educated in your country, but I assure you that his morals and underlying character have been indelibly shaped by his family affiliations and the culture of his tribe. Are you prepared to do what has to be done?"

I paused for a moment, trying to think of any other conceivable options, then I grudgingly nodded. I couldn't believe that my exciting desert adventure had suddenly turned into a deadly serious conspiracy where two people's lives lay in the balance.

7

———

Laila and I waited until we heard Amir snoring under his blanket, then she roused each of the girls, telling them about our escape plan. Everybody got up and tiptoed through the sand toward the camels, then we tethered them together and mounted them carefully, slowly leading them away from the rest of the livestock herd.

"What about the goats and the sheep?" I whispered into Laila's ear, who I'd paired up with on the lead camel.

"We haven't got time to gather them together and we can't risk disturbing Amir–"

Suddenly I heard a man's voice yelling in the darkness, and I turned to see Amir rising from his sleep and begin chasing after us. Laila kicked the sides of her camel and the whole train burst into a gallop, creating a dusty trail behind us. Amir screamed and shook his fists as he tried to catch up with us, but he was no match for the fleet group of camels, and within seconds he disappeared behind us in the thick cloud of dust.

"*Jesus*," I said to Laila after we'd put a few hundred meters between us. "Are you sure this is going to work? Now we're *all* unwitting accomplices in this sordid affair."

"We're at least three days' camel ride to the nearest village on the outskirts of the desert," she said. "It would take three times as long to cover that distance on foot. There's no way he can survive in this stifling heat for that long without water."

"And the *rest* of the animals?"

"They're a bit more hardy. We can come back for them a little later when the coast is clear."

I peered behind me to see the other girls following behind Laila's camel in single file.

"What will you and the others do now that you're no longer part of Amir's caravan?"

"I plan to send them back home to their families when we get to Algiers. This many camels will fetch more than enough money to arrange safe transit to their home ports."

"What about *you*? Won't people be looking for Amir at some point if he doesn't show up? Surely his family–"

"I plan to be long gone before anyone raises any suspicions. I've got some extended family in the Andalusia region of Spain where I can lay low for a while. I'm more worried about you. Did you tell anyone that you were going to join Amir's caravan? The local authorities won't take kindly to finding out you might have been involved somehow in his disappearance."

I paused for a moment trying to remember the details of the message I'd sent Hannah before I set off to see Amir at the cafe.

"Just my best friend back home," I said. "I gave her Amir's name and told her to alert the U.S. Embassy in Morocco if she didn't hear from me in a week or so."

"You'd best clear out of this region at your earliest opportunity then," she said. "It will be difficult for the local police to hold you to account once you're out of the country."

"But I didn't do anything–" I began to protest.

"We're *all* implicated now. If they find Amir's dead body, they could trace any one of us to the deed. Technically, we'd all be considered accessories to the crime."

"Christ," I sighed, feeling my heart suddenly racing at the implications of what we'd done. "What the hell have I gotten myself into?"

"Don't worry," Laila said, patting my thigh reassuringly. "The desert soon buries anything that doesn't move. He'll never be found, and we'll all be long gone before anyone raises any suspicions."

"What about *Ali*?" I said. "Won't another caravan eventually find his dead body at the bottom of the well?"

"Perhaps, but with any luck it should be pretty decomposed by then. Whoever finds him will have difficulty connecting him to Amir's disappearance."

Suddenly I had a queasy feeling in the pit of my stomach, and I wrapped my arms around Laila's midsection, resting my head against her back as I peered at the never-ending hills of red sand dunes.

"How will you find your way through this wasteland all the way to Algiers?" I asked.

"The shadows of our camels will guide the way. It shows which way the sun is pointed, and all we have to do is head east and north until we reach the Mediterranean coast. From there, it should be easy to track our way to the city."

"You're a pretty smart cookie," I smiled, clutching her closely. "These girls were pretty lucky to have such a strong leader to get them out of this predicament."

"I hope they'll be happier now that they're freed from Amir's grip," she nodded. "But I'll be sad to see some of them go. I've grown quite attached to these girls after all this time we've spent together in the desert."

Twelve hours later, the sun began to fade over the horizon and Laila stopped the group to set up camp, laying out our bedrolls amongst the circle of resting camels. Most of our food was still packed in the saddlebags and we enjoyed a peaceful dinner of rice, cooked legumes, and sweet dates. Everybody seemed much more relaxed around the campfire, chatting and giggling amongst themselves in their native arabic.

When we finished eating, we retired to our beds but soon discovered in our haste to leave the previous camp that we hadn't brought enough bedrolls and blankets for everybody to sleep on separately. Taking charge of the situation as always, Laila nestled the blankets together then we lay down as a group, not bothering to take off our robes to protect ourselves against the encroaching desert chill. It didn't take long for everyone to snuggle together for extra warmth, and before long I felt the telltale sensation of someone's fingers sliding up the bottom of my smock.

I turned around and saw Fatima smiling at me in the soft moonlight, and she leaned in to kiss me. Whether she was trying to express her gratitude for my helping to save her or she was just curious about feeling my fair skin, I couldn't be sure. But either way, I was happy to accommodate her newfound intimate interest in me. As we began to kiss more passionately, intertwining our tongues and pressing our bodies together, she pulled my robe up over my hips, caressing the outside of my thighs and my round buttocks.

But when her hand curved around to my bald pubis, she gasped and uttered something in arabic. I heard Laila reply to her in the darkness on my other side, and Fatima giggled as Laila rolled over to sandwich me between the two of them. Suddenly I had two pairs of hands caressing my body from both sides, and I moaned as they slipped their fingers between my thighs, caressing my vulva from two ends. I pulled Fatima's smock higher, feeling her fluffy bush caressing my bare mound, and I groaned in her mouth as her fingers found my pleasure spot and she began rubbing my clit in soft circular motions. But when I felt Laila's fingers press inside my slit and begin fingerfucking me from behind, I began rocking my hips, moaning more loudly.

When the rest of the girls began to realize what the three of us were up to, it didn't take long for the entire group to devolve into a moaning, slithering mass of naked bodies writhing under the thick jumble of cotton robes and woolen blankets. I pulled Fatima's dress all the way over her shoulders and squeezed her bare tits while she played with my clit and moaned into my mouth. It didn't take long for the combined action of her manipulation of my clit and Laila's caressing of my vulva to bring me to the brink of pleasure. As the two women pressed their bodies tightly against mine, I felt my orgasm overtake me and I jerked my body spastically, gushing all over the two girl's hands.

Fatima said something again to Laila, and she responded in arabic, then Fatima moved her body down closer to my midsection, apparently fascinated by my unusual bare mound and my propensity to squirt when I came. When she spread my legs apart, the other girls stopped what they were doing to peer at my dripping bald pussy glistening in the moonlight. Before I knew it, I had a clutch of pretty young girls kissing and probing every part of my body as Laila propped her head up on her elbow, smiling at me.

"Holy shit," I said to her. "You weren't kidding about how these girls like to stay entertained when the men aren't around. I think I've died and gone to *heaven!*"

"Welcome to the club, baby," Laila said, leaning in to kiss me as I felt a deluge of tongues and fingers converging on me while they sucked and nibbled on every square inch of my body. The multitude of erotic sensations soon brought me to the edge again, and I screamed in ecstasy as my whole body convulsed in another intense orgasm. Fatima suddenly pulled away from licking me while the whole group watched my pussy twitching and squirting my juices all over her face and my bare legs.

"Oh my God," I purred to Laila, after I came down from my high. "I could seriously get used to this. Are you *sure* you want to disband this group of horny young vixens?"

"Not for a couple more *days* at least," she smiled, rolling her body on top of me, grinding her dripping mound into my pliant face.

As I began to eat her pussy, the girls swarmed over top of me like a bunch of buzzing bees, rubbing their wet pussies and hairy bushes over whatever open flesh they could find on my pinned body. One of them positioned herself between my legs, pulling her pussy tight against mine and began scissoring me in a prone 'X' position while some of the other girls sucked my nipples and toes. Before we all fell asleep in a steaming pile of sweaty flesh, I must have come at least a dozen more times sucking, caressing, and fucking every one of the girls in one position or another.

As I lay on the soft desert sand surrounded by the bevy of beautiful women, I looked up toward the sky at the cloud of stars shimmering above me like a blanket of sparkling sequins. Suddenly the troubles at the previous camp seemed a hundred miles away, and I smiled at one of Amir's last comments to me. *The desert gives and takes away indeed*, I thought, as I drifted off to sleep.

8

For the next couple of days, we rode slowly through the desert, stopping periodically to relieve ourselves and snack on dried dates and flatbread. At night we reassembled the blankets in one large group and resumed our wild orgy under the stars until we all fell asleep, completely spent and satiated. I almost regretted seeing the dusty buildings on the edge of Algiers as we approached the city from the west, and I squeezed Laila's tummy softly to express how much I dreaded the thought of leaving her.

She parked me and the rest of the girls out of sight behind a tall dune so as not to arouse suspicion, then she led the camels three at a time into the local trading market, where she sold them at a relative bargain. It was approaching dusk by the time she returned to fetch all of us, then she took us down to the docks to arrange clandestine travel for each of the girls to return to their original towns. She gave each of them enough money to pay for the remainder of their passage, then the two of us walked along the waterfront while we talked about our next steps.

"That looked easier than I *thought* it would be," I said after all of the girls had boarded their individual ships to head home.

"These merchant seamen will transport anything for the right amount of money," she nodded.

"What about the harbormaster? How did you manage to bypass all the usual paperwork and document controls?"

"The protocols for onboarding and offboarding passengers on cargo ships are far looser on the North African coast than in Europe or America," she said, sliding her fingers and her thumb together to indicate the payment of a bribe. "Nobody seems to have a problem looking the other way as long as you grease their palms a little bit."

"How can you be sure the ships' captains will *complete* the transaction now that they've already been paid?"

"Because I promised to have them paid an *equivalent* amount once the girls safely complete their journey on the other end."

"All of this is made possible from the selling of a few *camels*?"

"Um-hm," Laila nodded. "Amir paid to take us *away* from our homes, now he's indirectly arranged to pay for them to get back."

"I'm not sure this was exactly the way he envisioned it," I frowned, trying not to think about how much he was suffering in the middle of the desert without any food or water.

"I suppose not," she chuckled. "Though I don't think *any* of this went down the way he imagined."

"So what now?" I said, peering over the Mediterranean as the sun began to set on the horizon.

"We pretend like none of this ever happened," she said. "You go back home to America, and I slip across the sea to start a new life in Spain. It shouldn't take long for us to put all of this unpleasantness behind us."

"It hasn't *all* been unpleasant," I said, grabbing her hand and pulling her into an alley to give her a long, passionate kiss. "I'll have far more *happy* memories to hold onto than this one unfortunate affair."

"Mmm," she nodded, pressing her body up tightly against me.

"Well isn't *this* a happy little reunion," a familiar man's voice suddenly cackled from the shadows.

Laila and I swung around to see Amir blocking the exit to the alley, brandishing his glinty curved knife.

"I knew the two of you were up to no good the moment I saw you ogling each other during the belly dance performance in my tent. And now it's time for the lot of you to be held to account for your transgressions. Right after you tell me what you've done with the other girls."

I stared at Amir with my mouth agape in a mix of shock and confusion.

"How—"

"Did I manage to get all this way on foot?" he said. "Your first mistake was leaving me with all the livestock. Their milk and meat can sustain a man for a long time in the desert. Plus, I was lucky enough to catch another passing caravan after a couple of days. If you two hadn't dawdled taking your time crossing the desert, you might have made a clean getaway by now." He paused, running his eyes up and down our bodies. "Of course, I didn't have any *other* distractions encouraging me to pause for a little entertainment in the evenings."

"So I suppose you've alerted the elders by now and arranged for us to be taken before the council to be properly punished?" Laila said, stepping in front of me and placing her arm around me protectively.

"In due course," he said. "First I needed to *find* you before you slipped away. I'm afraid your fate, along with the rest of my little harem, has already been sealed, Laila." Then he turned toward me, clucking his tongue. "As for my pretty Western friend, I'm sure we can find a dark prison somewhere in the bowels of this medieval city to let her rot away the rest of her miserable life."

Amir lurched forward, placing the knife under Laila's neck.

"Now *tell* me where the rest of the girls are!" he sneered.

Suddenly, Laila reared back, kicking Amir as hard as she could between his legs and he hunched over, dropping the knife onto the ground. She quickly picked it up and before he could regain his composure, she sliced it across the front of his neck in one quick and silent motion. He clutched his throat, looking at us with wild eyes, then he fell to his knees, collapsing onto the cobblestone pavement. As a thick pool of blood seeped out of his jugular vein onto the darkened stones, the life slowly drained out of his eyes, and he suddenly became still.

"Holy *fuck*, Laila," I gasped. "You *killed* him!"

"It was either him or us," she said nonchalantly. "He got what was coming to him."

"What the hell do we do now?" I said, looking around frantically to see if anyone else had witnessed the scene. "We can't just *leave* him here. He can be traced back to us."

Laila paused for a moment as she peered around the wharf to get her bearings, then she nodded toward a nearby dock.

"We'll have to drag him to the edge of the jetty and dump him into the water. There's no one around and it's dark enough for us to dispose of the body. Grab a leg and help me pull him toward the pier."

I shook my head, hardly believing how fast our plan had unraveled and wondering what would happen if anyone saw us. But I knew Laila was right. Between the front desk attendant at my hotel in Morocco and my email trail to Hannah, there was more than enough circumstantial evidence to connect me to Amir's disappearance. The best chance for both of us to get away before the police caught wind of any malfeasance was to dispose of the body and exit as quickly as possible.

We each grabbed one of Amir's legs and after checking to make sure the coast was clear, we carefully dragged his body the thirty feet or so across the narrow roadway lining the wharf and dropped his lifeless body into the murky water at the edge of the pier. We watched his body slowly sink into the deep water, then we ducked into another alley to decide what to do next.

"So what do we do now?" I said, shivering from a combination of shock and the encroaching chill.

"You've still got your travel bag and papers," she said, nodding toward my clutch case. "You need to get changed back into your Western clothes as soon as possible and catch the earliest flight out of the country. With any luck, you'll be long gone before anyone finds any evidence of foul play. I'll pay for safe passage to the continent and try to slip into Spain undetected. Right now, we both have to get the hell out of here."

"Okay," I said, wrapping my arms around my body to keep myself from shaking. "But will I ever see you again? I hate leaving you this way..."

"It's best we make a clean break," she said, pulling me close against her breast. "We don't want anyone connecting us together after this. You'll be fine. I'll think of you whenever I'm sleeping alone under my woolen blanket."

I paused for a moment, darting my eyes across her pretty face. I hated the idea of leaving so abruptly, but I knew we didn't have any other choice. I opened my travel bag and scribbled my address on a piece of paper.

"This is my address back home in America," I said, handing her the paper. "Just do me one favor. Write me once you get situated in Spain and send me your address. It'll be safe to see you again once this all settles down. I'd love to be able to stay in touch."

"Okay," Laila said, folding the paper and tucking it away into her robe. "But you need to go now. I want you to catch the earliest flight out in the morning. I'll contact you once I get settled."

She leaned in towards me, clasping the sides of my head with both hands.

"This has been the most amazing adventure of my life," she said. "I'll never forget these few days we've shared together, my beautiful sweet, American girl. Safe travels, my love. We'll talk again soon."

Then she turned and walked briskly down the wharf into the inky darkness without looking back. I watched her robes billowing in the cool evening breeze until she disappeared in the mist, then I changed out of my thawb in the darkness of the alley and put my Western clothes back on, hailing a cab to the airport. I was lucky enough to catch the seven a.m. flight to Paris with a connecting flight to Chicago later that day. As my jet lifted off the runway and turned north over the Mediterranean Sea, I peered down at the wide expanse of sparking blue waves, smiling at how it reminded me of the golden sand ripples in the desert.

After I got home, a few months passed without hearing from Laila, and I began to fear that she might not have made it out of the North Africa. But when I received an airmail letter postmarked Seville, Spain, I tore it open and read the contents breathlessly.

Jade,

I hope this letter finds you well and fully recovered from our little desert adventure. I've thought of you often since we departed so suddenly in Algiers and miss having your smooth, supple body snuggling up next to me. You may be happy to know that I've grown quite accustomed to your Western-style grooming habits and I always think of you whenever I touch myself on dark, lonely nights. If ever you find the time to come visit me, I've enclosed my new address below.

Love always, Laila

Oh my God, I exhaled, happy to hear that she'd made it out safely. And the fact that she still had fond memories of our time together and even thought of me whenever she touched herself intimately made my heart dance and my panties moisten. As I sat in my chair rereading her letter over and over again and smelling the delicate scent of jasmine and lemongrass infused in the paper, my fingers trailed a path down between my thighs as I separated my legs slowly.

Maybe this won't be the end of my arabian adventure after all, I smiled to myself.

Ready *for more erotic chills and thrills? Enjoy the next volume in* Jade's Erotic Adventures:

I hadn't expected the scenery on this cross-continent trip to be quite this breathtaking...

Sneak peek:

I looked around me to see if anyone else could see what she was doing, but fortunately all the other guests were sitting snugly against their windows, either reading a book or quietly gazing outside. Because we were the only two people in the compartment sitting on the outside edges of our booths, we had a direct view of each other. At first, I sat dumbfounded watching her play with herself, shocked at her audacious display of carnality, but as my panties grew wetter and wetter watching her, I looked around me to make sure the coast was clear, then I lifted my ass off my seat and pulled my panties down over my ankles, placing them inside my purse. Then I pushed my hand under my dress and slid my fingers up my thighs until they reached my sopping sex...

READ MORE...

VOLUME THREE

THE DOMINATRIX

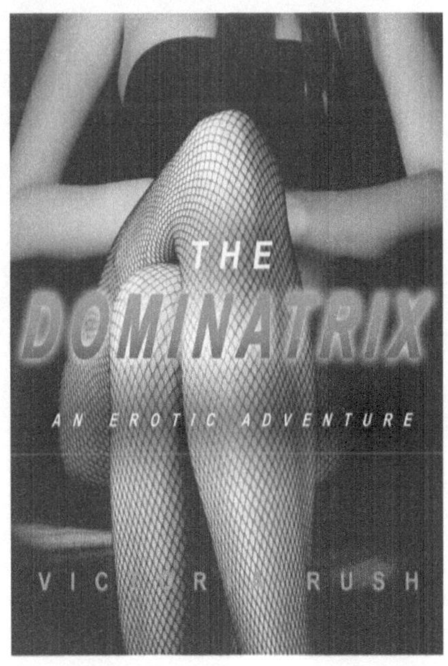

1

———————

BRAVE NEW WORLD

After my personal training sessions ended, I felt a new void in my sex life. Kate was incredibly hot and sexy and had pushed me past my limits in so many ways. She'd not only helped me restore my youthful body shape, she'd helped me realize that I could accomplish anything with the right motivation and workout plan.

But there was something else missing. I missed her guidance, her *commands*. There was something about the way she directed me through my paces that I found exhilarating and arousing. Even though she'd set me up with a self-directed routine to maintain my muscle tone, it wasn't nearly as much fun without her sexy body standing next to me, barking out orders to push out one more rep.

I needed a new life coach—one who'd push me beyond just my physical limits. I wanted a sex partner who'd fully take charge and *control* me. All I knew about BDSM was that it had something to do with bondage and domination. It was time to explore a new dimension to my sexuality.

I sat down in front of my computer and typed in the search box: *where to find a sexual master*. Near the top of the listings was a heading titled *Mistress Directory — Professional Mistresses and Dominatrix*

Contacts. I clicked on the link and a website popped up with a gallery of sexy women dressed in provocative leather outfits holding whips and chains. I scrolled through the images until I saw a sexy redhead named Mistress Velvet.

When I opened her page, my eyes widened as the screen toggled between a series of full-screen photographs of the redhead in various stages of undress. Each pose revealed more and more of her voluptuous figure. In the first slide, she lay on a white leather settee in a red push-up bra and garters. Her large natural breasts overflowed her top, with the edge of her pink nipples peeking over the seam. In the next slide, she lay facedown in a shiny black body suit with her legs playfully elevated. I stared at her tight round ass, fantasizing about burying my face in her deep sensuous cleft. The third panel showed her on her hands and knees in a corset and nylons, with her knees suggestively splayed over an assortment of sex toys. My pussy fluttered imagining her lowering herself over me.

Even more tantalizing than her centerfold-perfect figure was her incredible beauty. Her dark eyes peered at me under long eyelashes as her plump crimson lips pursed in a beckoning pout, her waist-length auburn hair cascading over every sensuous curve and valley of her magnificent figure. Whatever this vixen was selling, I wanted a piece of it. I clicked on her Profile tab where an introductory paragraph described her services:

Welcome to Velvet's Place. My name is Mistress Velvet, the supreme Sex Goddess and Dominatrix. My mission is to deliver the ultimate sensual experience and take you to new heights of pleasure through my unique style of sexual domination. I'm highly experienced with most fetishes and forms of BDSM. My specially-equipped pleasure chamber is equipped with state-of-the-art bondage furniture and stimulation equipment designed to tease and arouse you until you beg for mercy. Call now or click the chat box below for more information...

Bondage furniture? Stimulation equipment?
I had no idea what she had in mind, but I liked the idea of teasing

me until I begged for mercy. By the time I finished reading her profile, my panties were soaked all the way through imagining what it would be like to be her sex slave. I scanned toward the bottom of the page and clicked on the chat box, hoping somebody would be available at this late hour. My fingers hesitated over the keyboard, unsure how to initiate the discussion.

Is anyone there? I typed.

After a few seconds, three dots popped up in the reply window, indicating someone was responding on the other end.

Hello! someone named Velvet replied. *Welcome to Velvet's Place. How can we stimulate your senses today?*

Is this Mistress Velvet? I responded, hardly believing my luck getting hold of the proprietor on such short notice.

It is indeed. Although some people like to call me Goddess, Master, or Glaminatrix Velvet. I'm here to please. What's your kink?

What's my kink?! I thought, sitting back in surprise. *How do I respond to that kind of invitation?*

Well I'm kind of new to this whole thing, I typed, *so I'm not sure what to look for. I just kind of like the idea of someone 'taking charge' in the bedroom.*

Look no further, Velvet replied. *Though I don't do outcalls. And my sex chamber resembles more of a dungeon than a boudoir.*

That sounds kind of scary. Is there any kind of torture or pain involved with your services?

Torture is in the eye of the beholder, she responded. *I inflict just enough pain to elevate your perception of pleasure. The withholding of pleasure can be exquisitely agonizing in its own right. By the time I finish with you, I guarantee you'll reach new heights of ecstasy.*

Just enough pain? Withholding of pleasure? It sounded like she was going to place me in some kind of torture rack. But she definitely had my interest. As I imagined her teasing and punishing me, I unzipped my jeans and thrust my fingers under my panties and began to play with my clit.

What kind of tools and restraints do you use? I typed. *Can I stop it if it gets too intense?*

Not to worry, Velvet replied. *When you arrive at my chamber, we will carefully discuss your interests and boundaries, then your session will be custom-designed to meet your individual needs. All your limits will be respected in a safe, mutually agreed upon way so your enjoyment is guaranteed. We'll sign a mutually binding waiver, and every session will be recorded to ensure everyone's rights are respected.*

Recorded? I suddenly had visions of my kinky S&M session going viral over the internet.

What do you do with the recording? I wouldn't want any of my intimate details being shared with the public...

It's for our mutual protection. I use old-school analog tape, so nothing can be copied. Upon satisfactory completion of the session, the tape is yours to keep. Many of my clients enjoy watching replays of our engagement to relive the moment long after they leave. No other record of the proceedings is taken beyond this.

I paused for a moment. Making a tape actually made a lot of sense. I could see how these sessions could get out of control from both sides, and having a record of the proceedings would ensure quick legal recourse if either party had a grievance. This Mistress Velvet was smart *and* sexy. My hand began moving faster between my legs at the thought of watching myself on videotape with the sexy redhead.

Will I be restrained? I enquired.

Half of the fun of BDSM is not being in control. I have special bondage chairs and harnesses that limit your range of mobility. I will stimulate you with a variety of appendages including whips and feathers and other sensual equipment. Sometimes it's more fun not being able to touch yourself or your partner while the final consumption is withheld.

Whips and feathers? The idea of being teased and tortured by someone while holding off the final release was getting me increasingly worked up. I spread my legs further apart, beginning to feel the pleasure radiating through my body.

Do you leave—marks? I typed with one hand.

Just minor localized inflammation in the form of temporary welts, she said. *I use a special leather whip that doesn't cut the skin. I think you'll find there's nothing like a little pain to heighten the feeling of pleasure.*

I stabbed at the keys while rubbing myself with increasing intensity.

So there'll be opportunities to experience pleasure as well?

Yes, Velvet replied. *It's just that it will be on my terms, and when I choose to allow it.*

Damn. I like the sound of that. I strummed my clit faster at the thought of her bringing me to the height of pleasure, only to make me beg for release.

So I'll be tied up?

Absolutely. I'll have you bound and stretched as wide as your body will allow so I can have my way with you.

Fuck me, I thought. I tore off my jeans and panties and thrust my fingers into my steaming tunnel. This Velvet goddess was already torturing me online.

Will I be able to touch you?

Only insofar as I take the initiative to touch you first. I enjoy touching my clients' bodies and having them touch me. But there will be limited ways in which you'll be able to engage with your hands and your feet while you're bound in the harness.

I smiled at the thought of Velvet having her way with me while I could only watch.

So you get off watching me squirm in restraints?

Absolutely. That's what being the domme is all about. As my slave, your role is to satisfy any of my curiosities and sexual whims. My clients get off just as much watching me get sexually aroused as when they finally have a chance to achieve release themselves.

The thought of watching this sexy redhead pleasure herself while I helplessly looked on elicited the familiar pangs of escalating pleasure from my core.

Do allow your clients to satisfy themselves in the end? I panted, stabbing spastically at the keyboard.

Yes, in a matter of speaking. But I'm the one who's always in control. Your release comes on my terms with my choice of apparatus. I assure you that after an hour of teasing and gentle torturing, your climax will be like no other.

"God! I" gasped, as my orgasm suddenly took hold of me. The image of this sexy redhead fucking me with some kind of contraption while I whimpered for release wrapped up in a ball of chains took me over the edge. I jerked softly in my chair as the waves of passion consumed me, reading what she'd written.

I believe you, I typed, pecking at the keys.

I paused for a moment to consider the next steps.

What are your rates and how soon are you available?

I charge four hundred dollars per hour, with a fifty percent deposit payable on booking and the remainder due at the start of the session. I'm booked solid for this week except for a small window this Saturday between ten a.m. and noon. If you'd like to reserve this spot, please fill in your online profile and complete the credit card details under the bookings tab.

That works for me, I typed. *If you can fit me into your Saturday slot, this is much appreciated.*

I'll block it off pending completion of your payment. May I ask your first name so I'll know who to expect?

I paused, contemplating whether to give her my real name.

It's Jade, I said, using the pseudonym that had become so intimately intertwined with my real identity.

Outstanding, Velvet replied. *Girls are a real treat from my usual parade of uptight guys.*

I smiled, knowing that she had a strong affinity for women.

See you Saturday, Velvet, I typed. *I mean Mistress Velvet,* signing off with a winking kiss emoji.

Saturday morning wasn't the only slot of hers I planned to fit into, I thought, as my juices dripped down over my hand still inserted deep inside my tunnel.

2

———————

BONDAGE

On Saturday morning, I drove to Mistress Velvet's studio with a mix of trepidation and excitement. I was intrigued about being with a more dominant sexual partner, but I definitely felt uneasy about the idea of being tied up. As long as I remained in her clutches, I'd be completely at the mercy of someone who professed to enjoy inflicting pain.

As I drove across town, I kept shaking my head, unsure if I wanted to go through with it. I told myself that I'd check out her operation and that if I wasn't feeling entirely comfortable, I'd walk away. We'd have a long conversation about ground rules, and even if it ate into a portion of my paid session time, I needed to be sure I'd have final control over what happened to my body.

But something told me that this dominatrix was far more interested using me for her *own* pleasure than in watching someone else suffer. Anybody who was that concerned about protecting her safety with written contracts and session recordings must have long ago learned where to draw the line. The closer I got to her address, the tighter my thighs squeezed together, pinching my buzzing clit.

When my car's navigation system indicated that I'd arrived at my final designation, I looked around trying to locate Mistress Velvet's storefront. The street address comprised a long strip mall and there was no visible signage revealing her service location. I drove into the half-empty parking lot and stopped my car in front of the indicated unit number. A large plate-glass window covered the storefront with closed horizontal blinds.

Something didn't feel right. Everything was just too quiet and secluded. It would be the perfect location to torture and hold someone captive while you had your way with them. I was just about to turn around and drive away when I saw a young mother and child enter another shop a couple of doors down. I looked up and read the adjacent signs. There was a health clinic and a pet store on either side of the unmarked address. As a steady stream of patrons began to file in and out of the stores, my heart rate slowly returned to normal.

I got out of my car and walked up to the unmarked door to Unit Fourteen. Peering through the glass, I saw the familiar logo of Mistress Velvet dressed up in a naughty bodice riding a unicorn. Near the bottom of the sign was an arrow pointing down a long flight of stairs.

Of course she wouldn't broadcast her services for just any random passerby, I thought. *Who knows what kind of weirdos this kind of operation would attract? This is exactly the kind of service that should be by appointment only.*

I pulled on the handle and found it locked. I squinted at the side of the door and saw a small buzzer with a handwritten note reading *Press for Attendant.* I pressed the button and after a few seconds a female voice responded.

"Hello?" the voice said.

"My name is Jade," I replied. "I have a ten a.m. appointment with Mistress Velvet."

The door clicked and made a loud buzzing sound, and I pulled it open and scampered inside. The place had a strange musky scent, like a gym with slight undertones of lavender. The long flight of stairs led down to a closed door with a larger sign displaying Mistress Velvet's emblem. I walked down the steps and hesitated in front of the heavy door. There was a small peephole at eye height and I rapped on the surface with my knuckles.

A shadow flickered behind the peephole, then the door swung open. The beautiful redhead from Mistress Velvet's website smiled at me wearing a shiny vinyl trench coat with black fishnet stockings and high heels. Her huge breasts thrust against the reflective coating as her long curly locks cascaded over her shoulders. She was even more beautiful in the flesh, with high cheekbones, full pouty lips, and dark penetrating eyes.

"Welcome, Jade," she said, motioning me into the room. "I've been expecting you. Step into my dungeon."

When I entered the room, my eyes opened as wide as saucers. An assortment of whips and chains hung across the exposed brick walls. In each of the four corners rested a strange padded contraption. One could have passed for a conventional massage table, except for the wrist and leg cuffs strapped to either end. In the next corner stood a long padded board balancing on some kind of see-saw apparatus, with long leather straps running across the width of the board in one foot intervals. In the opposite corner rested a tall wooden throne-type chair with metal arm and foot restraints. In the final corner lay some kind of leather harness with a jumble of hopes and chains. Near the middle of the room, a long lever extended up from the floor, directly under a series of hooks and pulleys hanging down from the ceiling. If it weren't for a lone table holding an assortment of dildos and sex toys, I would have thought I was in some kind of medieval torture chamber.

"I see why you call this a *dungeon*," I said, nodding my head slowly. "It looks like more of a torture chamber."

"Everybody's a little taken back the first time they see my sex palace," the redhead nodded. "It looks scarier than it really is. I assure you, everything in this boudoir is designed to take you to new heights of pleasure."

"Only mine?" I said, noticing a huge strap-on dildo resting on the sex toy table.

"That depends on the client," she said, running her eyes up and down my body. "Under the right circumstances, we *both* can have a little fun."

I peered around the room at the assortment of bondage paraphernalia and narrowed my eyes.

"This is my first time doing something like this," I said. "Do you mind if we take a few minutes to discuss exactly what will be involved before we begin?"

"Of course," Velvet nodded. "I'd have it no other way. There are a few necessary preliminaries. Just keep in mind that I have another appointment at eleven. So we'll want to dispense with the formalities as quickly as possible in order to give you the maximum attention you deserve."

"Is there somewhere we can sit down?" I said. "I mean other than the torture rack or the throne chair?"

"Absolutely," Velvet chuckled, motioning in the direction of the sex toy table. "There are some comfortable chairs in this corner."

Velvet opened a collapsible chair and waited for me to sit down before sitting kitty-corner across the table. When she lifted her leg to cross her knees, I caught a fleeting glimpse of a black garter between her legs.

"What concerns do you have that I can assuage?"

"Well, mostly," I began tentatively, "I'm concerned about being tied up and having no ability to—*defend myself*. Will I be able to stop the proceedings at any time if I begin to feel uncomfortable?"

"Of course," she said, batting her long dark eyelashes. "We live in a civilized culture, after all. You'll always have the final say. I'm here to make you feel stimulated and excited, not to inflict unmitigated pain."

"So all I have to do is say 'stop' or 'no' when I want it to stop?"

"Technically, yes. Though I prefer each client to have a more elegant code word to terminate the proceedings. Just keep in mind that if you choose to deny me for any reason, that will automatically end the session and you won't be eligible for any refund of unused time. What would you like your code word to be?"

I paused to think of something less harsh than simply 'stop'.

"How about arrêtez? It means the same thing in French."

"That'll work," Velvet nodded. "But try to use it sparingly, since you can only say it once. I think you may find that the less control you have and the more uncomfortable you feel, the more invigorating the session will be. The whole point of BDSM is in giving complete control to your domme and in embracing the slave role."

My pussy pulsed at the mention of the word slave. I kept staring at the giant strap-on dildo on the other end of our table, thinking what Velvet had in mind for me.

"I understand," I nodded. "Where do we begin?"

Velvet reached into a drawer and passed a piece of paper and a pen across the table.

"I'll just need you to sign this waiver. And your credit card to process the rest of your payment."

"Of course," I said, reaching into my purse and passing her my card.

As Velvet processed my payment, I quickly scanned the contract. It was mostly standard boilerplate, limiting liability in the event of a dispute over the nature of services rendered. I was happy to see the clause referencing the recording of the proceedings and that I would be given the only tape upon successful completion of the session. The contract reiterated that Mistress Velvet would have complete and total authority to do whatever she pleased with me, so long as I didn't utter the agreed upon code word.

"Does everything appear satisfactory?" Velvet said, handing me the credit card voucher to sign.

"Yes, I think so," I said. "Although I'm a little confused by what 'satisfactory completion' of the session means."

"That's more for my protection than yours. It simply means that as long as I'm not physically threatened or harmed, you'll be given possession of the recording upon completion of the session. Not that I'm worried about you. But some of my male clients like to play pretty rough." Velvet pointed to a dark glass window on the far wall of the room. "Until then, everything will be securely filmed behind that wall."

I looked at the dark window and chuckled nervously.

"How do I know there isn't also some weirdo peeping at us behind that wall?"

"Fair question," Velvet said, beckoning me toward the door. "I like to be completely transparent at all times."

She punched in a code on the keypad lock, then swung the door open for me to look inside. I peered into the closet-sized room and saw an old VHS video camera on a tripod, pointed toward the window.

"I like your style, Miss Velvet," I said, appreciating her abundance of caution.

"Shall we begin then?"

"Yes, I feel comfortable now."

Velvet stepped into the video room and pressed a button on the side of the camera and a red light begin to flash. Then she pulled the door closed and we returned to the sex toy table, where I signed the contract.

"Right then," she said, suddenly changing her tone. "From this point forward, you are to address me only as Mistress Velvet or Master. I will refer to you simply as Slave. Repeat the code word that you wish to use to cease all proceedings one last time. In the absence of this code word, you are to obey all of my commands. Is that understood?"

"Yes—Master," I smiled. "The code word is arrêtez."

"Good," Velvet said. "Now strip off all your clothes."

"Everything?"

"Everything."

I unbuttoned my blouse and slowly pulled it off my shoulders.

"Where shall I put them?" I said, looking at Velvet demurely.

"Hand them to me. I'll place them in a safe location."

I handed Velvet my blouse then unclasped my bra and passed it to her. Although she maintained a steely expression as she peered back and forth across my naked breasts, the quickening pace of her breathing as evidenced by her heaving breasts above her corset, betrayed her excitement.

"Now your pants," she ordered, glancing below my waist.

I unzipped my jeans and lowered them slowly to the floor. Then I pulled off my sneakers and handed them to her. Finally, I pulled down my panties and held them out with an outstretched arm.

"What about you?" I said, running my eyes over her curvaceous figure hidden under her trench coat.

"I'm the one giving orders here, slave," she barked. "Now stand still while I appraise your figure."

She ran her eyes up and down my body, pausing for a long moment to stare at my bald hips and mound, then again at my nipples, which seemed to get harder and more erect the longer she stared at them.

"Not too shabby," she said, narrowing her eyes. "Now turn around."

I turned one-hundred-and-eighty degrees and stared at the dark window, smiling for the video camera.

"Spread your legs shoulder width apart and bend over ninety degrees."

As I followed Velvet's command, I felt the moisture beginning to accumulate on the inside of my labia.

"Very nice," she said. "Now turn around and face me again, with your legs spread shoulder width apart."

I turned around, and Velvet lowered her head to gaze at the bare folds of skin outlining my pussy.

"You'll do fine," she said. "I'm going to have a lovely time using and abusing your girlish figure. Wait here while I retrieve your harness."

Velvet hung up my clothes on a hook next to some whips and chains, then she disappeared behind me where I heard some rustling of clothes and equipment. When she returned to face me, she'd taken off her trench coat and was carrying a tangled assortment of leather, ropes, and chains. She kneeled down on the floor and spread out the equipment into a star shape, with the ropes angling out in four directions from a perforated leather harness.

When she stood back up, I ran my eyes wildly over her body. Her

D-cup breasts spilled over the top of a black leather half-corset, with her large brown nipples pointing sensuously toward me above the seam. Her waist tapered to a narrow midsection, before flaring to wide, curvy hips, framed by a crotchless black leather garter supporting fishnet stockings with long thin black straps running up the front of her bare thighs. Her pussy, like mine, was entirely bare, revealing a large nub between her legs. I sagged at my knees, gasping at her gorgeous body.

"Lie down on the harness," Velvet commanded, directing her eyes to the floor.

"Can I just—" I pleaded, wanting a few more seconds to take in her magnificent figure.

"Lie down!" she commanded.

"Yes, Master," I demurred, kneeling down on the floor. "How do you want me—"

"Place your ass at the bottom of the harness, then lie back with your head toward the ropes. I'll take care of the rest."

I did as I was told, lying back against the cold perforated leather. The harness looked like a small hammock with large holes to permit maximum access to the recliner's skin. Velvet kneeled down and straddled my waist, and my pussy throbbed as I envisioned her rubbing herself against me. But instead she reached over my head and grabbed the ropes splayed out on the floor and began wrapping them tightly around my tits. She encircled each breast with the nylon cord, then ran a figure eight across the front of my chest and tied the two ends securely around the back of my neck.

My eyes widened at the thought of having a rope tied around my neck, but I began to relax when I realized the pressure point was behind my shoulders rather than over my throat. I peered down at my tightly bound boobs, noticing how they'd already swelled from the constricted circulation. My areolas had turned a dark shade of purple and my nipples stood out almost a full inch, tingling in arousal.

Velvet paused for a moment to appraise her handiwork then peered into my eyes with a sexy grin.

"Do you like that, my sexy little slave?" she purred. She grabbed my tits with her two hands and squeezed them roughly. "Because your nipples are definitely saying yes."

"Yes," I squeaked, arching my hips to press against her body.

Velvet spread her knees wider apart, placing her full weight on my abdomen, thumping my body back onto the floor. Then she lowered her head and sucked hard on each of my erect nipples for a few seconds, making a loud popping sound each time she removed her mouth. Her wet pussy writhed against my bare stomach as she pinned her body over mine.

"Fuck yes!" I exclaimed, letting her know in no uncertain terms that I was enjoying her attention.

Then she shimmied her hips over my hard mound and hipbones, spreading her juices over my midsection like she was marking me.

"I'm going to have a lot of fun with you before we're finished," she said. "But first I need to get you properly restrained so I can have my way with you."

She waddled up my body until her pussy rested just above my face, then she grabbed my arms and tied the ropes at the top of the harness tightly around my wrists. Then she threaded the loose ends through two eyelets and tied secure knots to hold my arms high above my head. When she finished binding my hands to the harness, she peered down to see me staring at her glistening labia. I extended my tongue trying to touch her throbbing clit, but she kneeled just far enough away for me not to reach her.

"You want to lick my pussy, slave?" she taunted. "You'll have to beg for it. But don't worry, there will be plenty of opportunities for you to satisfy me soon enough. Let's get those pretty little legs of yours pulled up with your arms. I want to have unfettered access to your sweet, moist kitty."

Velvet lifted her knee and turned around so she was straddling me in the other direction. She leaned forward, revealing her pink rosebud and dripping labia. When I lifted my head trying to reach her, she shifted her body in the other direction, toward my hips. She paused for a moment over my bound breasts and rubbed her pussy over each of my distended nipples until both of my tits were thoroughly coated with her sex juices. There was something incredibly sexy about her spreading her wetness all over my prostrated body while I could only stand there and watch. My hips twisted and convulsed, trying vainly to produce some friction against my aching clit.

When she reached my midsection, she straddled my hips again and titled forward at the waist, giving me another premium view of her tight rosebud and wide-open lips. Then she grabbed my legs and wound the other two ends of the loose ropes around my ankles while spreading my legs apart. When she finished, she stood up and pulled the ropes as far as she could toward my head, binding my ankles to my hands. I was now stretched as far into an accordion position as my body allowed, with my legs splayed and pulled behind my head. I looked between my legs and saw that my pussy was wide open, with my labia spread apart and my juices dripping down the crack of my ass.

"Now we're talking," Velvet smiled, standing over me, nodding approvingly. "It looks like you're already getting excited about the idea of being hog-tied for my amusement. But you haven't seen anything yet."

She stood over me for a moment, straddling my waist in her six-inch stilettos, then stepped slowly up toward my head. I peered nervously out of the corner of my eyes, fearing she might pinch my skin with her sharp heels, but she simply sneered as she got closer and closer to my breasts. When she reached my armpits, she spread her legs on either side of my shoulders and paused to let me peer up her long and magnificent body. Her legs seemed to go on forever, and above the sensuous cleft between her legs, her tits jutted out like ripe melons from the dark stem of her corset.

Her pussy was glistening in obvious excitement, and as I watched her juices begin to run down the inside of her thighs, I hoped they might eventually reach the sides of my body. But just as I envisioned she might let me have a small taste of her body, she stepped over my head and grabbed the top of my harness and fastened three chains with hooks to the top and two sides of my harness. Then she lifted the three ends of the chains toward a large metal hook hanging from the ceiling.

"What the—?" I muttered, realizing she intended to lift me up onto the hook.

"That's right," Velvet sneered. "I'm going to hang you from the rafters like a piece of meat. Then you'll really see who's in charge here."

She connected the ends of each chain to the large overhead hook, then she grabbed the lever poking up from the floor and began thrusting it forward and back. The slack in the chains tightened, and I began to feel myself lifting off the floor. Most of my weight was supported by the black leather harness, but I could definitely feel my arms and legs stretched tighter and wider with each pull of the lever. When my ass elevated to Velvet's hip level, she stopped cranking the lever and looked down at me. Every part of my body was pulled as high and far apart as possible. I peered down my midsection, seeing my tits squeezed into tight pyramids and my hips curled up toward my face, revealing the separated parts of my puffy lips spread into a wide and gleaming crevasse.

Velvet reached up onto the two chains supporting the sides of my harness and suddenly pulled them down, angling my body forty-five degrees forward.

"Do you like that, my sweet?" she said, looking deep into my eyes, stepping forward and rubbing her bare mound tantalizingly against my splayed pussy.

"Yes, Master," I said. "Please fuck me now. I want you to have your way with me."

"Oh I will, my slave. Don't you worry. When I'm finished with you, I'll have sprayed myself all over your tight little body and you'll have licked every square inch of me."

Velvet walked slowly around my suspended body until she was standing behind my head. Then she reached up and yanked down on the chain supporting the other end of my harness. I suddenly tilted forty-five degrees in the other direction, until my head dangled just under her dripping pussy. Then she turned around and planted her ass on my face.

"Lick my rosebud, slave," she commanded. "I want you to clean me with your tongue."

3

———

DOMINATION

For a moment, I panicked. I imagined Mistress Velvet subjecting me to an increasingly demeaning series of sex acts where I'd have no ability to extract myself from my helpless state. My face was buried in the cleft of her ass and I had very little freedom of movement. I considered twisting my head and crying out my safe word, but then I remembered the contract said my session would end as soon as I did. I'd signed up for this crazy idea; the least I could do was give her a chance to explore my limits.

Besides, her anus didn't smell nearly as bad as I thought. In fact, it smelled kind of pleasant, with hints of lemongrass and vanilla. Velvet had obviously already cleaned herself with some kind of scented soap.

Of course, I thought, *she wouldn't make someone lick her unclean ass. That would be a little over the top. This was a business after all, and her success relied in large part upon repeat business.*

"What's the matter, slave?" Velvet said, rubbing her cheeks against my face. "Have you never licked a beautiful woman's rosebud before? You never know if you might like it until you try. Don't worry—I won't bite. It's time to pay tribute to your master and kiss my ass."

I tentatively extended my tongue and felt the fleshy folds on the insides of her cheeks. It was soft and smooth, not rough and gritty like I imagined. There was no appreciable taste other than the slightly salty flavor of fresh sweat that I'd experienced while running on the treadmill at the gym. Beyond the faint smell of lemony soap, the only scent that penetrated my nostrils was a sexy musk aroma, similar to the pleasant smell of a woman's freshly washed pussy.

"That's right, sweetheart," Velvet purred. "Lick my ass. Run your tongue over my rosebud and make your master feel good."

I titled my head up a few degrees, moving my tongue closer to her anus. The closer I got to her puckered hole, the more I could feel the gentle folds of her skin on my sensitive tongue. When I reached the deepest part of her pit, I closed my eyes and pursed my lips to prevent the intrusion of any undesired elements. But to my surprise, there was no change in taste or smell, and I found myself enjoying the sensation of probing her most intimate parts with my tongue. Before long, I was swirling and lapping up her bare flesh like an ice cream cone.

"Now you've got the idea," Velvet panted, as she pressed her ass down further and began to hump my face. "Be a good little slave and lick my ass all the way from my tailbone to my pussy."

As Velvet tilted her hips up and down, giving me freer access to the full length of her undersides, I opened my mouth and savored the sexy mixture of my saliva and her bodily fluids coating her ass. Every few seconds, she'd angle her hips far enough forward to allow me to see her rubbing her clit furiously with her right hand. Seeing her touch herself while I licked her most sensitive areas sent a charge through me, and I buried my face deeper into her chasm as I motorboated her tight ass cheeks.

"Yeah baby," Velvet moaned. "That's what I'm talking about. Have your way with my ass. Make Mistress Velvet cum all over your face."

My eyes suddenly flung open in surprise.

She was going to let me make her cum this way?

This bondage thing had already exceeded my expectations. The feeling of pleasuring my partner while balled up in restraints suspended from the ceiling was more erotic than I ever imagined.

When Velvet shifted her ass down my face and positioned her soaking pussy over my mouth, I moaned into her crevasse.

"Do you like that, slave?" she said. "Do you like burying your face in my sweet pussy? Lick my cunt and taste my juices. Hold still while I fuck your tongue with my slit."

I extended my tongue as far as I could into her hole, curling it to make it firmer and harder. She began to flex her knees up and down, and I penetrated her deeper. Her labia spread wider and wider apart until my entire mouth and chin was embedded in her cavern.

"Fuck, yes," Velvet moaned. "Fuck my pussy with your tongue. Make Mistress Velvet gush all over your pretty face."

As the pace of Velvet's movement on my face increased with the volume of her commands, I knew it wouldn't be long before she came. I pressed my tongue deeper inside her, trying to reach her G-spot. Suddenly, she tilted her hips down and I felt a fleshy proboscis snap into my mouth. For a moment, I was unsure what she had inserted into me until I felt the telltale throbbing of firm flesh.

It was her clitoris. She had a huge, oversized clit. It must have been almost three inches long, and freestanding like a man's cock. Firm and pointy, it felt like a red chili pepper in my mouth. I'd never seen or felt a woman's clit like this, and as I sucked it deeper into my mouth, my own clit pulsed in excitement.

"Yeah, baby," Velvet moaned. "Suck Momma's big cock. Do you like my big fat clit?"

"Umm-hmm," I murmured, wrapping my tongue around the shaft and head-banging her with my face.

"Suck it, slave," Velvet panted. "Suck my flute until I come. I'm getting close."

I could feel her juices streaming all over my face as she face-fucked me with her meaty phallus. I opened my eyes and saw her butt cheeks shaking in a spasm above me and knew that she was close. I began flicking my tongue over the sensitive end of her big clit, then she pulled out of me and planted her ass over my mouth.

"Fuck, yes!" she screamed. "Tease my anus while I come. Make your master cum, slave!"

As I flicked my tongue over her puckered opening, I watched with amazement as her hips writhed and shook over top of me. Her anus seemed to open slightly, and for a moment I worried that she intended to defecate on me in a final perverted denouement to our session. But instead, she pressed down harder onto my face and in one final thrust, let out a primal scream.

"Uhnnn," she groaned. "Fuck my anus, baby. Fuck my hole while I cum all over you."

I curled my tongue again and Velvet pressed it into her hole as her hips and buttocks shook in spastic delirium. To my surprise, I still didn't taste or smell any sign of unpleasantness, as I realized that she'd cleansed her insides also. I peered down between her cheeks and saw her long pointy clit flicking up and down in spastic jerks, like a man does when he comes. The multiple assault on my senses was simply too much, and I suddenly gushed a geyser out of my upturned pussy as I came hard watching and feeling her come.

"Oh! Oh! Oh!" Velvet moaned, as I felt her anus clamping down over my tongue in repeated contractions. This was something I'd never shared with anyone before, and I spasmed along with her for many long seconds before I felt my juices running back down along my elevated thighs and upturned ass. Velvet jerked and moaned with my face still buried in her ass, and I dribbled like a baby as my saliva and her pussy juices washed all over my face.

My first experience with bondage and domination felt more like a baptism than a persecution.

4

———

DENIAL

When Velvet finally finished cumming, she turned around and grabbed the sides of my head with two hands and pulled my face roughly into her snatch. I peered up at her still-erect clit with wide eyes, amazed at the size of her twitching womanhood.

"Good job, slave," she said. "You're a natural at this. You know how to give good head. Do you like my big girl-cock?"

"Yes," I murmured under the slick folds of her throbbing pussy.

"Do you want me to *fuck* you with it later?"

As I nodded my head enthusiastically, my pussy pushed out one last spasm of love nectar. Velvet peered up and noticed the coating of juices over my legs, then she narrowed her gaze and shook her head disapprovingly.

"What's that?" she said. "You didn't come too, did you? Because I haven't given my permission. You're only supposed to satisfy *me*."

"I'm sorry," I said. "I couldn't help it. It was just too much of a turn-on watching you—"

"*I'm* the one who decides when you're allowed to feel any pleasure. You've been a naughty girl, and now you'll have to pay the price for breaking the rules."

Velvet paced to the far wall where she removed some items hanging on the hooks on the exposed brick surface, then she lifted a collapsed director's chair and placed it on the floor in front of me. She unfolded the chair and placed the paraphernalia on the seat, then reached down and lifted two stainless steel clasps and held them up in front of my face.

"You'll have to experience a little bit of pain to pay amends for stealing some unauthorized pleasure. Do you know what these are?"

"Um," I hesitated, looking at the devices with wide eyes. "I can guess—"

"That's right," she said. "They're nipple clamps. This will teach you what it feels like to disobey your master."

Velvet pressed the front of my harness down a few inches as my head tilted toward the floor. Then she squeezed the clasps open one at a time and placed them over my erect nipples and slowly spread her fingers. As the pressure of the clamps squeezed tighter and tighter against my nipples, I groaned in pain.

"Does that hurt, baby?" Velvet said in a taunting voice. "Don't worry, you'll get used to it soon enough. You might even grow to like it. Many of my clients find the pain only heightens the pleasurable feeling of being bound and controlled."

I grimaced as I watched my nipples turn a ruddy shade of purple from the constricted circulation. But inside, I had to admit seeing the metal clamps standing firmly attached to my erect nipples was turning me on even more.

"But don't get too excited about having your erogenous parts stimulated," she said. "Because I have so many other ways to punish you."

Velvet grabbed the side of my harness and swung me around one-hundred-and-eighty degrees until my ass was facing her once again. Then she pulled the front of the harness down so I was tilted up just enough for me to see her midsection. As I watched her still-throbbing woman-cock, for a moment I thought she intended to fuck me with it to teach me a lesson. But instead, she sat down on the director's chair and picked up a long wand that looked like some kind of horse whip. Staring between my legs, she snapped it in the air in front of my exposed pussy.

"That's a very pretty kitty you have," she said. "What kind of implements do you think it might accommodate for me today? I have such a broad selection of equipment..."

Velvet slapped the leather strands at the end of the wand on top of my chest, and I flinched as I watched the strands splay out across my breasts.

"Did that hurt, baby?" she said, pinching her eyebrows together in mock empathy. "Because we're just getting started."

She slowly pulled the whip down the front of my body until the leather strands ran between my legs and spilled over my pussy. I shuddered at the first sensation of direct contact against my private parts and raised my hips begging for more.

"Do you like that?" Velvet said, raising an eyebrow.

She raised the whip over her head and held it menacingly over my quivering snatch. Then she suddenly arced the wand to the side of my hips and snapped the leather straps against the bottom of the harness. I yelped when I felt the sting of the straps on my bare ass through the holes in the harness and instinctively tilted my hips in the other direction.

"Sorry," Velvet teased. "I didn't mean to strike you quite so—*softly*."

She snapped the whip again and struck me a few inches lower on my buttocks on the same side of the harness. I winced in pain and twisted the harness as far as I could away from her.

"There's nowhere you can go, my sweet," she said with a sneer. "You're just going to have to lie there and take your punishment. But don't worry, my whips are specially designed to inflict maximum pain with minimum bodily harm. This is an equestrian whip, designed with wide, smooth-edged strands of leather that won't puncture your skin. Doesn't it feel sublime?"

Velvet shifted the wand to her other hand and suddenly snapped the whip against the other side of my body. My body jerked from the unexpected attack on my unblemished side.

"I can't hear you," Velvet said, snapping the whip in the same area, stinging my left buttock cheek.

"Yes, Mistress," I groaned weekly.

Velvet snapped the whip harder, striking me on the same tender part that was still smarting from her last lash.

"Yes, Master," I squealed, louder.

I struggled to form the right words to describe the sensation.

"It feels...tender, yet sensitive. I see what you mean by heightening my sensations."

A wide smile formed on Velvet's lips.

"Exactly. Doesn't the pain so close to your most sensitive zones make you tingle all the more in other areas?"

"Yes Master," I said, unsure if by agreeing it would be more likely to increase or decrease her flogging.

"Well then, let's finish getting you properly tenderized. It will make the next stage all the more enjoyable."

"For you or for me?" I said, wondering what she had in store next.

"Silence!" Velvet barked. "I'll tell you when you can speak. Speak now!"

She snapped the whip three times in rapid succession against the underside of my harness, each time getting closer and closer to my exposed pussy. Each time I squealed out loud, half in real pain and half in overreaction, hoping she'd have mercy and strike me more softly.

For another minute or so, she struck me repeatedly, flogging the entire underside of my back and buttocks, until she leaned over and placed the whip on the floor. I was glad that she'd spared my front side, not least because my breasts were already tender from the clamps still pinching my tender and extended nipples.

Velvet glanced up at the clock on the adjacent wall, then reached down beside her chair to pick up a new object that was outside my line of sight. It was ten-forty. I couldn't imagine another twenty minutes of this kind of punishment before our session ended.

"Have you learned your lesson, slave?" she said. "Do you think you've felt enough pain for today?"

"Yes, Mistress," I said, wondering what she intended to do with our remaining time.

"Alright then," she said, suddenly standing up. She lifted her arm and waved a long feather boa in the air. "Let's see if we can torment you with a different kind of pain. Sometimes it's the softest of touches that can be the most cruel."

Velvet lowered the boa toward the floor and traced it along the sides of the harness as she walked slowly around my suspended body. I shivered at the soft sensation of the feather against the tender welts where she'd flogged me with the whip. When she reached the other side of my body, she placed the feather at the top of my head and slowly lowered it over my face. I closed my eyes, feeling the soft fringes flow over my cheeks and jaw, raising my chest instinctively to welcome it on the lower portion of my body. When she reached my neck, she angled the boa sideways and drew it across my throat in both directions. The feathers tickled me slightly, and I giggled softly.

"It tickles, does it?" Velvet said, smiling at me gently. "Maybe this will tickle your fancy even more."

She dragged the large boa slowly over my chest, stopping to encircle each of my clamped nipples with the most delicate touch. I arched my back, enjoying the exquisite softness juxtaposed against my stinging nipples enclosed in the tight clamps.

"There now," Velvet purred. "Doesn't that feel better? Mistress Velvet isn't all about pain, you know. Don't you agree that pleasant feelings are magnified in the presence of pain?"

"Yes," I sighed, rolling my breasts across the feather to increase the stimulation.

"Shall we test this theory by stimulating your more erogenous areas now?" she said, glancing in the direction of my upturned pussy.

"Yes please," I panted, tilting my aching pussy further up in the air.

Velvet chuckled as she moved the boa onto the undersides of my upturned legs. Then she slowly waved it down my thighs toward my throbbing snatch. Even though my back and buttocks were still smarting from the flogging she'd just meted out, the feeling of the soft feather on my untouched skin made the little hairs on my legs stand up in excitement. It was true what she'd said about pleasurable sensations being magnified in the presence of pain.

But when the boa reached the base of my thighs, instead of drawing it inward toward my pussy, she tilted her arm and drew it softly across my back. The feeling of the soft feather touching my painful welts somehow multiplied the tenderness of my skin, and I grimaced as she fluttered it over the inflamed surface.

"It's strange feeling pleasure and pain at the same time, isn't it?" Velvet said, smiling at my discomfort.

I nodded softly, not wanting to encourage her too much.

"Let's see if it feels any better on the untouched parts of your body," she said.

She dragged the feather along the underside of my body toward my buttocks, then drew it up between the crack of my ass and over my pussy. She watched my legs quivering as my pussy dribbled down my crease.

"Yes," Velvet smiled, noticing the wetness between my legs. "Your body seems to agree. Are those cries of sadness or pleasure?"

"Pleasure," I whimpered, as she tilted her hand up and down, drawing the feather up and down my folds. I wriggled my hips wildly, trying to increase the friction of the feather against my burning clit, but Velvet seemed to enjoy steering it just at the edge of my love button.

"Please," I blurted out, forgetting that I wasn't supposed to speak unless spoken to.

"Do you want *more*?" Velvet said, smiling at me with a sinister sneer. "Or would you like something a little *firmer* touching your pretty little twat?"

"Yes please," I nodded enthusiastically.

"Let's see if we can find something a little more—*satisfying*."

She leaned over and picked a new object off the seat of the director's chair. When she held it up for me to see, my eyes widened and my pussy pulsed uncontrollably. It was a Magic Wand, one of my favorite vibrating sex toys.

"You've used one of these before, I see," she said, plugging the device into an extension cord snaking from the wall.

I nodded softly, twisting my hips in a beckoning motion.

"Perhaps not quite the way I intend to use it though," she said.

Velvet flicked the ON switch on the side of the handle and the ball-shaped head of the vibrator began to buzz and shake. Then she leaned over and held the vibrating head against each of my nipple clamps. I gasped at the sensation of the snaps buzzing against my tender nubs.

"Pleasure and pain," Velvet smiled, looking into my eyes. "Isn't it exquisite?"

I nodded excitedly, rolling my body in excited convolutions.

"Something tells me you might like it even more somewhere *else*," she said, glancing at my twitching pussy.

She pressed the head of the wand against the underside of my knee and slowly traced it down my right thigh until it hovered next to my quivering labia. As I felt the vibrations radiating into my core, I twisted my hips to press the vibrator closer to my aching clit.

"Do you want more *direct* contact?" Velvet teased, peering into my eyes.

"Yes, Master," I moaned. "Please—Mistress."

"Your wish is my command."

She slowly lowered the vibrator until it sat between the crack of my ass, then she pulled it forward until it rested over my anus. Feeling the vibrations directly against my rosebud while my pussy quivered in excitement was something I'd never experienced before. I began to feel the familiar urge rising up inside me and could have easily come from the stimulation to this sensitive area of my perineum, but Velvet suddenly lifted the wand off my skin when she noticed my breathing escalate.

"You see?" she said. "The anus is indeed an erogenous zone. It's not just *guys* who like to have that area stimulated. But it's too early to let you release all that pent-up energy. I have other plans for you."

I turned my head to glance at the clock on the wall. It read ten-fifty-five. There was only five minutes left in my scheduled session, and I was aching to come.

"Please, Mistress," I begged. "Let me come. I'm burning up inside."

Velvet sat down on the director's chair and lifted her thighs over the armrests, spreading her bare pussy apart.

"Is *this* what you want?" she said.

She placed the head of the magic wand over her slit then rubbed it up and down her opening, pausing for a long moment to stimulate her anus, then she pulled it back up and inserted the thick ball inside her dripping pussy. As she wiggled her hips and moaned softly, I watched her clit once again rise and extend from her body. When it had reached its full three-inch hard angry state, she pulled the vibrator out of her pussy and pressed it firmly against her twitching digit with two hands.

"Do you think you can come again, watching me get off?" she asked, peering at me through dewy eyes. "Because I'd like to watch you gush all over your thighs and ass while I come."

I shook my head, unsure if I could come again without direct stimulation. But the sight of Velvet jilling herself with two hands on the vibrating wand held against her big chili pepper clit, soon changed my mind. Within seconds, I felt the familiar pangs of a rising orgasm welling up within me, and I tilted my head to look at my twitching pussy lips.

"Yes, Master," I groaned. "I'll happily come with you."

"Good," she said. "This time I'm going to watch your rosebud pucker and spasm when you come. I'm getting close. Are you ready?"

"Yes," I panted, feeling the first waves of my orgasm beginning to wash over me. "I'm going to cum, Master."

"Uhnnn," Velvet moaned. "Cum with me, baby. Let me see your sweet hole smile and pucker for me. Here it comes!"

Velvet suddenly screamed out my name as her arm muscles tightened and she began jerking wildly in her chair.

"Jade!" she yelled. "Spray your cum all over your master's tits and cock. I'm cumming!"

As soon as Velvet uttered those words, I lost all control and my pussy and anus began clamping down hard, as all the built-up fluid inside my upturned pussy sprayed out in a wide arc directly in front of Velvet. As she spasmed in her chair, my juices spread all over her giant tits and girl-cock. For almost a full minute, the two of us faced each other, thrashing and moaning while we watched each other have one of the most powerful orgasms of our lives.

5

CONSUMMATION

After Velvet finally stopped cumming in her chair, she stood up and walked over to me. She placed her palms on the underside of my upturned legs then drew her hands down over my dripping skin and smeared my juices all over her breasts. As if winking at me, her big pink clit still stood on end, twitching between her legs.

"You're been a good girl," she said. "You know how to satisfy Mistress Velvet like a proper slave."

She noticed me glancing at her huge clit and smiled.

"But something tells me you're still not satisfied. Do you want something inside that pretty pussy to feel like a complete woman?"

"Yes," I said, peering up at the wall clock. It was two minutes before eleven. The last thing I needed was another client walking in and seeing me hanging in the air covered with my own sex juices.

"But aren't you expecting—"

"There's been a cancellation. I've got another free hour if you'd like to use it. I'm willing to offer it for half the regular rate if you're interested."

Whether she'd told me earlier that she had another appointment to encourage me to take the last open slot of the week, didn't matter to me. Right now, I desperately needed to be fucked, and I would have paid twice the going rate if she'd demanded it.

"I'm definitely interested," I panted, swiveling my hips in front of her fluttering clit.

"Good," she said. "We can take care of the payment at the end of the session. Was there anything in particular you had in mind?"

I licked my lips as I stared at her giant twitching pudendum.

"I want you to fuck me with your big girl-cock," I said, spilling out my fantasy.

"I bet you do," Velvet said. "You've never been fucked by a real ladycock, have you?"

At this point, I was hardly in a position to quibble about whether any of my previous transgender experiences qualified.

"No," I said. "Please fuck me, Mistress Velvet. I want to feel you inside me while I cum all over your pretty clit."

Velvet hesitated for a moment while she ran her eyes over my bound-up body.

"We might be able to arrange that," she said. "But first, I want you to suck me. Let's see what kind of head my pretty slave can muster up for her master."

She swung the harness around again until my face was between her legs. Her vulva was slick with a mixture of our juices, and her large erect clit waved in the air above my mouth.

"First, I want to fuck your throat to remind you who's the master. If you're a good slave and make me cum hard enough, we'll see about filling that pretty little pussy of yours with an appropriate tool."

I was disappointed that she wasn't going to fuck me yet with her big clit, but I was excited about the prospect of feeling it inside my mouth. She stepped forward until she was standing directly over my face, then she tilted my head downwards and forced my jaw open. Then she thrust her wet chili pepper all the way into my cavity.

At first, I almost choked on the sudden intrusion, but when I realized that her cock wasn't long enough to touch the back of my throat,

I relaxed and closed my lips around the shaft. It was strange feeling the pointy phallus in my mouth. It was thinner and shorter than other cocks I'd had, and it was comforting to know that she couldn't gag me with it or fill my mouth with salty cum. I wrapped my tongue around the fleshy stem and bobbed my head against her undercarriage, trying my best to give her a memorable blowjob.

"That's my girl," Velvet said. "Suck your master's girl-cock. Feel me twitching inside your pretty mouth."

She grabbed the sides of my head and pulled me harder against her vulva and began thrusting her cock deeper inside my mouth. Far from feeling used, there was something incredibly sexy about feeling another woman's wet vulva mashing against my face while she fucked my mouth like a man. As Velvet thrust her cock deeper inside me, I pursed my lips to increase the pressure on her shaft and began to swirl my lips around the pointed end.

"Fuck yes," Velvet panted. "Suck the head of my dick, slave. Just like that. Make your master cum in your mouth."

She tilted her hips down a few degrees to press deeper inside me, and I opened my eyes to see her buttocks spreading apart, revealing her twitching rosebud. As she increased the speed of her thrusting into my mouth, I could see her hole widening as she approached climax. I found it fascinating to watch this previously unexplored organ go through the same cycle of arousal, plateau, and orgasm that I was so familiar with from my own pussy.

Velvet's commands suddenly elevated in pitch and urgency, and I knew she was on the edge.

"Yes, Jade," she moaned. "I'm going to cum inside your pretty mouth.

"Ohhhh!" she suddenly groaned.

Although she wasn't cumming inside me like a regular man, there was no doubt that she was in the throes of a real orgasm, as I watched her pretty pucker spasm and clench in repeated strong contractions.

"Uh-Uh-Uh," she panted in synchronicity with each of her contractions.

I sucked as hard as I could on her twitching cock while she gushed all over my face and neck. The feeling of being prostrated underneath her while she had her way with me just added to the eroticism of the experience. Though I didn't come with her this time, my pussy throbbed and pulsed in sympathy with each of her contractions. I could feel myself leaking once again out my slit, and in my reclined state, my juices began running down my stomach and over my tightly bound breasts.

Velvet kept hold of my head, jerking softly against my face, until her rosebud finally stopped spasming, then she pulled out of me and held her twitching clit over my eyes. I watched in fascination as the pointy appendage jerked and throbbed with each new beat of her heart. She held herself over me for a moment, running her eyes all over my upturned body, nodding in approval.

"That was heavenly," she panted, still out of breath. "You sure know how to give good head, little girl. I think it's time you had a proper reward."

She peered up my body at my twitching hole.

"Are you ready to see what it feels like to have a big girl-cock inside your pussy now?"

"Yes, master," I said. "I'm so ready for you to fuck me."

"So am I," Velvet said. "I want to bury my dick deep in your cunny. Are you ready for me to fuck you like a man now?"

"Yes, master. Fuck me with your man-cock."

Velvet swung the harness around again, then angled it down until my hips were just under hers. I tilted my head up and was glad to have a clear line of sight all the way down her upper thighs. But instead of stepping forward and inserting her ladycock into my hole, she turned around and leaned over to wiggle her ass in my face.

What is it with this anal obsession of hers? I thought. As sexy as it was, I need some direct stimulation. *If she doesn't trib me or fuck me right now, I'll go out of my mind.*

As if reading my mind, Velvet suddenly lowered her hips onto mine and began swiping her wet lips over mine.

"God, yes," I moaned. "Rub your pussy against me, Miss Velvet. That feels so good."

"Mmm, yes," Velvet purred. "You're so wet. Your lips are so soft and puffy. Have you been getting pumped up watching Mistress Velvet having her way with you?"

"Yes," I panted. "I've been throbbing the whole time I've watched you. I'm ready to burst at the seams."

"I like the sound of that. Will you gush inside your master's pussy this time? I want to feel you spray all over my ass when you cum."

"Fuck yes," I moaned. "I'm gonna squirt all over your pretty rosebud."

Velvet tilted her hips toward me, and I felt her clit slip inside me.

"Yes, master," I squealed, thrilled to finally feel her inside me. "Fuck me with your big ladycock."

As Velvet began humping my hips up and down, I tilted my head forward to watch her pointy appendage pistoning inside me. The feeling of having her hot clit inside me while she mashed her pussy lips against mine felt sublime. I'd been holding off for so long feeling any direct stimulation on my pussy that it didn't take long for the passion to quickly well up inside me.

"Mistress Velvet," I moaned. "You're going to make me cum soon. I can't hold it any longer. Fuck me hard with your big cock."

Velvet picked up the pace of her pounding against my vulva, then she tilted her hips down a bit further and I felt the tip of her pointy cock tickling my G-spot. My orgasm suddenly crashed over me with the power of a tsunami.

"Fuck, yes!" I screamed. "I'm cumming! Pound me, Mistress Velvet. Pound my sweet pussy while I cum all over your pretty cock and ass."

I tensed my neck muscles to keep my head tilted forward and watched a geyser erupt from my upturned pussy as I sprayed all over Velvet's tight pucker.

"Oh God," she screamed. "I feel you cumming all over my ass."

As she pressed her hips against me with one final thrust, her buttock muscles twitched and spasmed as she jerked her hips forcefully against mine. With each strong contraction of my orgasm, I sprayed four or five powerful squirts directly up the crack of her ass. My juices bounced off her buttocks and redirected over the front of my body, reaching as far as my face a couple of times. I wailed and thrashed my hips against Velvet as she held her long clit inside me for many long seconds. When we finally came down from our highs, she pulled her appendage out of me then she turned around and licked all the way up my vulva from my anus to my clit.

"That was good, baby," she said, winking at me with a sly smile. "Did you enjoy having your master's cock inside you?"

"Yes," I panted. "Thank you, master. I really needed that. Thank you for letting me come."

"It was my pleasure, believe me," she said, glancing up at the clock. "But we still have almost a full half hour left in your session. What shall we do with you with your remaining time?"

I looked at her with wide eyes, shaking my head. Whatever it was, I hoped it would involve more of this type of pleasure than the previous pain.

Velvet peered at my twitching pussy and paused. Then she steepled her fingers together and inserted her hand all the way into my hole up to her knuckles.

"As much as I enjoyed fucking you with my girl-cock," she said, "something tells me you're used to having *bigger* objects inside your tight cunny. Are you ready for a real man-sized cock now?"

I pinched my eyes at Velvet, unsure what she meant.

"No—I don't have a real man standing by to pleasure you," she laughed. "But I might have the next best thing."

She walked over to the far wall and lifted a blanket off a long piece of furniture nestled behind the throne chair. It was a square box with a long shaft extending horizontally out the end, with a giant dildo attached to the end. She grasped the metal shaft with one hand and tilted the box up on its end, then rolled it over in front of me.

"Have you ever tried one of these?" she said. "It's a fucking machine. My clients find it can be quite satisfying once they're properly warmed up. Do you think you can accommodate a slightly larger penis inside you?"

I looked at the giant dildo attached to the end of the rod and shook my head.

"That's a mighty big penis," I said. "How exactly does that thing work?"

"I'm sure you've experienced plenty bigger cocks than mine before," Velvet sneered. "It works just like a man does, providing forward thrust and pumping action. Let me show you."

Velvet pulled the device closer to my body, then strolled over to the handle in the middle of the floor. She pushed it away from her a few times, and my body ratcheted closer to the floor. When my pussy was about level with the height of the sex machine shaft, she returned to the box and flipped a switch on its upper surface. The metal bar began slowly pushing in and out of the box as the dildo thrust inches away from my dripping pussy.

My body instinctively turned away from the automated device as my eyes widened in fear. I wasn't quite ready to be fucked by a machine over which I had little control. Besides, the phallus attached to the end of the pushrod had to be at least ten inches long and three inches thick. I wasn't even sure it could fit inside me.

"What do you think, slave?" Velvet taunted. "Are you ready to be dominated by a new kind of master?"

"I'm not sure," I said, tentatively. "Exactly how deep and fast does this thing go?"

"That's entirely up to *me*," she said, lifting a remote-control device off the top lid and thumbing the control wheel forward.

As Velvet's smile grew progressively wider, the dildo began pumping faster and faster. Although my head was shaking no, my pussy was spilling a steady stream of love juices all over my ass.

"At least *one* part of you seems to like the idea," she said, noticing the cataract running between my legs. "Are you ready to give it a try?"

I nodded my head slowly, and Velvet pulled the device closer to me until the tip of the phallus was pressed against the entrance to my hole. Then she sat back on her chair and inched the flywheel forward with her thumb. I felt the dildo press harder against my opening, pressing my lips wider apart. Slowly, it inched further forward, spreading me wider apart. My eyes widened as I watched the huge cock slowly slide inside me until it was buried to the hilt. I moaned as it filled me up, surprised I could take its full length and girth.

"There now," Velvet said. "Doesn't it feel better to have a full-sized man cock inside you? Are you ready to be properly fucked now?"

"Yes," I nodded slowly.

I still wasn't sure I was ready to be fucked by such an imposing device while being tied up and in complete lack of control. But then I remembered I could utter my safe word at any time and stop the proceedings. Besides, Velvet would ultimately be in control of the device, and so far, she'd demonstrated reasonable restraint in subjecting me to unpleasant acts.

She pushed the control wheel forward, and the dildo began slowly pushing in and out of me. The silicone composition of the phallus made it soft and pliant, making it feel like a real man's penis. Before long, I began lubricating more freely and swaying my hips in tandem with the dildo's movement.

"I see you like being fucked by a *man*-cock too," Velvet smiled. "It looks like you swing both ways. Are you enjoying being filled up by a life-size penis?"

"Yes," I panted, feeling the big dildo spreading me open with each new thrust. "Fuck me with your man-cock, Mistress Velvet."

Velvet pressed the control wheel further forward, increasing the thrusting speed of the dildo. As I began writhing and moaning in my harness from the rising pleasure between my legs, Velvet placed her free hand around her erect clit and began jerking it up and down like a man.

"Fuck yes," I said, watching her get off watching me being fucked by her robot proxy. "Rub your big clit for me. I want to watch you cum again while I get fucked by this big cock."

Velvet slid down in her chair and spread her legs further apart as she thumbed the wheel forward another inch. The big dildo was now pistoning rapidly inside me, and I arched my back preparing to cum.

"Velvet," I panted. "Fuck me with your robot cock. I'm going to cum soon. Pound me harder."

Velvet pressed the flywheel forward as far as it could go as the dildo began cavitating rapidly inside me. With her mouth opened wide and her eyes glazed over, I knew she was on the precipice with me.

"Cum, baby," I said, temporarily forgetting the protocol of master and slave communications. "Let me see your pretty clit twitch and jerk with your orgasm."

Velvet removed her hand from her cocklet and she arched her back as she lifted her hips in the air. As I watched her ladycock flutter in spasms, I pressed my cunt forward as far as I could to press the big dildo against the back wall of my cavern. As it continued to pound in and out of me, I clamped down hard over the phallus and groaned out another long hard climax. Velvet watched me twist and jerk in my harness, her big chili pepper twitching and jerking as if applause of my accomplishment.

Suddenly, she reached down beside her chair and stood up holding a strap-on dildo. She quickly fastened it around her waist, then inserted her throbbing clit in the hollow end of the tube, then she turned off the fucking machine and yanked on the floor handle to ratchet me up to her height. Then, without warning, she thrust her big dildo inside me and began fucking me wildly. I was still coming down from last orgasm but the sight of her fucking me with the strap-on dildo quickly resurfaced the tingling between my legs and I soon felt another orgasm beginning to well up within me.

"Yes, Velvet," I screamed. "Fuck me harder. Make me come again, master. It feels good."

Velvet's eyes opened wide and she peered deeply into my eyes, looking at me like a wild animal. The hollow dildo was obviously providing some kind of direct friction for her also, and I could tell from her panting and hip action that she was on the verge with me.

"I'm going to cum again, master," I said. "Cum inside my hot cunt. Fuck me!"

Velvet grabbed the side of my harness and suddenly pulled me tight against her body as she pushed forward in one final powerful thrust.

"Uhnnn," she groaned, as I sprayed one last long stream of love juices all over her bare lips and asshole.

When we both finally stopping cumming, Velvet pulled out of me and watched me swinging helplessly above the slippery floor. For the first time in almost two hours, I felt all the tension and stress of being bound and suspended in thin air slip away. I'd become fully satisfied being her submissive slave.

R eady for more erotic chills and thrills? Enjoy the next volume in Jade's Erotic Adventures:

Sometimes the best fantasies happen with strangers...

Sneak peek:

Are you touching yourself? I said.

Yes, Holly replied. *Are you?*

I am now.

I wish I could touch you the way you're describing right now.

If I could reach out through my screen, believe me, I would. I'd love to show you what it feels like to make love to a woman.

Can I see your breasts? They look very full and sexy.

I thought you'd never ask...

READ MORE..

VOLUME FOUR

PAINT ME

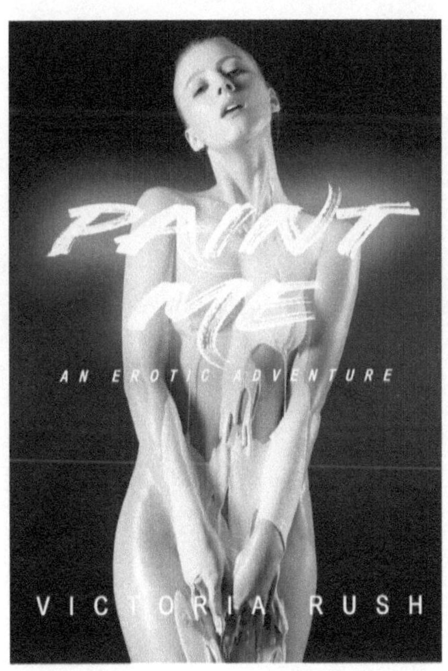

1

CREATIVE LICENSE

It had been weeks since I'd felt the live touch of another woman and I was beginning to feel restless. There was only so long I could go relying on my own devices for fulfillment, even with the help of live online partners. I needed to experience the excitement of a warm body next to me, one who responded to my touch just as I was to hers. I wanted to feel her hot breath on my skin, her moisture on my lips, and her moans in my ear.

One recent day after clearing through the checkout line at the grocery store, an intriguing poster caught my attention on the bulletin board near the exit. It had a photo of a buxom beauty dressed in a Wonder Woman costume with the headline *Looking for a New Adventure?* I stopped my cart and leaned in to admire the girl's curvy figure. Her uniform was so intricately detailed and form-fitting, it almost looked like it was painted on her. The stylized 'W' emblem on her chest arched over her firm breasts and her star-spangled briefs hugged every curve of her hourglass-shaped hips.

I'd never seen a woman in costume look so sexy and striking. As I squinted at the picture ogling her centerfold-perfect figure, I gasped when I recognized the telltale dimples and bulges on her body. At the edge of the black outline surrounding her chest emblem there were two raised nubs located in the center of each breast, and in the middle of her gold belt buckle was a little indentation right where her belly button should be. Even in the crotch of her tight blue shorts, I could make out the tiny appendage of her clitoris poking seductively between her splayed legs. I grasped the handle of my grocery cart, suddenly becoming weak at the knees.

That's not a uniform she's wearing, I thought. *She's naked! That costume is actually painted on her body!*

As I began reading the banner description to see what it was all about, my panties flooded with moisture:

Embrace your inner superhero—join our nude body painting workshop and experience the thrill of living out your wildest fantasies in the flesh. Explore your artistic side using the beautiful human form as your canvas. You can choose to be either the painter-voyeur or the model-exhibitionist. Bring a friend or partner up with one of our like-minded muses at our private studio. Either way, you'll find this to be an unparalleled experience. Find more details at nudebodypainting.com.

By the time I finished reading the ad, the front of my jeans was soaked with a giant wet spot. I found the idea of painting a beautiful naked body up close and having someone do the same to me incredibly arousing. If their customers looked anything like the Wonder Woman model, I couldn't wait to lay my brush—or my hands—on her naked body. This forum was a perfect fit with my graphic design skills. Except this time, I'd be exploring my passion for illustration with live brush and oil.

Holding my cart close to my hips to conceal the stain between my legs, I wheeled the buggy to my car and quickly drove home to gather more information about this intriguing class. When I opened the website, I was greeted with a gallery of colorful men and women bodypainted in a variety of themes. Some were covered in nature motifs with beautiful flowers and foliage covering every square inch of their bodies. Others appeared to be wearing professional uniforms that looked as authentic as the real thing. And there were plenty more superhero costumes, ranging from Batman and Superman to Catwoman and Elastagirl.

In every instance, the designs were so detailed and intricate that it was difficult to separate their naked private parts from the rest of their figures. Extra embellishment was added to their erogenous zones in a concerted effort to disguise their nudity. But as I zoomed in on each picture, it was impossible not to notice the little shadows betrayed by their bare nipples and navels. Most of the men appeared to be wearing a codpiece, but at least one brave model painted as *The Thing* let it all hang out with the creative placement of orange-colored stones coating his genitals.

As I scrolled further down the page viewing more pictures showing artists applying their brushes to the naked figures of their models, my panties clung to my rapidly moistening vulva. I imagined caressing my model's nipples with the soft brush hairs, watching them harden and elongate as I swirled the dye around her areolas. What a turn-on it must be to feel the wet oil being dabbled on the most private areas of your body! I slid my hand down my panties and rubbed my fingers along my slick lips, trying to imagine the sensation.

But I still had many questions about how the program worked. *What happens if the model gets excited while they're being painted? How could anyone not feel aroused with someone caressing your private parts with a soft, moist brush?* I imagined the studio filled with soft moans and sighs as the male models' penises hardened and the female models' hips gyrated from the pleasurable sensations.

And what becomes of the models when the artist's composition is finally finished? I thought. It would be a shame to have to wash it all off before leaving the studio. I'd want to take my newly fashioned super-hero into a private room and have my way with her as I fantasized about her using her superpowers on me. Suddenly, a Live Chat box opened in the lower corner of the website window, and an ellipsis appeared, indicated someone was sending me a message.

Hi, I'm Eva, the attendant typed. *Can I answer any questions you might have about our program?*

I removed my wet hand from between my legs and wiped it on the front of my jeans, then placed my fingers over the keyboard.

Yes, I began. *What happens if I come to the studio alone? How do I pair up with a partner?*

My clit throbbed in anticipation as I watched Eva typing her reply.

We try to schedule even numbers of participants for each session to ensure everybody has a partner. But in the event there's a last-minute cancelation or no-show, the workshop instructor will stand in for anyone who's orphaned.

Stand in? I thought. If the instructor looks anything like the gorgeous Wonder Woman model on their poster, I'd volunteer to be one of the orphans any day.

How long is each session? I asked. *Do both partners get painted by the time it ends?*

We schedule two hours for each session, Eva replied. *Most clients need the full allotment of time to cover a complete body with a detailed design. Although some artists can work more quickly, our customers find it's more relaxing and rewarding to devote all of their attention to one partner at a time. We offer a discount for follow-up sessions to encourage you to take your time and use the full allocation to create a truly memorable experience.*

Memorable experience indeed, I thought. I could only imagine how worked up both the artist and the model would get after two full hours of worshipping their partner's bodies in such close quarters.

Are we allowed to use any design of our choosing?

Absolutely. We encourage our artists to be creative. But if you have trouble finding inspiration, you can choose from a large number of interesting templates we have in our design catalogue.

My mind had already begun racing ahead with risqué ideas for my models.

I'm an experienced graphic designer, so I probably won't need too much help with that aspect of the procedure. But what happens if my partner needs some assistance?

That's what the workshop coach is for. She's available for coaching support during the duration of the session. Even if she's busy with her own client, you can still ask her questions at any time and she can pull away to provide personal help.

I smiled, imagining how far the 'personal help' might go in such a sexually-charged atmosphere.

Are the models always fully naked?

It's generally more fun to have the full canvas to work with, but we don't pressure anyone to be entirely naked. If customers wish to cover up their private areas with tight-fitting undergarments, that is their prerogative. Oftentimes it's difficult to tell they're wearing any clothing once the design is fully blended in.

I pinched my eyebrows wondering how safe it would be to allow paint to invade our private spaces.

What kind of paint do you use? Is it non-toxic and hypoallergenic?

We have three different types of paint, depending on how long you wish for it to remain on your body. The easiest to work with is an oil-based paint that goes on smoothly and is quick to wash off. But some clients like to wear their design a little longer and carry it home under loose clothing to show their friends and lovers. For this, we have a latex-based paint that hardens to a rubbery coating that you can peel off. We also have a vegetable-based paint that enables your partner to remove the coating in a more exciting manner. In all cases, the paint is fully hypoallergenic and non-toxic.

Edible paint? Holy shit! I thought. That would really allow me to let my imagination run wild with my superhero muse. But I wondered if the studio environment would be appropriate if my partner and I wanted to go that far.

How open are the workshop participants to that kind of activity, or is that something that's meant to be reserved for the privacy of one's own home?

Most of our customers find the experience of having their naked bodies painted by someone else to be highly stimulating. Plus, it takes a certain kind of free spirit to disrobe in front of a bunch of other strangers and allow your most intimate areas to be touched in this manner. We find that most clients are quite open to the unrestricted exploration of their bodies before, during, and after the actual painting process. But if you want more privacy, we also have private cubicles and showers in the change rooms for your personal use.

I began to feel my panties sticking to my thighs and looked between my legs, seeing another wet patch forming in the crotch of my jeans. The whole idea of painting nude models in the open space of a group studio was incredibly erotic. The thought of licking my muse clean after I finished painting her with a beautiful design was just the icing on the cake. I quickly wrapped up my online chat so I could attend to more pressing matters.

I think you've convinced me this is something I'd like to try, I typed with trembling hands. *How do I go about making an appointment?*

Just choose an available date and time, then fill in the online booking form under the Appointments tab and make your payment. Feel free to book either a couples session or a solo appointment. Either way, we'll make sure you're partnered up with a like-minded partner. But keep in mind that sessions fill up quickly since we limit each class size to ten participants. Hope to see you soon!

I booked an appointment for next Saturday, then signed out of the chat session and ran downstairs, scrambling through my kitchen cupboards looking for some kind of makeshift body paint. The best I could find was a few small tubes of food dye and a small jar of blackberry jam. Then I smiled when I noticed a large tub of peanut butter in the pantry. I stripped off my clothes and rubbed the batter all over my tits and stomach, watching myself in the hallway mirror. As I swirled the paste into a faux bodice and panty design mimicking the sexy Wonder Woman figure on the bodypainting poster, I spread my legs and rolled my burning clit between my fingers. In a matter of seconds, I came hard imagining myself licking the sticky substance off my moaning partner.

2

———

PAINTING OUTSIDE THE LINES

When I arrived at the bodypainting studio on the day of my scheduled appointment, I was trembling in excitement. I still wasn't sure exactly what to expect, but I knew it was unlikely to be anything like any of my previous art classes. I'd done a few nude studies before, but this took the idea of illustrating a naked body to an entirely new level. This time I'd be touching my model up close and personal, using her body as my very own canvas.

As customers streamed into the salon, I sized up each person as a potential partner. Most of the participants wore full-length clothing, so it was difficult to imagine their bodies naked and exposed under the bright lights of the studio environment. But I saw enough curvy hips and shapely breasts under their tight jeans and blouses to rekindle the memory of my body plastered in peanut butter.

Unfortunately, most of the visitors appeared to be already paired up as couples. Three of the pairs were young men and women who were obviously looking for a little adventure to spice up their love life. But one of the couples was a middle-aged lesbian pair who peered at me expectantly as they entered the room. The chunky blue-haired butch eyed me up and down, but her pretty girlfriend smiled at me as her partner led her by her hand. She couldn't have been much older than me, and I felt myself blushing as I checked out her slim dancer's figure in her skinny jeans.

That left me the odd woman out watching the hostess greet each new couple as they entered the studio. She looked to be in her early 30s with long blonde hair tied back in a ponytail. Her bright green eyes and pretty smile reminded me of the actress Charlize Theron, but her figure was all Sofia Vergara. Her full breasts created a deep cleavage in her tight-fitting blouse, and her curvy hips swayed seductively as she greeted each new guest. I glanced up at the clock, remembering the online chat attendant saying each session was limited to ten participants. With only a few minutes left, I squeezed my thighs together in anticipation of being paired up with the instructor.

But just as she moved to lock the front door behind the blacked-out windows, a young girl who barely looked out of her teens squeezed through the entrance. The moment I looked at her, she took my breath away. With shimmering auburn hair, large radiant eyes and pale freckled skin, she looked like the consummate girl next door. Fresh-faced and perky with an infectious smile, I was instantly smitten by her, quickly abandoning the notion of partnering up with the instructor. Besides, I thought, she had a more suitable palette for the design concept I'd been mulling over for my model the last few days.

With all the scheduled participants now accounted for, the hostess latched the front door and moved to the front of room.

"Good morning, everyone," she said, peering around the room. "My name's Molly and I'll be your facilitator for today's class. Thank you all for coming. I think you'll find this workshop to be a unique and exhilarating experience. It looks like everybody's already paired up except for Jade and Brianna, so if you two would like to introduce yourselves, we can get started in just a few minutes."

I looked over in the direction of the pretty redhead and she glanced back at me shyly. She seemed frozen in her corner of the room so I strolled over and introduced myself.

"Hi, I'm Jade," I said, extending my hand slowly.

"I'm Bree," the girl said in a gentle voice. "Pleased to meet you."

When our hands touched, I could feel the perspiration on her palm. I wasn't sure if she was more nervous about the prospect of getting naked in front of a bunch of strangers or from being one of the only orphans along with me. As a show of solidarity, I held her hand as I turned back to face Molly.

"Before I explain some of the logistics and protocols for our workshop," she said, "does anyone have any general questions? I know this can seem a bit daunting at first, since I believe this is a first-time experience for all of you."

One of the couples asked a question about how easy it was to remove the paint from their bodies, and I absent-mindedly glanced around the workshop. There were five distinct stations positioned about ten feet apart, each with a large easel and table carrying an assortment of bowls, paint canisters and different-sized brushes. The easels had a large sketchpad overlaid by a roll of cellophane sheets depicting various characters and images from the public eye. Some of the pictures displayed familiar superhero characters, while others showed famous reproductions of classical portraits from painters ranging from Picasso to Warhol to Vermeer. I smiled, remembering the unique design that I had envisioned from one of my own favorite artists.

"Right, then," Molly said when she finished answering the last of the participant questions. "If each of you wants to stake out a position next to one of the easels scattered around the room, let me explain how to use the materials. You'll find a variety of bowls and brushes at each of your tables, together with a collection of different colored paint canisters. These aren't the typical oil paints you find in the art store. Because you'll be painting on a larger and smoother canvas, i.e. your own bodies, we use a special fluid-acrylic type that spreads and binds more easily to naked skin.

"I suggest that you pour small quantities of each color you wish to use into the empty bowls, then select the fineness of each brush depending on how detailed your design. The broad brushes allow you to cover more area with a uniform pattern, and the thin brushes allow you to apply more detailed designs. There's also a bowl filled with clear water to clean your brushes when changing from one color to another. You also have an easel to draw some preliminary sketches if you wish and a variety of design templates to peruse for inspiration. I'll be circulating around the room and offering assistance whenever you need it, but feel free to shout out any questions as they come up. We've intentionally kept our group size small so I can give you more personalized attention.

"All you need to do now is decide who's going to start off being the painter and who will be the muse. Take your time and have fun. You'll likely find you need the full two hours to finish painting your partner's full body, in which case you can swap positions at our next class. There's a clean smock on each table, which I highly encourage the painter to use to protect your clothing. Now let's get this party started!"

Bree and I stepped toward the nearest painter's station and glanced at each other uncertainly. I didn't have any hesitation about stripping naked in front of other people, but I could tell that she was feeling a bit nervous.

"What role were you thinking you'd like to play first?" I asked.

Bree raised her eyebrows and frowned.

"I'm not much of an artist," she said, peering at my gym-toned body. "I'm afraid I wouldn't be able to do your beautiful figure proper justice."

"Not to worry," I smiled, happy she was giving me an opportunity to touch her first. "I've actually got a little experience in this area, so it might be easier for me to go first." I stared at her little buds poking under her tight t-shirt, trying to contain my excitement. "That is, if you don't mind taking off your clothes..."

Bree hesitated for a moment, glancing down at the floor.

"Do you mind if keep myself partially covered?" she said. "I've got a tight sports bra and some thong panties that shouldn't get in the way too much—"

"No worries," I squinted, disappointed that she wasn't going to give me complete access to her girlish figure. "We can make it work either way."

"Okay. Where do you want me to stand?"

I surveyed our workspace and nodded toward the area in front of a small stool next to the table.

"I suppose right here would work best. The shorter the distance from the paint and the brushes, the less mess we'll make." I paused for a moment, sizing up her figure. "Did you have any particular design in mind that you wanted me to paint?"

"Not really," she said. "If you're an experienced artist, I don't want to get in the way of your creativity. Were you thinking of anything special?"

"I had something in mind that I think perfectly suits you," I nodded. "But I'd rather keep the design a secret until I'm finished. I think it'll be all the more exciting for you to see the finished product once it's on your bare body."

"Okay," Bree said, with a curious grin. "Do you need to prepare anything?"

Sensing that she wanted a little distraction while she disrobed, I glanced toward the bowls and brushes on the side table.

"Why don't I prepare the paint while you get yourself ready?

As I opened the canisters of paint and filled five bowls with the primary colors, I listened to the rustling of Bree's clothing while she stripped. Glancing around the room, I watched each of the other models removing their clothing. Most the women chose to go completely nude, including the pretty lesbian girl on the other side of the room. The solo male model stripped down to a skimpy jockstrap covering his crotch.

Always the double-standard, I thought, shaking my head in dismay. *Perhaps his partner will be able to entice him out of this last bit of protection before they're finished.* I knew that I certainly had similar designs on my muse.

I tied the white smock around my waist then turned around to see Bree standing half-naked with her arms clasped tightly by her side. She was wearing a plain-white, one-piece bra and matching thong panties. Her pale alabaster skin looked so delicate, from a distance another observer might think she wasn't wearing anything at all. Her small but perky breasts thrust firmly against the stretchy fabric, producing two sensuous points where her aroused nipples stood. I glanced down her body and noticed the small cleft in her panties where the tight fabric hugged the indentation of her vulva. I nodded approvingly, realizing her sparse undergarments would blend in nicely with my planned design.

"You're beautiful," I said. "The perfect canvas for what I had in mind."

"You don't think the seams will interfere with your composition?"

"They might distract my *mind* a little," I smiled. "But I think we can make it work."

Bree glanced at my bowls of paint and pinched her eyebrows.

"That's a lot of yellow and black. Are you going to paint me as a leopard?"

I smiled at her and shook my head.

"Nice try, young lady," I said. "You're not going to get it out of me that easily. Though you will be nicely speckled by the time I'm finished."

"More than I already am?" she frowned self-consciously. "Don't you think I've already got enough spots?"

"Don't be silly," I said, noticing the little line of freckles running along the tan lines on her chest and hips. "You can barely see them. But in any event, they'll be all covered up by the time I'm finished. The patches I have in mind are a little more—*stylized*."

"Well now I'm intrigued," she said, spreading her legs, inviting me to begin with her lower half. "Where do you want to start?

"Let's begin at the top with your pretty face. It'll be the focal point of my composition, after all."

"Okay," Bree said, shifting her weight with a worried expression. "I didn't realize—"

"Don't worry, sweetie. I'm not going to cover you up too much. I just want to highlight certain areas of your face to add a little drama to the rest of my scheme."

I dipped a fine-hair brush into the red paint bowl and dabbled a small patch onto my palette plate, then swished it in the water bowl before adding some blue to the compound. Just then, Molly circulated by our table, watching me mix my colors.

"It looks like somebody knows her primary colors," she said, noticing Bree looking nervous as I swirled the purple mixture into my brush. "Did either of you have any questions or concerns?"

I nodded at Molly, happy that she'd arrived at an opportune moment.

"Actually, there was one thing I was wondering about. How *flexible* is this acrylic paint when it dries? I'm concerned about applying it to areas of Bree's face where changes in her expression might crack or break it."

"Good question," Molly said. "While all of our paint is safe to use on the face, if you were thinking of applying it around her eyes or mouth, you might want to consider an alternative material. We have different colors of powdered eye shadow and mascara available, as well as a full range of lip gloss colors."

"That might work a little better," I nodded. "I'll take some pink lip gloss and light purple eye shadow if you have it. And maybe a bit of rose-colored blush for her cheeks."

"Coming right up," Molly said. "I'll be back in one sec."

"*Pink and purple*, hmm?" Bree said, raising an eyebrow. "Are you painting me as a flamingo? Or a peacock, maybe?"

"Ha!" I teased. "Keep guessing—you're just going to have to wait until the end. But I can tell you that I'm not painting you as any kind of animal."

"I figure if I just keep asking these kinds of closed questions, by the time two hours have passed I'll have figured it out simply by the process of elimination."

"You can try, girl. But this is a pretty unique design. I'll be surprised if you've seen it before."

"How do you know I'll like it then?"

"Because it's one of the most beautiful pieces of art every created. And it suits your body tone and shape perfectly."

"So it's a recognizable piece of art? Are you going to paint me as the Mona Lisa?"

"I'm not *that* good an artist," I laughed. "It's pretty hard to match Da Vinci's level of skill. Besides, you didn't sound too thrilled about my painting your face, and that picture is all about the face."

Molly returned placing a small makeup kit on my table and asked if I needed anything else. I shook my head and she circulated around to the next table where the man with the jockstrap was being covered in a liberal coating of black paint.

Batman, I nodded. *Not very original, but I suppose it's every little boy's dream to play their favorite superhero fantasy.*

I flipped open the dish of eye shadow and drew the brush over the powdery paste then stood up directly in front of Bree.

"Close your eyes for a moment," I said.

"Normally I use a soft green," Bree said, lowering her long eyelashes.

"Who's the artist here?" I teased. "You'll have your chance soon enough to mess with me. For now, just stand still and let me do my job."

"I'm looking forward to it," she grinned.

I swiped the brush over each of her eyelids to create a light dusting of lavender color, then reached over to the table for the lipstick cylinder. Bree opened her eyes and smiled at me as I leaned in to apply the gloss.

"I feel like a movie star being primped for the big show. Shall I vamp while you're preparing me?"

I suddenly felt a warm rush between my legs. I was beginning to fall for this girl's personality. Her saucy attitude belied her initial sense of modesty.

"Just shut up while I attempt to make you even prettier than you already are," I said.

As I pressed the tube against her soft lips, Bree opened her mouth, exhaling her cool breath onto my face. My panties suddenly moistened and I flushed slightly.

Bree looked me straight in the eye as her pupils dilated wide as saucers. Apparently, *both* of us were getting turned on by my intimate touch. It took every ounce of my willpower not to close the short distance between us and kiss her on her mouth. The wet gloss hung seductively on her rosebud lips, and I had to bite my tongue to force myself to pull away. When I turned around to retrieve the compact containing the blush, I leaned over at the waist to give her a premium view of my tight ass.

Two can play this game, I thought, turning my face to disguise my widening grin.

When I stood back up with the blush pad in my hand, Bree smiled at me, recognizing how excited I was.

"It looks like one of us doesn't need any help in this department," she said, peering at me through half-closed eyelids.

"You're just getting me all flustered with your sassy attitude. I bet the Mona Lisa didn't give Da Vinci this much trouble while she posed for him."

"He had fewer distractions, as I recall. Wasn't she full clothed?"

"So you have some familiarity with classical art, after all," I said, patting the blush pad gently on each side of her face.

"Just a little. I had to take one course in art history as part of my liberal arts program."

"Where are you studying and what's your major?"

"UC, Public Relations."

My mind suddenly wandered to my last webcam chat with Holly, who was also a student at the University of Chicago. With her red hair and little freckles, Bree even looked at bit like her. I pinched my thighs together imagining her naked with her legs spread apart playing with her wet pussy while I watched her on my computer.

"Is everything okay?" Bree said, noticing my sudden distraction.

"Yes. It's just that you reminded me of someone I know."

"Another one of your muses?"

"In a manner of speaking," I said. "But let's get back to you. I need to concentrate on the matter at hand."

Bree looked at my trembling hand still holding the blush pad and clasped her fingers around my wrist.

"Your hand looks a little shaky right now. Do you need to take a little rest?"

"I'll be fine," I hesitated. "This next part doesn't require the same degree of...personal contact."

I turned back to the mixing table and poured a small amount of red paint into the yellow bowl and blended it with a stir stick. Then I dipped the widest brush I could find in the gold mixture and began swiping the front of Bree's body. As the brush flipped over the edge of her sports bra, it splattered a few drops under her chin. I reached for a towelette on the table and dipped it in the water then wiped her neck with a frown on my face. Bree noticed the other couples painting their fully nude partners, and she grabbed my wrist again.

"You know what?" she said. "This is silly wearing all this getup for a bodypainting class. It's just getting in the way and making a mess. Everybody else doesn't seem to mind getting naked. Why don't I lose the bra and panties? You'll just be covering me up soon enough anyway, right?"

"Um—yes," I said, feeling my heart begin to race at the prospect of seeing her fully naked. "By the time I finish adding all the intricate details of my design, it will be almost impossible to tell that you're actually naked."

"What the hell. Let's do it then."

Bree hooked her thumbs around the side of her one-piece bra and stretched it down and over her body to avoid spilling any gold paint on her face. Then she bent over at the hips and pulled her panties down to the floor, stepping out of them nonchalantly. When she stood back up, I couldn't help ogling at her beautiful figure. Her perfectly bald pussy was framed by slender but shapely hips, and her small breasts were capped with large pink areolas that looked like little cupolas atop her half-domes. To top it all off, her pointy nipples extended almost another full inch from the surface of her skin, echoing the Cathedral of Florence with its pointy lantern atop its peach-colored dome.

Perhaps I should have stuck with a Renaissance-themed design after all, I thought, admiring her classical beauty.

"Still think you can disguise this under all that yellow paint?" Bree said, raising another eyebrow at me.

"I think so. But it's almost a shame to cover you up. You're already a masterpiece just as you are."

"Stop—you're swelling my head," Bree smiled.

"That's not the *only* body part that swelling around here," I joked.

"If you're talking about my funny-shaped breasts, I'm already self-conscious enough about them. I'll be glad when you have them covered up again."

I peered into Bree's eyes, wanting to hold her.

"You shouldn't be the slightest bit self-conscious about your breasts. Believe me, I've seen quite a few in my day, and those are some of the sexiest and prettiest ones I've ever encountered. If I were you, I'd be showing those off every opportunity I could."

"I guess I'm not quite as experienced as you are. I'm still getting comfortable in my own skin."

"Well, let's paint some clothes on you then so you don't feel so uncomfortable."

I dipped the big brush in the gold paint bowl then slowly swiped it over Bree's torso and upper thighs, stopping just below her knees and over the edge of her shoulders. As I watched the hairs of the brush separate over her pointy breasts, I imagined it was my fingers caressing her instead. I was glad that I was wearing a painter's smock to disguise the inevitable wet patch that I was sure was spreading once again in my tight jeans.

"Is that better?" Bree asked.

"Much," I purred. "It's smoother and slicker. Not to mention *sexier*. Which is perfect for the character I'm painting."

"So you're painting a yellow dress on a red-headed model and it's a recognizable portrait of a famous artist. Can you at least tell me in which *century* it was painted?"

"I think I've already told you too much," I said. "If you've taken a course in art history, you could probably narrow it down pretty fast if I told you that."

"What about the *style* of painting? Is it expressionist, cubist, realism, or something else?"

"There's no way I'm giving you any more details. Though if you've seen this painting before, you'll probably figure it out pretty quickly once I start adding the details."

"Do you want me not to look down while you're painting me to maintain the surprise?"

"Yes, please. There must be plenty of other distractions around the room to keep your interest."

"Mmm, yes, I noticed. There are some pretty interesting designs taking shape. You might have some serious competition."

"Well it's not really a contest," I said, dipping my brush into the black paint bowl, "so I'm not too worried about that."

As I sat down on my stool and started to paint the vertical stripes on her stomach, I began to wonder about Bree's sexual orientation.

"But now that you mention it, which ones do you find most interesting?"

Bree took a minute to scan the room, then paused for a long moment peering into the opposite corner.

"Superheroes seem to be a popular theme. There's a Batman, Wonder Woman, Supergirl, and a Catwoman. It looks like we're the only outliers in the room."

I glanced up at Bree's face and noticed her staring intently at one of the models.

"You seem fixated on one in particular. Who are you looking at right now?"

"The two ladies in the far corner. The pretty one is being painted as Catwoman."

"You're not attracted to the naked Batman at the station next to us?"

"He's interesting too. But there's something about that woman's figure. She looks incredibly sexy with her naked body all covered in black."

I dipped a fine hair brush in the red bowl and leaned in to circle Bree's areolas with a flower petal design.

"Do you find yourself attracted to women particularly?" I said, fishing for details.

"I hadn't thought about it very much before today," she said, drawing a slight gasp when I touched her sensitive nipples. "But I have to admit these women look especially sexy dressed up in their naked costumes."

I cleansed my brush in the water bowl, then dipped it in the blue paint and dabbled it softly over Bree's pointed buds.

"Is it turning you on?"

Bree sighed as I circled her nipples with my moist brush, and she began to sway her hips unconsciously.

"Not as much as what you're doing to me right now."

"I'm just getting started," I said. "We've still got a lot of ground to cover. I haven't even gotten to your most interesting parts."

"I'm already buzzing in anticipation."

The further I moved down Bree's body with my brush, the more her hips gyrated in excitement. By the time I began painting the floral arrangement on her mound, I noticed thin rivulets of lubrication streaming down the inside of her thighs.

"Have you ever been with another woman?" I probed.

"Only in my dreams. I've never actually been with *anyone* before."

I glanced up from my stool, surprised to hear that she was still a virgin.

"Is that why you came to the body painting workshop? To explore what it would be like to feel the touch of another woman?"

"Maybe," she said. "I thought it would be a safe place to watch and explore other people's bodies without the pressure of having sex."

"I see your point," I said, facing directly in front of Bree's crotch. "I find it incredibly sexy too." I sensed that she was ready for the last stage of my composition. "Can you spread your legs for me a little bit so I can apply the finishing touches?"

"So soon?" she said. "I'm enjoying this far too much for you to stop now."

"We can always come back for more at the next session. Besides, I have a feeling you might like this next part."

As Bree shifted her legs apart, I pressed my brush between her thighs and drew the soft hairs over her glistening labia. She closed her eyes and moaned softly, tilting her mound upward. I dipped my brush into the bowl of red paint, then flicked it gently over her swollen clit.

"Oh!" Bree panted. "That feels so good. Caress me more with your soft brush, Jade."

Even though I'd covered most of Bree's body and had pretty much finished my design, I lingered for a few moments longer in the sensitive area between her legs. Gently stroking her clitoris with circular motions of my brush, I gradually increased the pressure and speed on her sensitive nub. As I listened to her soft moans and sighs above me, her hips swayed in increasing intensity along with my movements. I was incredibly turned watching her get off from the simple touch of my brush, and I fought the urge to lean in and press my face closer to her.

Suddenly, Bree grasped the top of my head with two hands and began jerking her hips directly in front of my face. I could hear her grunting softly above me, trying not to draw too much attention to our corner of the room. I squeezed my legs tightly together under my painter's smock and enjoyed a long, silent orgasm along with her. I waited until she came down from her climax before withdrawing my brush, then I looked up seeing the flush roll over her face.

"Did you enjoy that, baby?"

"God, yes," she panted. "I want you so bad. I can't wait to touch you at our next session. I've been fantasizing this whole time about how I want to caress you in return."

"We don't necessarily have to wait that long if you want to continue our partnership. I feel exactly the same way about you."

Bree looked down and smiled at me.

"I suppose we should finish up here first. Are you just about done?"

"Just a little bit of final clean up," I said, noticing the yellow paint running down the inside of her thighs. I reached for the moist towelette and rubbed the streaks falling below the hemline of her painted skirt, then reapplied some last-minute touch up where the paint had rubbed off between her legs. As if on cue, Molly moved to the front of the room to address the group.

"It looks like everyone is nearing completion of their compositions," she said. "This is always one of the most exciting parts of the workshop, where each partner gets to reveal their finished work. If you're feeling comfortable sharing, who'd like to go first?"

The Wonder Woman couple raised their hands, then moved their easel out of the way for the rest of the room to see. The model spread her legs and crossed her forearms in the famous pose, as the rest of us cheered. Just as in the poster, the black and gold outline of the "W" emblem across her chest disguised the girl's naked form, but we could still make out the shape of her breasts from the shadows cast by the overhead lights. She was wearing a short blue skirt to cover up her private parts, but she still looked stunning with her painted-on high red boots and epaulets.

"That one looks familiar," Molly said. "Very nice work. I particularly like the golden tiara painted on her forehead. Very convincing. Who's next?"

The Supergirl model stepped forward with a simple blue top and red skirt ensemble and famous red "S" emblazoned across her bare chest. She raised her arm in the Supergirl pose and flapped her cape, giggling her bare breasts under the S emblem.

"We have lots of strong female role models, today," Molly nodded. "I like your use of props to complete the package. Very pretty." Molly turned to the Batman couple and smiled. "I see we have another famous superhero in our midst."

The Batman hunk growled as he assumed the famous pose with his fists clenched by his sides. He'd brought a rubber cowl and cape to match the rest of his uniform and looked every bit the part of the Christian Bale character from the movies. The only distraction in his costume was where his codpiece protruded in his painted-on blue shorts, but we all cheered him on nonetheless.

Next to present was the pretty lesbian woman in the Catwoman costume. Unlike the other models, she was completely nude and painted in black from head to toe. We all ogled her sexy figure, paying particular attention to the sexy cleft between her legs where we could see the slit in her pussy when she spread her legs. Bree wasn't kidding when she said she was the hottest model in the room.

But when it came our turn to present, everyone gasped when I moved the easel blocking Bree's design. We were the only ones with a portrait concept, and everyone oohed and aahed at the intricate composition. I'd been careful to disguise Bree's private regions with floral designs, but you could still tell she was completely naked if you looked closely enough. She seemed to revel at everyone staring at her, but she still didn't know what she'd been painted as.

"Another exquisite piece of work," Molly nodded, admiring our design. "Now I think it's only fair for each of the models to see their partner's handiwork," she said, wheeling a large wardrobe mirror to the front of the room. "If each of you would like to take turns in front of the mirror, I think you'll be pretty impressed with the finished product."

As each of the models stepped up in front of the mirror, their eyes widened at the realism of their designs. They primped and posed as their partners took pictures of them for posterity. Nobody seemed the least bit self-conscious that a bunch of strangers were watching them stand buck naked as they channeled their superhero alter-egos.

When it was Bree's turn to view herself in front of the mirror, she smiled a huge grin when she recognized the familiar image of Gustav Klimt's famous painting titled The Kiss. She looked absolutely shimmering in the gold and black motif, with red- and blue-colored floral arrangements embellishing her golden tunic. Although she was completely nude, the strategic placement of the black and colored patches made it almost impossible to distinguish her private spots from the rest of her body.

"I had a feeling this was what you were painting," she said, turning her body from side to side. "With the gold and black paint and all the hints you were dropping, I knew it had to be Klimt."

"Are you disappointed I ruined the surprise?" I said.

"Not at all. It's a gorgeous design. You're a very talented painter,

Jade. Can you take a photo of me with my phone? I want to remember what this looks like before I have to wash it all off."

I held Bree's phone up and snapped a few pictures, then I handed it to the Catwoman model who'd moved in closer to admire Bree's figure.

"Would you mind taking a picture of the two of us?"

I asked Bree to kneel on a nearby stool, then I moved behind her and dipped my head down over her shoulder and kissed her face just like in the famous original composition.

"What a perfect way to end our class," Molly said, as everyone cheered. "If you'd like to clean yourself up before you leave the studio, we have special lotions in the changing room to help you remove the oil-based paint. Feel free to use the private cubicles if you need any assistance from your partners. I hope to see you all again soon where you can switch roles and paint your other partner with equally pretty bodypaint designs."

As I continued holding Bree in my arms in the kiss pose, I whispered something into her ear.

"Did you need any help removing all this getup?" I asked.

"Yes," she sighed, peering deeply into my eyes. "I want to feel the *rest* of you touching my naked body."

As I pressed my hips against her bare pussy, her tunic design imprinted onto my smock, making us appear as two unified lovers surrounded by the golden fold of her gilded cape.

Soon, my love, I thought, feeling her warm body pressing against mine. *Soon we can dispense with this play acting and be real lovers.*

3

HIDING IN PLAIN SIGHT

After our session ended, Bree and I showered together in the change room where I helped her remove her body paint. While it was disappointing to remove the intricate design, we enjoyed rubbing out bodies together as we channeled the two lovers kissing in Klimt's portrait. I gave Bree two more powerful orgasms running my fingers over her smooth pussy under the warm shower spray.

While we waited impatiently for our next scheduled body-painting class, we texted back and forth exchanging ideas about what design theme she'd like to use when we switched roles. We searched together online for ideas about how best to highlight my fuller figure while still maintaining a little mystery about my naked form. The trick seemed to be in adding extra detail around the private parts to distract attention from all the extra curves and bulges.

Bree fantasized about painting me as Mystique from the first X-Men movie. She thought Rebecca Romijn's body looked hot and well-camouflaged under the thick layers of dark blue paint. I preferred more playful themes, my favorite showing two hound dog faces painted over one model's huge breasts, with their red noses hiding her erect nipples. But as I scrolled through the nude models on Google Images, all I could think about was Bree's unusually puffy nipples resting atop her perky little breasts. I must have cum a hundred times remembering how it felt sucking on them in the shower of the bodypainting studio.

By the time our next session rolled around, I felt closer than ever to Bree and couldn't wait to feel her caress my naked body with her brush. When we arrived back at the studio on our appointed day, I was happy to see a new lesbian couple had joined our group. Bree seemed to have a special affinity for the female form, and I was hopeful the extra distraction would elevate her interest in deepening our relationship.

As with the first session, Molly greeted each couple as they arrived, then she locked the door and closed the window blinds to preserve our privacy. When she addressed the group, she announced a new theme for today's class.

"Welcome back to our returning couples, and to our new couple, Jenna and Lexi."

I noticed Bree sizing up the young lesbian couple, and when one of the girls smiled back at her, I felt a tinge of jealousy.

"Today," Molly continued, "we're going to work with a different type of paint called liquid latex. It goes on thicker and is more durable, so you can wear it longer and even wear it home to show your loved ones. It also can also be fashioned to look like clothing, so it makes the perfect camouflage if you're looking to create an optical illusion. Some of our clients even leave the studio wearing nothing but their body paint to test the realism of their designs."

One of the young lesbian girls raised her hand with a question.

"Yes, Lexi?" Molly said.

"Is that the same kind of paint that was used to design Mystique's costume in the X-Men movie?"

"As a matter of fact, yes. And if you've seen that movie, you might remember how good a job the paint did hiding the fact that she was completely naked in all of her scenes. I must warn you though, that this paint is harder to remove than the oil-based compound we used in our last session. You'll need to use a special body wash to loosen the film, then peel it gently off your skin. Also, if anybody is allergic to latex, you'll want to avoid contact with it. Otherwise, this new paint form can be a lot of fun to work with. As before, choose a painting station to work at, then decide which of you will be the painter and who'll be the model. I'll be floating around offering suggestions and providing assistance as needed. Just let me know whenever you have any questions or need anything. Have fun and let your imaginations run wild!"

Bree and I chose a spot near the window next to the Batman character from our previous session. He smiled at Bree remembering her sexy Kiss design from last time, and she blushed slightly, turning away.

"So, have you thought any more about how you'd like to paint me?" I asked, stealing her attention away from the hunky guy. "Maybe you didn't have such a bad idea about the Mystique character from the X-Men movie after all."

Bree paused for a moment, glancing at some of the design templates hanging from the easels scattered around the room, then flipped through a few posters on our tripod. She stopped at a picture showing a sexy woman wearing a painted-on business suit. Although the design highlighted every curve of her figure, the lapels and seams of the suit provided just enough camouflage to make it seem at first glance that she wasn't naked.

Bree raised an eyebrow and smiled at me.

"The instructor said that some people choose to wear their designs right out of the studio. Something like this might be kind of fun to test people's reactions outside the workroom. Plus, it doesn't look overly complicated for a newbie artist like me."

I glanced at the design on the easel and felt my pussy beginning to throb, imagining myself walking buck naked down the street dressed as a business executive.

"That could work," I said, trying to conceal my excitement.

Bree noticed my erect nipples poking against my thin blouse, then she peered back up at me.

"If you're going to show this to people outside the studio, did you want to wear anything underneath or do you want to be entirely naked?"

"You've already seen me in my birthday suit," I smiled. "I might as well go au naturel in my new business suit."

"I was hoping you'd say that," Bree said, running her eyes over the rest of my body. "I've barely been able to keep my thoughts off your gorgeous figure ever since we shared that sexy shower after our last painting session."

"Oh?" I said, feeling my panties beginning to moisten imagining Bree fantasizing about me while we were apart. "Did you touch yourself while you were thinking of me?"

"Many times. I couldn't wait to get my hands back on you."

"Or at least your *brush*," I said, glancing at the array of painting equipment on the worktable.

Bree looked into my eyes with a lopsided grin.

"From what the instructor said, you're going to need a lot of hands-on help removing the paint when we're done. It could be kind of fun removing your sexy outfit at the end of the day."

I hadn't thought about that aspect of the procedure until Bree mentioned it. The idea of her peeling off my clothes to reveal my naked body underneath sounded like almost as much fun as the business of painting it on. It would also be the perfect pretense to take her home with me and spend some more quality time with her.

"Okay," I said. "You've talked me into it. Why don't you prepare your materials while I get myself ready?"

As I began to disrobe, I watched the other models around the room removing their clothes. The butchy girl from the older lesbian pair had large pendulous breasts, and I wondered what theme her partner would use to highlight her fuller figure. I resisted the temptation to suggest the hound-dog faces, chuckling to myself imagining how it might look on the chunky woman. The Batman couple had also decided to switch roles, and my eyes widened as I watched his sexy girlfriend undress. She had a pretty ballerina's figure and I couldn't help staring as she wiggled her tight ass out of her skinny jeans.

One station further away, the other couple from our previous class had also switched positions, and this time the young man chose to go fully naked for his bodypainting experience. As I watched his large, semi-erect dong swinging between his thighs, I wondered how his partner could possibly disguise his oversize package with any kind of realistic design.

The new lesbian couple were cute and young, and I would have been happy to see either one of them strip naked and display her body for the rest of the group to see. When the dark-haired beauty stepped out of her loose pantsuit, I was surprised by how large and firm her breasts were. I was glad they'd positioned themselves at the opposite corner of the room where they'd be less of a distraction to Bree. I wanted her attention only focused on me, and I shifted my position a few feet to my left to ensure her line of sight would have minimum diversions.

When she swiveled around on her stool and saw me standing buck naked in front of her, she gasped.

"God, Jade," she panted. "You're even more beautiful than I remember."

"Really?" I said. "It's not like you haven't seen me naked already."

"Well yes, but that was in the close confines of the shower stall while we were standing up washing each other." I watched her eyes dart across my bare mound and flicker between my thighs. "I didn't realize how smooth your skin is. How do you manage to keep your-self so perfectly bare down there?"

"With a little help from my dermatologist," I chuckled. "Laser hair removal is a wonderful thing. If frees you up from having to undergo those frequent painful waxings at the esthetician's office. I'll never have to worry about growing unsightly hairs anywhere in that region ever again."

Bree leaned in to examine me closer.

"And there's no stubble or bumps either. You've given me a perfectly smooth canvas on which to draw my masterpiece."

I looked down at Bree with a mischievous grin.

"If you do a good enough job, I might even let you tear it off me later too."

"I can't wait. But don't distract me. I'm going to need my full concentration to do a worthy job painting this gorgeous piece of sculpture."

She turned to study the picture of the businesswoman on the easel then peered back at me.

"Do you have a preference for what color of suit you'd like?"

"Well, if I'm going to walk out of here in this getup, the least we can do is match the shoes with the outfit. I always carry a pair of black pumps in the car in case I break a heel, so either black or dark blue might work."

"Let's go with navy blue," Bree said. "I'm going to channel that sexy Rebecca Romijn body one way or the other."

I smiled at Bree's flattering comparison.

"You're going to have your work cut out for you disguising my body as well as her makeup artists did, but I'm up for it if you are."

"Do you prefer a pantsuit or a jacket-and-skirt design?"

"Let's go full pantsuit. It'll look a bit more convincing when I spread my legs. That is—if you think you can properly disguise my kitty."

Bree glanced between my legs and noticed my swelling clit poking out between the top of my labia, then peered up at me and smiled.

"That could be a bit of a challenge, but I'm looking forward to giving that particular part of your body a little extra attention." She motioned to her side table filled with bowls of paint. "You're the expert artist here. What colors do I mix to create navy blue?"

I looked at Bree's collection of bowls arranged with the same colors I'd set up from our last session.

"You can either mix black or orange with lighter blue. But you'd need an intermediate step to create orange by mixing red and yellow, so try black first. Pour a little bit of black paint into the blue paint bowl then mix it up to see how it looks. You can always add more if necessary."

Bree did as I suggested, then lifted the contents of the blue bowl for me to see.

"How's this?"

"Still a little too blue," I said. "I think we need just a touch more black to create true navy."

Bree poured a bit more black paint into the blue bowl and mixed it with the wooden paddle.

"How about now?" she said, tilting the edge of the bowl toward me.

"Perfect," I nodded.

"This first part shouldn't be too hard," she said, glancing at my naked body. The only question is what you want to wear under your suit. Do you want to go bare-chested and reveal maximum cleavage, or shall I also paint a blouse under your jacket?"

"Well, if we're going to take this outside, I suppose the less bare skin showing, the better. It's going to be difficult enough to disguise that I'm nude without drawing extra attention to my bosom."

"Okay," she said, not sure how to blend the two elements. "Should I paint the blouse or the jacket first?"

"I think you'll find it easier to paint the blouse first. You can cover the top half of my chest with white paint, then use the blue paint to draw a V-shape over it to simulate the open lapels of the jacket."

"Will you guide me along the way so I don't screw up too badly? I'm going to need a little help around the neck and with the seams to create an authentic-looking shirt."

"No worries," I said. "Just start by drawing a little band of white paint around the back of my neck, then when you get to the front, create a little V to make it look partially unbuttoned."

"What about the collar? How do I create the little flaps pointing down to the sides?"

"I'll help you when you get there. Don't worry about making it perfect. Most of the fun is in drawing it on the skin, remember? Besides, you can always wash off the paint while it's still wet if you make a mistake. Just go with it. Trust your eye."

Bree tensed her mouth into a little frown, then dipped a medium-width brush into the bowl with the white paint. Then she stood up and moved around my backside as I felt the wet brush slide along the back of my neck. She moved slowly at first, trying to create a perfectly straight line around the diameter of my neck, then exhaled heavily when she turned around to face me again.

"Whew," she said. "It's harder than I imagined drawing a straight line on a curvy surface. Now for the tough part."

She paused for a moment, looking at my neckline and large breasts, trying to imagine how a real blouse would look on my chest.

"How much cleavage do you want me to show?"

"Just enough to maintain interest but not enough to draw undue attention to that part of my anatomy."

"Okay," she said, holding the brush with a trembling hand next to my collarbone.

"Just taper the line gently into a closed V," I said. "Remember that an open blouse has a bit of a naturally wavy line anyway, so it doesn't have to be perfect."

Bree inhaled a deep breath, then slowly drew the brush down the front of my chest over the top of my breasts. I tried to remain still while she painted me, but I could feel myself shaking as the most hairs of the brush slid over my bust.

"Now for the other side," she said, repeating the process on the left side of my chest.

When she finished, she stood back and appraised her work, nodding softly.

"I think that looks about right. Now I just need to fill in the side panels and the collar."

As Bree continued to work on me, Molly circulated around the room and joined our group. She glanced at the design Bree had chosen on our easel, then looked at her work-in-progress on my upper body and smiled.

"Looks good so far," she nodded. "Did you need any help, Bree?"

"Actually, yes," Bree said. "You arrived at the perfect time. I'm trying to paint a faux blouse on Jade's chest, but I'm not sure how to create the proper edges to form the points of her collar. Can you help me?"

"Absolutely," Molly said. "The key is to adjust the shades ever-so-slightly to create the illusion of shadows at the edges of each element. Why don't I do the right side for you while you watch, then I'll guide you as you do the other side?"

"That would be perfect, thank you," Bree said.

"If you look closely, you can see that the first coat of white paint has a slight pink tinge to it from Jade's bare skin beneath. All you have to do is paint over the area in question with one or more coats to brighten the whiteness. Let me show you."

Molly chose a finer-point brush from the table then dipped it into the bowl of white paint. Then she leaned in close to me and drew a short V-shaped design pointing down to my left breast. She seemed laser-focused on drawing the design, and I was disappointed not to see her gaze stray at any time down toward my naked breasts. She repeated the sequence a couple of times, painting over the same area to brighten the white color. Then she mixed a bit of black paint with the white on the mixing palette and drew a small outline around the edge of the collar.

"Using just a little bit of light gray color around the bottom edge of the collar simulates a natural shadow effect and makes the fold stand out a little more prominently."

She stood back and surveyed her work then looked at Bree.

"What do you think? Does it look like a realistic collar?"

"Absolutely," Bree said, with wide eyes. "That's incredible how easy you made it look. Can you stay and watch me while I try the other side?"

"That's what I'm here for," Molly said. "I think you'll find it's easier than it looks."

Bree picked up the fine white brush and began slowly drawing it over my right collarbone. I could see that she was holding her breath the whole time as she got redder and redder in the face, then she looked up at me as she drew away. I blew her a gentle kiss and mouthed the words 'you're doing great'. She stood back comparing the two sides and squinted her eyes.

"I can see it beginning to take shape," she frowned. "But it still doesn't look as natural as your side."

"You just need to add a bit of gray shadow around the corners, like I did," Molly said. "You might go a few more centimeters further around the edges though, to mimic the deeper shadow coming from the other side of her body."

As Bree touched up the other side of my collar with the gray brush, I watched Molly's eyes as the darted up and down my chest from my exposed breasts back to Bree's brush. I smiled when I caught her eye and wondered if we'd have a chance to see her naked before we finished our bodypainting program. I remembered Liz mentioning in our original online chat that we might have a chance to work with edible paint at some point, and I hoped that there might be an odd number of participants at our next session so I'd have a chance to see her naked body close-up.

After Bree finished applying the gray shadow around the edge of the collar, she stepped back and furled her brows in disappointment.

"It still doesn't look as natural as your side," she said, shaking her head. "What have I done wrong?"

Molly took the brush from Bree's hand and stepped back in toward me.

"You just need to feather the grayness slightly as you move further from the tips of the collar, like this."

I felt Molly draw the brush gently down the front of my chest closer toward the top of my breast, then she glanced up and smiled knowingly at me as she assessed the design.

"What do you think?" she said to Bree. "Does that look a little more convincing?"

"It's perfect," Bree said. "Can you come back a little later when I get to the jacket lapels and seams? I might need your assistance to create the proper shading with the blue paint also."

"No worries," Molly said. "Just remember to paint over the areas you want darker and use a slightly modified shade to create the necessary shadows. I'll come back in a few minutes to see how you're doing."

After Molly left, Bree looked at me with wide eyes and exhaled through puffy cheeks to emphasize how difficult the painting process was.

"You're doing fine, girl," I said. "If the painting expert says it looks good, I'm sure it will pass the man-in-the-street test. Just keep doing what you're doing and it will come out fine. I'm just enjoying watching your pretty face contort into all these sexy expressions while you're touching me with your little brush."

"Isn't it supposed to work the other way around?" she said. "I want to make your face contort into sexy expressions while I'm touching *your* naked body."

"All in due time," I said. "I'm enjoying the buildup. Believe me, I'm getting incredibly turned on watching you do your handiwork."

"Maybe I can make you feel a little more so as I move lower down your body," she said, winking at me seductively.

Bree moved on to highlight the two sides of the seam running down the separated halves of my blouse, then dabbled a bit of gray into the white paint to draw the buttons on the placket. Then she grabbed the widest brush and dipped it into the navy blue bowl and began swiping it over my breasts.

"Now we're getting to the fun part," she said, peering into my eyes as they glazed over in pleasure.

"Yes," I purred. "Paint me, Bree. Slap that wet brush all over my tits. God, how I wish I could fuck you right now."

"All in due time," she said, mimicking my taunts from our last session. "We still haven't gotten to the interesting parts."

"Mmm, I can't wait," I said, continuing our little game of cat and mouse.

Bree continued swiping the thick brush down the front and back of my body, pausing briefly around my wrists and ankles to draw a straight hemline at the bottom of the sleeves and pant legs. Then she selected a finer brush to draw the V-shape at the front of the jacket outside the edges of the white blouse she'd painted earlier. I could feel the white paint starting to harden as it stuck to my breasts, feeling like a stretchy rubber film on my skin. I looked down and saw that my nipples were swelling, stretching the film into two shiny, frosted teats.

If this is what it feels like for a guy to wear a condom, I thought, *this isn't such a bad feeling.* I was getting more and more turned on as Bree covered my body with this sexy second skin.

When she finished painting the basic outline of the pantsuit, she paused for a moment, studying the picture of the model on the easel. She glanced again at the shading around my blouse collar, then chose another fine-point brush and dipped it in the black paint bowl. Then she leaned in closer to me and traced a diagonal line from my left shoulder over my left nipple, toward the center of my chest.

"Whatever you're doing now, I like it," I sighed, feeling the wet brush tickling my erect nipples as it flicked over my raised points.

"I'm highlighting your jacket lapels, so be still so I can get the lines right. I'm trying to use the black shadow to disguise your big nipples, so no one will know you're actually naked."

"They're not as big as yours," I said, glancing at Bree's chest covered by her splatted apron. "You have the most sensuous, swollen areolas I've ever seen. I can't wait to feel them back in my mouth when we're done with all this."

"It sounds like you've had a lot of girls' nipples in your mouth," she said, glancing up at me briefly.

"Well, not really that many," I backpedaled nervously, as a blush fell over my face.

"Don't worry," Bree said, glancing over my shoulder at the nude model at the next station over. "Your secret will stay with me. I'm kind of glad you've got more experience with girls. It just makes you a better lover, where you can teach me all the tricks."

"You have *no* idea," I said, smiling at her devilishly. "I've only just begun to share some of my girl-loving secrets."

"I'll look forward to that," Bree said, noticing the blue streaks running down the inside of my thighs. "But right now, you better put your dick back in your pants. I need you to stay composed while I finish your wardrobe. At least until the paint dries."

"Yes ma'am," I said, staring at the front of her smock, trying to distract my attention from her pretty face.

For the next twenty minutes, Bree sat facing me on her stool as she used the black paintbrush to outline the front and bottom seams of my suit jacket. I could feel the brush sliding over my skin from the center of my navel toward the edges of my hips. She seemed to be finding her confidence now, moving more quickly as she leaned back periodically to appraise the unfolding design. But when she began drawing a straight line down the front of my mound to highlight the shape of the fly on the front of my pants, I couldn't stop moving my hips as my clit buzzed in anticipation. When she stopped just shy of my throbbing nub, I peered down at her, disappointed.

"I thought you were going to spend a bit more time down there," I said. "My love button is dying for some special attention. Doesn't it need a special disguise too?"

Bree paused, holding her black brush inches from my glistening pearl, trying to decide how to best camouflage the parted folds of my swelling labia.

"Spread your legs," she said. "I think I know just the trick."

I shifted my legs apart and Bree drew a straight line from the crack of my ass to the bottom of the fly seam just above my clit.

"That's it?" I protested. "That's all the attention you're going to give me down there?"

"I don't want you to get too excited. You'll mess up my perfect design. But I'm not quite done yet. Spread your legs a little wider so I can see what I'm doing."

I widened my stance another foot apart and inhaled slowly, thinking Bree was going to tease my love button with her brush from the extra room I was providing. But instead, she tilted her head and drew a fine line down the inside of both thighs all the way to the bottom hemline of both legs. Then she grabbed the gray brush and swiped it gently over the side of my shinbones. When she finished, she stood up and appraised my body from top to bottom. Molly rounded the corner and nodded approvingly at Bree's composition.

"Very nice, Bree," she said, admiring the design. "I see you've taken my guidance well on how to create the appropriate shading to highlight the edges of the lapels and seams. That was very clever the way you drew the jacket lapels over Jade's breasts to disguise her nipples. Did you have any other questions before we wrap up?"

"Just one thing," Bree said, focusing on the front of my chest with pinched eyebrows. "The lapels still look a little flat, like they're, well, *painted* on. I've tried outlining them already with a black color. Have you got any other ideas as to how I can make them look a bit more natural and realistic?"

"I think so," Molly said. "Once again, it's all about using different shades of the base color to create subtle shadows mimicking the natural fall of light on the different angles of the fabric. The lapels naturally curve over a woman's chest, reflecting more light from above. You just need to use a lighter shade of navy to create the illusion of the natural fabric. I'll demonstrate once again on Jade's right side, and you do the left."

Molly dabbled some navy paint into the mixing palette then dabbled a swish of white paint into the mixture to lighten it slightly. Then she took a medium-hair brush and swiped it a few times down the right side of my chest and stepped back.

"See how that highlights the lapel slightly, making it seem to bend and curve naturally in the light?"

"Yes," Bree said. "Thanks for your help. I think I can take it from here."

Molly looked up at the wall clock showing we only had only fifteen minutes left in our session.

"How much more time do you need?"

"Just a couple more minutes, then we'll be done."

Molly handed Bree her brush and she dipped it back into the mixture, then she carefully swiped the brush over the other side of my jacket lapel. She stepped back and nodded at the final result, then reached over for the fine-point brush on the table.

"It just needs one more finishing touch," she said.

She dabbed the brush into the bowl of white paint, then she leaned back in toward my chest and drew a thin horizontal line directly over my right nipple.

"Well it's a little too late for that," I sighed in mock disappointment. "But I'll take whatever I can get at this point."

"I think you'll be happy with the final result," Bree said, smiling into my eyes. "We can always have more fun playing with you later. Right now, I'm excited to show you the finished product. I think you look absolutely stunning in your custom-tailored business suit."

When everybody had finished painting their designs, Molly drew our attention to the front of the room and had each model pose once again for the group.

The chunky lesbian girl had been dressed as a clown, which actually looked superrealistic with her oversized circus shoes, spongy nose, and curly red hair. The batman couple had flipped roles, with the girl painted this time as Batgirl, which didn't seem terribly inspired, but nonetheless looked sexy on her slim and shapely frame. The guy with the big dick was dressed as a fireman, with a thick coil of hose painted over his shoulder. A loose section of the hose dangled down the front of his torso, with the open end strategically positioned directly over his thick organ. I nodded at the creative placement of the brass fitting on the end of the tube used to disguise the exposed glans of his penis. Someone would have to look twice to notice from a distance that he was stark naked. I smiled, thinking how much fun the couple might have with this design after they went home and charged up his firehose with a little extra pressure. The young lesbian couple chose to go with another cartoon superhero theme, this time using the Joker's quirky sidekick Harley Quinn as their muse. Bree and I both lingered for a few extra seconds ogling her girlish figure, recalling the sexy image of Margot Robbie from the recent movie, *Suicide Squad*.

When it came our turn to present, everyone commented on how realistic the suit looked on my body, and when I looked in the full-length mirror, I was floored at how good a job Bree had done. The shadows around the shirt collar and jacket lapels made the design seem to stand out in 3-D relief, and the positioning of the lapel edges and pant seams made it almost impossible for someone standing at a distance to notice my prominent breasts and bare pussy. She'd even added a white pocket square over my breast patch to help disguise my protruding nipples. I'd never been more excited in my life to show my naked body to someone, and I was eager to test how well it would pass the public scrutiny of strangers outside the studio.

"You did an incredible job!" I said, turning to give Bree a big wet kiss.

"Do you really think so? Do you think it's fairly realistic?"

"*Fairly?* I bet I could sit at the end of a boardroom table and hardly anyone would tell I was naked. Let's give it a try and see what people in the street think!"

"You mean walk out of here just like *that*?" Bree said with wide eyes.

"Absolutely. What's the worst that could happen? Get arrested for public indecency?"

"That, and a major traffic pileup from rubberneckers gawking at your gorgeous body."

"Only if they figure out that I'm actually naked. Come on, let's get out of here and have some fun!"

4

EN PLEIN AIR

Bree and I pranced out of the art studio giggling like two schoolgirls. I stopped to fetch my black pumps from my car, then we walked arm-in-arm down the sidewalk of the local street. A few oncoming cars passed by without any sign of recognition, then one of the drivers on my side of the street stepped on his brakes and craned his neck into his rearview mirror as he passed by. We stopped at an intersection waiting for the light to change, and someone on the opposite side honked his horn when the lead car paused unusually long at the green light. When we stepped onto the crosswalk, an older woman approaching from the other side smiled at us, then her eyes opened wide when she realized that I was naked.

"This is crazy," Bree said, looking at the stunned look on the faces of passing motorists.

"It's not so bad," I shrugged, turning my head to assess the oncoming traffic. "So far I've only noticed a couple of people recognizing me. This road is too quiet to do a fair test. Let's turn down this busier street and see how many heads turn. It's much more liberating than I imagined walking outside without any clothes."

"It'll only seem liberating until a cop pulls over and throws you inside his paddy wagon."

"You only live once," I said, hooking my other arm through Bree's and pulling her across the adjacent crosswalk. "Let's live a little dangerously!"

As we began to walk along the side of the busy boulevard, most of the motorists passed by without incident, but after a short time, more and more drivers slowed down and honked their horns when they realized what was going on. By the time we approached the next intersection, men were cat-calling at us through their open windows and weaving dangerously across the road. When we got to the light, I heard the sudden screech of tires and the sound of crunching metal behind me. Bree and I looked over our shoulders, and when we realized it was only a minor fender-bender, we scampered across the intersection to the other side.

"I *told* you we were going to cause a traffic jam," she said. "Haven't we had enough fun already? Let's get out of here before someone gets seriously hurt."

I glanced around me, noticing the accumulation of pedestrians staring at us from the other side of the intersection.

"Okay, but where can we go? It's at least a twenty-minute walk back to our car."

Bree heard the sound of a passing overhead train and looked up.

"Let's take the El to the next stop. It'll bring us closer to the studio, and at least get us off the street."

"And be packed in a sardine can with a bunch of leering passengers?" I said, beginning to feel increasingly self-conscious from so many prying eyes upon me.

"It shouldn't be too busy at this time of the day," Bree said. "We'll can find a spot in the corner and I'll stand next to you to provide cover."

She glanced over her shoulder at the two bickering motorists, pulling me toward the transit station entrance.

"Let's get out of here before the police arrive."

The station wasn't as busy as I feared, and we passed through the turnstiles without incident as other commuters hurried up the escalator to catch an incoming train. Bree stood below me on the moving stairs to block the view of other people riding behind, and I crossed my arms over my chest as passengers riding the opposite escalator gawked at my unusually tight-fitting clothes. I was glad we were able to step inside the arriving train as soon as we reached the platform. We found an empty corner of the carriage and sat on a side bench facing away from the rest of the compartment.

"Whew!" Bree giggled, squeezing my hand tightly beside me. "That was a close one. I was afraid that guy from the accident was going to blame you for the crash."

"We're still not entirely in the clear," I said, glancing nervously around the compartment. "What if a transit cop sees us? I'm pretty sure riding in the nude on a public train is against the rules."

"Just be cool," Bree said, noticing the other passengers scattered around the car staring at their phones. "Nobody's noticed you yet, and we're all alone on this side of the car."

She looked down at my crossed arms and legs and smiled.

"You know, I've barely had a chance to look at you from a distance since we left the studio. Do you mind if I sit on the opposite side of the aisle and take a few pictures? It'll be kind of cool to have some photos of a nude businesswoman riding the train to work."

"What the hell," I shrugged. "Might as well milk this thing for all it's worth while the going is good. Just don't leave me alone if more passengers come down this way."

"Don't worry," Bree said, smiling at me reassuringly. "I'll protect you from any peeping Toms."

She stood up and walked over to the adjacent bench seat and reached into her purse. Then she held up her camera and tapped the screen.

"Don't look so stuffy," she said. "Uncross your arms so I can see your pretty tits. There's no point going out in public like this if you're not going to flaunt it a little bit."

I uncrossed my arms and placed my hands in my lap, not knowing where to put them. In my haste to get away from the studio, I'd stowed my purse and other belongings in my car. It felt strange to be sitting in a public venue without my phone or any other personal effects, making me feel even more exposed.

"That's good," Bree smiled, as she tapped her screen to take a few pictures. "Now spread your legs a little bit. Imagine you're riding to work and you're trying to steal the attention of a pretty girl on the other side of the train."

"Like *this* one," I said, nodding toward Bree as I parted my legs.

"Exactly. Imagine she can see between your legs and notices you're not wearing any panties. See if you can get her to squirm in her seat while she looks at your sexy naked body."

I parted my knees further and placed my right hand on my crotch as I began to rub my nub under the dry latex paint. The coating felt strange to my touch, like when I was washing dishes wearing rubber gloves. But this sensation was a whole lot more enjoyable than cleaning dishes. As I felt my button begin to swell under the tight film, the buildup of juices around my pussy made a seductive squishing sound.

"*Yes,*" Bree said. "Just like that. You are so turning me on. Can I take you home with me when we're done here? I've been fantasizing about fucking you ever since our first painting session. I want you to teach me all your girly moves."

I smiled at Bree, pointing my toes to spread my legs wider.

"If I wasn't covered in this tight film of paint, I'd show you one right now," I said, wanting to plunge my hand into my sopping pussy and finger-fuck myself while she watched me. But I was thankful to have the coating of paint protecting my bare skin from all the germs on the public transit seat.

Just then, the train roared into the next station and the doors opened as more passengers streamed into our end of the car. I shook my head at Bree, wondering if she wanted to exit at this stop. She noticed a folded newspaper in the corner of her seat and quickly threw it across the aisle to me. Two passengers took positions on opposite sides of each of us, and I unfolded the paper and crossed my legs, holding the tabloid over my chest.

With the paper concealing most of my upper body, neither of the new passengers seemed to notice that I was sitting bare-naked directly in front of them. Bree looked at me and smiled with a devilish grin. I was beginning to enjoy this process of play-acting like a regular commuter, and Bree tilted her head sideways, encouraging me to uncross my legs again. I furrowed my eyebrows, watching the pretty girl next to her clicking her thumbs on her smartphone.

Bree frowned and mouthed the words *'You only live once'* to me.

I lifted my knee and slowly parted my legs, shuffling the paper to distract attention from my shifting position. But the noise caught the attention of the girl next to Bree, and she looked up from her phone and did a double-take when she noticed the deep cleft between my legs created by my swollen labia. I froze in terror, realizing that she'd found me out, then she looked up and smiled at me before tapping on her screen with increased urgency. It was obvious that she was texting someone about what she'd just seen and I glanced at Bree, rolling my eyeballs to my side to indicate that her seatmate had discovered me. Bree looked down out the corner of her eyes at what the girl was tapping on the screen and smiled at me.

'She thinks you're hot!' she mouthed.

Suddenly Bree's brows furrowed and the color went out of her face as she realized the girl was opening the camera app on her phone. She held her fists out in front of her chest and raised them a few inches, signaling for me to cover my face. When the girl tilted her phone toward me, I crossed my legs and spread the paper as wide as I could to conceal my identity. As much fun as I was having playing this little game of striptease, the last thing I needed was for an image of me sitting naked on the subway going viral all over the internet.

When the train rushed into the next station and the doors opened, I stood up and rushed toward the exit. I'd had enough of sharing my body with a bunch of strangers, I just wanted Bree all to myself. She followed me out of the car and we paused on the platform to discuss our next step.

I noticed a taxi dropping someone off at the station entrance below the platform.

"Let's grab a cab and go home," I said. "I think I've had quite enough of this exhibitionist routine. It's time to get out of these clothes and feel your naked body next to mine."

"I was thinking the exact same thing," Bree said. "Do you want to go to your place or mine?"

"I need to go somewhere safe and comfortable. Do you mind coming to my place? We can always go back to the studio to pick up our cars a little later."

"I'm in no rush," she smiled. "Except to feel your bare skin again."

As soon as we got to my place and I closed the door behind us, I turned around and pinned Bree against the frame. As I pressed my body against her and kissed her passionately, I rubbed my burning clit against her hip.

"Fuck, that was hot," I panted. "That has got to be one of the sexiest things I've ever done."

"No kidding," she said. "Did you see the look on that girl's face when she realized you were naked?"

"I almost had a heart attack when I realized she was trying to take a picture of me. What was she typing on her phone?"

"Something about this hot babe sitting naked in front of her on the train. She told her friend you were gorgeous and that you were turning you on."

"Did that get you turned on too?"

"Are you kidding me? I almost came when you started touching yourself."

"Let's go upstairs," I said. "Help me get this stuff off so I can properly make love to you. I'm damp as a dishrag under all this plastic coating."

"Can we leave it on just a little longer?" Bree asked. "I want to fantasize about the business executive having her way with me before you go back to your normal identity."

She lifted her finger to my mouth and pulled my bottom lip down.

"You still have a few open bare patches where we can have some fun."

"As long as you help me peel this off all the *other* spots where we can have even more fun."

I took her by the hand and led her upstairs to my bedroom, then laid her atop my comforter.

"Now it's *your* turn to spread your legs," I said. "I've been dreaming of sucking your pussy ever since I covered you in yellow paint at our first workshop. Let me show you what it feels like to be properly made love to by a woman."

"Yes, boss," Bree grinned. "Teach me the right way to do the job."

I pushed Bree's torso down on the bed, then began to unbutton her blouse. It was lightly splattered with blue paint around the collar, and I smiled remembering how pretty she looked as she concentrated on painting me.

"The first thing to remember," I said, getting back into character for our play-acting scenario, "is to not rush an important task like this. The key is to tease your subject, so her arousal level slowly builds up until she's begging for you to touch her."

Bree looked at me with a playful expression.

"What if she's *already* seriously turned on from all the foreplay we've just been through?"

I paused, peering at her with a lopsided grin, then I grabbed the two sides of her blouse and ripped it apart, revealing her bare breasts.

"Then you dispense with any unnecessary effort and seize the opportunity when it reveals itself."

"Hey!" Bree protested in mock indignation. "That was one of my most expensive blouses. Now you're going to have to give me a raise."

"Oh, I'll give you a *raise*, alright," I sneered, leaning down to suck her puffy areolas into my mouth.

As I sucked on her teats, I could feel them swelling in my mouth, and after a few moments I lifted my head and stared at her unique double-domed breasts.

"That's my girl," I panted. "God, how I love your pointy breasts. Do you like it when I suck on your pretty tits?"

"Yes," Bree sighed. "Show me how to properly lick a woman's breasts. I want to learn everything from you so I can return the favor when it's your turn."

"Mmm, yes," I smiled. "Soon enough. But since this is your first time, I think it's only fair that I spend a little more time with you. Lie back while I worship your beautiful temple."

I placed my mouth back over Bree's swollen nipples and circled my tongue around her tips as I felt them harden and press further into my mouth.

"That feels so good, Jade," Bree moaned. "Don't stop. Suck my big pink nipples. Hold me like the lovers in Klimt's painting."

"I couldn't touch you the way I wanted while I was painting you," I said, moving up to kiss her lips. The brush can only accomplish so much. You've got to lose yourself in your painting in order to truly appreciate it's beauty."

"Yes, Jade," Bree panted. "Lose yourself in me. I want to feel you become one with me just like the lovers in the painting."

Seeing the flush in her pale cheeks, I bent down and began kissing her down the front of her torso. As I passed her breasts, I reached out one last time and squeezed them gently, rolling her thick nipples between my fingers. I could have spent all day playing with her tits, but her gyrating hips told me she wanted my attention elsewhere.

When I reached her navel, I unfastened the button at the top of her jeans then I unzipped her pants and pulled them off her legs. She was wearing gold-covered lace panties, and I smiled remembering what it was like to touch her there while I painted her at the studio.

"You shouldn't have," I purred, looking at her bare skin under the lacy threads.

"This time you can *remove* the yellow from my body rather than covering me with it."

"That's exactly what I was thinking," I said.

As I curled my fingers under the top of her panties, she lifted her hips off the mattress and I pulled them softly down her thighs. This was the first time I'd seen her pussy fully exposed from below, and I gasped when I saw how delicate it looked. She had the prettiest puffy folds of symmetrical lips running along both sides of her slit and not a single hair follicle in sight. With her pale, perfectly bald skin, her cunny almost looked like a little girl's, and I felt the latex covering sticking to my snatch as my pussy began to water like an open faucet. I could see the head of her clit poking out from its sheath, throbbing in the glistening overhead light.

"God damn, Bree," I panted. "Just when I thought you couldn't possibly get any sexier. That's the prettiest pussy I've ever laid eyes on."

"I'm glad you like it. I spent a lot of time today getting myself properly prepared. I know how you like it smooth and bald."

"I do," I said. "It's as smooth as a baby's bottom."

"Lick my bare pussy, Jade. Show me how to make love to a woman."

"Oh, Bree," I said. "You have no idea how much I've wanted to do this. Just lie back and enjoy."

I lowered myself onto the bed between Bree's legs and began kissing her thighs up toward her mound. The closer I got to her pussy, the wetter her skin became as her lubrication streamed down her legs. I moaned, remembering the image of the yellow paint running down the inside of her thighs when I brushed her bare vulva in the workshop. I lapped up her sweet nectar and closed my eyes savoring the fresh scent.

When I reached her pussy, I flattened my tongue and licked the front of her slit like an ice cream cone up and down a few times, as Bree made soft mewing sounds. Then I closed my lips around her soft labia and sucked her flesh into my mouth. Bree spread her legs wider for me, and I nibbled my way up toward the apex of her folds. When I finally reached her burning clit and closed my mouth around her, she gasped and pressed her mound into my face.

"Oh God," she moaned. "It feels incredible to feel your lips around me. I'm going to come, Jade. Hold me close."

I was surprised that Bree was ready to climax so quickly, but I knew that this was her first time experiencing cunnilingus, and I was thrilled she was so turned on by my touch. Her hips jerked softly against my face as she grunted above me, and I pressed my tongue against her bud, feeling it tremble in my mouth. I held her gently while she came down from her high, then I pulled myself up beside her and peered into her blushing face.

"That was fast," I said.

"I've never felt anything like that before," she said. "That's way better than doing it by hand."

"Even with a wet brush?" I said, smiling into her eyes.

"Well you were giving me a little more focused attention down there this time. Speaking of which, I promised you more of that at the studio. Can I return the favor now?"

"By all means," I said. "But I think you'll have to help me off with my clothes first. I'm probably covered in who-knows-how-many germs from the subway seat."

Bree peered back at me and smiled.

"Maybe I only need to remove a little flap over your strategic areas. Let me enjoy this little fantasy for a little longer."

I kissed Bree softly, feeling the wetness building up in my crotch.

"Okay, but I have a feeling you won't need any special moisturizer to loosen things up down there. I'm already soaking wet between my legs."

As Bree wiggled her body down beside me, she kissed and licked the sticky paint covering my torso. When she reached my breasts, she squeezed them gently and flicked her tongue around my nipples just I'd done with earlier.

"What does it feel like underneath all this paint?" she asked.

"Kind of strange, actually. I can feel you touching me, but everything is kind of desensitized."

"That's not what your *nipples* are telling me," Bree said, noticing my teats pushing up against the stretchy film.

"Maybe this is what it feels like for a guy wearing a condom," I mused. "He can get hard, but it doesn't feel the same as going au naturel. I've always enjoyed the touch of bare skin far more."

"We can arrange that," Bree smiled, noticing my hips beginning to gyrate in excitement.

She lifted herself up and positioned herself between my thighs, then paused for a moment to study her handiwork.

"It almost seems a shame to take this off," she said. "I drew the paint seam so perfectly right over your crot—"

"If you don't tear these off me soon," I interrupted, "I'm gonna jump you and fuck you, pretty pants or not. I'm dying to feel your sweet mouth on my bare lips."

Bree looked up at me with a devilish grin.

"I'm just playing with you. You told me earlier that the key to making love to a woman is to tease her until she's begging for you to touch her."

"You're a quick study, girl," I smiled back at her. "But I think you've gotten me properly warmed up. Now get down there and show me some love."

"Yes boss."

She spread my legs further apart, then she dug her fingernails into the sides of my vulva and drew them down toward my bottom. I could feel the rubbery film stretching, then I felt a rush of cool air as the seal broke over my wet pussy. It was an exhilarating feeling being exposed in this raw condition to Bree, but I worried that the lack of fresh air to my covered pussy over the last couple of hours might create an unpleasant smell.

"It feels so good to let my pussy breathe again," I said. "But it must stink down there after being all closed up this long."

Bree moved in closer and began to peel the layer of film away from my perineum.

"Not at all," she said, inhaling a deep breath through her nose. "You just smell...*sexy*."

"At least it should be *clean* down there," I said. "Nothing else has touched me since I showered this morning."

"Let's see if we can remedy that situation."

When I felt Bree's lips touch my pussy, I moaned as I tilted my hips up to meet her lips.

"God, I needed this so bad," I hissed. "I feel like I've been freed from a cage. Suck my pussy, baby. Make your boss cum with your pretty lips."

She proceeded to nibble and tease my labia as I'd shown her earlier, then she placed her lips over my raging clit and sucked me into her mouth.

"Yes, Bree," I panted. "Suck my clit. It feels so good."

Bree circled my pearl with her tongue, then she began flicking it up and down in a repeating pattern. I lifted my head and pulled her head up gently.

"Don't forget to mix it up a bit, baby," I said. "A girl likes to feel like she's being worshipped down there, not trilled by a teenage boy. Pretend you're licking a lollypop. Sometimes you suck on it, sometimes you lick it, and sometimes you roll it around in your mouth. It's the *variety* that turns your partner on."

"Sorry, Jade," she said, looking up at me with her wet face. "This is all so new for me. I'm glad you're teaching me. I want to learn how to satisfy you. Keep telling me what you like while I lick you."

She placed her face back between my legs and rolled my nub around her mouth, alternating between licking and sucking. As I began to feel my passion rising, I rolled my hips on the bed and moaned in excitement.

"That's perfect, Bree," I panted. "I'm getting close. Make love to me with your mouth."

I reached down with my two hands and pulled her face tighter against my pussy. It didn't take long for me to reach the point of no return, and I lifted my hips off the bed as I cupped Bree's face in my hands.

"I'm going to come for you baby," I groaned. "I'm gonna cum so hard in your mouth."

When the wave finally poured over me, I whinnied like an injured animal from the pleasure rolling over me.

"Uhhn," I moaned. "I'm cumming, Bree! Taste me, baby."

As the explosion of built-up lubrication inside my pussy poured out of me, I felt my juices spraying against the side of my thighs and all over Bree's face as I held her tightly against me. My contractions lasted for almost a full minute while I jerked and heaved my hips in the throes of climax. When I finally collapsed my body back onto the bed, Bree lay transfixed watching my vulva continue spasming until I exhaled heavily, signaling the end of my powerful orgasm.

"That was so hot!" she exclaimed, shimmying up excitedly beside me. Her looked like she'd devoured a messy watermelon. "I didn't know a girl could squirt like that. You almost *drowned* me with your juices."

"Sorry, baby. I can get pretty wet when I'm turned on. I think I had quite a bit pent up inside me from all the foreplay leading up to this. When you made me cum so hard, it just gushed all out of me."

"So I did a pretty good job for my first time, boss?" she said, smiling at me.

"Yes, baby," I said, peering into her pretty green eyes.

I placed my mouth over her glistening lips and tasted my sweetness coating her face.

"And next time," I said, remembering that we'd be using edible paint at our next painting session, "I'll be the one eating you all up."

5

FORBIDDEN FRUIT

I made love to Bree all afternoon, bringing her to multiple new highs worshipping her tender body. I wanted her to spend the night, but she was beginning to experience cramps from all the powerful orgasms she'd experienced, and she had mid-term exams the next day. In the intervening days leading up to our next body-painting class, we texted back and forth like lovestruck teenagers, teasing each other about what we planned to do at the next session.

I went online and scrolled through hundreds of images of nude bodypainting models, but by the morning of our class, I still wasn't sure what theme I'd like to use. It was Bree's turn to be the model again, and I was looking forward to playing out our fantasies in front the whole class. I wasn't sure how far Molly would allow us to explore our partners in full view of the other participants, but I had a feeling the addition of edible paint would create some strong temptations.

When Bree and I arrived at the studio, three of the couples from the last session were already there and they asked us about our experience testing our business suit design in the street. The young lesbian couple seemed particularly interested in where we went, and when we told them about our train experience, their eyes widened in excitement. Everybody seemed more charged up than usual for today's class, but I noticed the fireman stud from the previous session kept tapping his phone while he glanced out the front window impatiently. As we neared the appointed start time, Molly asked where his girlfriend was and he said they'd had a fight and wasn't sure she'd attend. When she offered to step in to be his painting partner for today's session, he took one look at her sexy body and nodded sheepishly.

At ten a.m., she looked outside the front door then latched it shut and slowly pulled the blackout blinds over the windows. I was glad she was being more careful than usual, because I knew if any passersby had any inkling as to what was going on inside, they'd be pressing their noses to the glass. When she was certain we had complete privacy, she went to the front of the room to address our group.

"As I mentioned at our last class, today we're going to change things up with a different type of paint. This time, we're going to use a special type of edible paint that will allow you to have a little more fun when I comes time to clean up. But I should warn you that this paint isn't quite as durable as the oil and latex paint we used previously, so it can get a bit messy and runny if you leave it on for too long.

"Also, in the interest of sharing the spoils with everybody, I encourage you to switch roles halfway through the session so that *both* partners will have a chance to be participate in the fun. As always, all your necessary materials are laid out for you at your respective painting stations, and you've got additional design ideas to browse through on your easels."

Molly looked over at the fireman stud and smiled.

"It looks like Brett will be on his own today, so I'll be pairing up with him for today's session. But if any of you need any help at any time, just give me a shout and I'll pull away for a few moments. Before we get started, do you have any questions?"

One of the young lesbian girls put up her hand.

"Yes, Lindsey?"

"What exactly is the edible paint made from? I mean, how safe is it to—*eat*?"

Molly nodded her head with the familiar question.

"You might be surprised to find that it's made from the same ingredients as store-bought Jello pudding. It's a blend of milk, sugar, cornstarch, butter, and vegetable-based food dyes, totally non-toxic and safe to eat. Although it might be a little cool to the touch at first, since it's been kept refrigerated to keep it from spoiling. But that just makes it all the more titillating to apply. Were there any other questions?"

The girl from the Batcouple pair raised her hand timidly.

"Yes, Kate?"

"Are we allowed to, you know, *sample* our creations from time to time as we work on them?"

Molly's lips curled into a sly smile.

"That's the whole point of using edible paint. Half the fun is in removing it once you've finished your design. We realize that some of you may find it difficult to contain your excitement as you're being painted. If you want to explore your creation more closely at any time, we've tried to provide a safe and open environment to do so."

Molly paused as she looked around the room.

"But if anybody is going to feel uncomfortable about seeing others touch their partner's body in this way, now is the time to say so. We don't want anyone feeling self-conscious about either watching or being watched as we explore this fun facet of the bodypainting experience. Of course, if you want some additional privacy, you're also welcome to use our private change rooms in the rear."

Molly paused to make eye contact with each workshop participant to be sure everyone was comfortable with the rules of engagement.

"Does anybody have any more questions before we get started?"

Everybody looked at their partners and nodded with crooked grins on their faces. Bree and I moved to the nearest painting station and flipped over a few design panels on the easel to generate ideas. The themes seemed to be divided between the main food groups. Most of the male models were painted in fruit or vegetable themes, with the strategic placement of various tubers and legumes used to disguise their hanging genitalia. Many of the female models were painted in dessert themes, with cherry-topped sundaes and other sundry pastries used to disguise their private parts. But we both paused when we saw a picture of the sexy Latin actress Carmen Miranda wearing a skimpy costume of grapes and berries with a fruit bowl perched atop her head.

"What do you think?" I said, looking at Bree. "Are you hungry for the main course, dessert, or a little appetizer?"

"As much as I like the idea of licking all those yummy-looking pastries off you, I think the vegetable and fruit themes might be a little easier to paint."

I glanced at the picture of Carmen Miranda and nodded.

"You might be right, but remember what Molly said. This session isn't so much about trying to create a perfect design as it is about having fun and enjoying the cleanup process. It's just going to get all smeared off soon enough, anyway."

"Mmm," Bree smiled, thinking back on how we rubbed our bodies together when she was at my place. "I like the idea of smearing it off each other. Who should go first?"

I turned to the front of the room and saw Brett beginning to strip in front of Molly.

"Why don't you go first so I can guide you along the way? I have a feeling Molly's going to have her hands full for most of this class. Besides, I've got a little surprise embellishment that I have planned for the end."

"Oh?" Bree said, widening her eyes in curiosity. "I thought you'd already showed me all your tricks when I was at your place."

I smiled at her with a raised eyebrow.

"A good lover likes to mix it up from time to time, remember? Plus, I like to save the best for last. Kind of like the cherry atop the ice cream sundae."

"So you were thinking of painting me in a dessert theme? I've been dying for you to lick my cherry again."

"You'll have to wait and see," I said. "Just try not to melt until I finish. This particular surprise will require a stiff upper lip, so to speak. Go get yourself ready while I strip."

"Yes, boss."

As Bree popped the lids off the glass jars of pudding paint, I glanced around the room to see how the other partners were progressing. The Batgirl at the next station over had chosen a meat theme to paint on her hunky boyfriend as she began to paint sinewy slabs of steak over his bulging pecs. The young lesbian couple was going with the pastry theme, as I watched one of the girls lean in closely to paint pretty pink cupcakes over her girlfriend's breasts.

The middle-aged couple had chosen a playful seafood-based theme, as the slender one began to paint an image of a school of fish swimming across her partner's undulating chest. Molly was painting another meat locker theme on Brett's gym-toned fireman's body. I glanced down at his thick Johnson swaying between his legs and noticed it twitching as she began moving her brush down his body.

"So, what'll it be?" Bree said, swinging around with her brush in her hand. "Citrus fruit up top and strawberries down below?"

"Sounds about right," I smiled. "Melons to cover my big parts and berries to cover the little ones."

"What do you think about grapefruits to cover your breasts? They're pink and sweet, and about the right size."

I paused, remembering some of the images I'd seen while surfing online to get ideas before the workshop.

"That could work," I said. "But did you know there's a special type of fruit grown in Southeast Asia that looks almost exactly like a woman's bare breasts? It's called milk melon, and it's incredibly erotic. Here, let me show you."

I reached into my purse on the floor and pulled out my phone, then tapped on my screen a few times.

"See?" I said, turning the screen around for Bree to view the images.

The picture showed a bamboo trellis with long flesh-colored bulbs hanging down from the vine. At the bottom of the spoon-shaped plants was a swelling with a darkened circle in the center that looked amazingly like a bare breast.

"It might be kind of fun to paint a bunch of these on my chest to make me look like I have multiple boobs. It would be hard to distinguish the real ones from the fake ones."

Bree took a look at the screen and jerked her head back in amazement.

"That's a *real* fruit?!" she asked. "They look exactly like a woman's breasts!"

"Yes, except for their elongated shape. But that just makes them look all the more erotic, like some kind of Salvador Dali painting."

"No kidding," Bree said. "Talk about a surreal image. I'm not sure if this is going to make you look more sexy or *creepy*!"

"It won't seem so creepy when you're sucking on those fake breasts once they're painted on my chest. Get to it girl. The clock is ticking."

"Okay," Bree said. "Just help me figure out how to blend the paint to create that unique color."

"Place equal parts of red, yellow, and blue on the mixing plate, then mix them together. You'll want to make it slightly darker than my skin tone so they stand out more clearly on my chest. If you need to lighten it, just add a bit of white to the mix."

Bree mixed the paint as I suggested, then dipped a medium-width brush in the blend and held it up to my chest.

"Here's goes nothing," she said. "Are you sure you're ready to have three breasts?"

"The more the merrier," I chuckled.

"All the more to suck on," Bree smiled.

She leaned in began slowly drawing the brush down from the base of my neck toward the center of my chest. When she reached the top of my cleavage, I could feel her moving the brush in circles as she stared intently at the design. Then she swiped the brush up and down the center of my chest a few times and stepped back and glanced at my phone to compare it to the photo.

"That was easier than I thought," she said. "It about the right color, and it stands out in nice contrast to the rest of your skin. Now I just need to add the fake nipple. Red and white makes pink, right?"

"You got it, girl."

Bree mixed the new shade, then used a finer-point brush to paint the darker nipple in the center of my new breast. She circled over it a few times to create the proper shading and shadow, then stepped back and nodded.

"Not bad, if I do say so myself," she said. "It almost looks like your real breasts."

"Just a lot more pendulous," I chuckled.

"Good point," Bree said. "We'll need to touch up your real ones a little bit to create the surreal effect from the image."

Bree leaned back over the mixing table and dabbled the brush in the flesh-colored paint, then turned around and began painting some lines above each of my breasts. Each time her brush reached the top of my tits, she paused and feathered the paint to blend in with the lighter shade reflecting from the lights overhead.

"I kind of wish we'd gone with the grapefruit theme," I frowned. "You're barely even touching my actual breasts this time."

"That's part of the *look*, remember? We're trying to mimic fake boobs alongside your real ones. They'll get plenty of attention later when I suck *all* of your breasts when we're done."

Bree proceeded to paint a few more faux breasts on the top and side of my chest, then she stepped back and compared her design with the photo one last time.

"I think I've got the gist of it," she nodded. "It looks pretty much just like the melons in the photo. Shall I paint the bamboo shoots behind them to simulate the look of a trellis?"

I looked up at the clock and noticed that forty-five minutes had already passed.

"I think you better move on to the lower part so we don't run out of time. I'm dying to feel your brush again on my clit. Besides, we still have to allow a bit of time at the end for the fun part."

"Oh yeah," she said. "For the *surprise*."

Bree glanced at the picture of Carmen Miranda on the easel, then began mixing a darker shade of pink to simulate the color of cherries. As she began painting the belt of hanging fruit around my waist, I glanced around the room again to see how the other teams were doing.

The Batcouple had almost finished painting the hunky guy in their deli-case theme, with mouth-watering cuts of ham, turkey, and beef covering his shredded abdomen. His girlfriend had cleverly angled a turkey roast over his crotch so that one drumstick extended down his thigh while the other one rested over his throbbing organ. I glanced over to the other side of the room, where the young lesbian girl sat on the edge of the mixing table with her legs spread apart as her partner kneeled in front of her painting a white cake with strawberries over her mound and pussy.

"Hurry up, Bree," I said. "I'm starting to get hungry. I can't wait to eat you all up."

Bree smiled at me as she dipped the fine-point brush in the pink paint mixture, then she sat down directly in front of me and began painting strawberries around my vulva. When her wet brush touched my clit and she began swirling it around in little circles to paint another berry, I sighed in pleasure.

"Keep doing that and you're going to make me come," I said.

"I better stop then," she said, smiling up at me. "I wouldn't want to ruin the buildup. I'm supposed to make you *beg* for it, aren't I?"

"I've taught you too well," I cursed.

Bree stood up and stepped back to appraise her creation, then she took a quick glance at the picture on the easel.

"Not quite as intricate as Carmen's dress, but I think it'll do in a pinch. You definitely look edible."

"Okay, *your* turn," I said, shifting her to the other side of the easel. "Now it's my chance to have a little fun with you."

"Were you thinking of painting me in a similar style?" Bree asked.

"With a slight variation," I said, winking at her. "I think I'll continue with the fruit theme, just with some different types of exotic fruit."

Bree looked at me curiously.

"Does this have something to do with the surprise you mentioned earlier?"

"Maybe," I smiled. "But just like with your Kiss painting, you're just going to have to wait until the end to see what it looks like."

"Damn, Jade, you're such a tease."

"Just like I taught you. Don't you find it makes for a more intense climax?"

"Yes, but maybe you can be a bit easier on me this time. It took three days for those abdominal cramps to go away after I last saw you."

"A lot of women would give their right arm to experience orgasms that powerful."

"I suppose you're right. I guess not *all* girl cramps are bad."

As I began painting my design on the front of Bree's body, she looked around the room, and I noticed a little stream of fluid running down the inside of her right thigh. She seemed particularly intent on watching the pretty lesbian couple in the far corner, and I wondered just how far along they'd gotten in appreciating their design. After another thirty minutes, I finished painting my composition and stepped back to admire the final product.

Molly had placed full-length mirrors on the opposite side of each workstation easel, and I motioned for Bree to step toward the back of the Batcouple's tripod to assess her completed design. When she looked in the mirror, she smiled at the level of detail I'd put into my concept. The horn of cornucopia tilted down the front of her chest, spilling it's bounty of fruit onto her bare mound and pussy.

"Mmm," she said. "I like how the bowl of fruit points to my kitty. But what's that purple-colored fruit right at the base of the bowl?"

"That's an eggplant."

"Isn't that a vegetable? It looks a bit like a—"

"Penis?" I chuckled, recognizing the familiar shape. "It's definitely a fruit. A very *tasty* fruit when cooked in the right way. But yes, it also makes a very sexy dildo when you're in a pinch."

I reached down into my purse and pulled out a real, eight-inch eggplant. Bree's mouth opened wide when she realized what I had in mind.

"You're kidding?" she said. "You put that thing *inside* you?"

"This one's big enough to fit inside *both* of us," I grinned.

Bree opened her eyes as big as saucers.

"You've been holding back on me," she smiled.

"Hey, a girl doesn't want to reveal *all* of her tricks on the first date."

Bree shook her head as she pinched her eyebrows at me.

"You weren't thinking—*right here*?" she said.

I looked around the room and saw that each of the other couples were locked in a passionate embrace as they kissed and licked each other's bodies. The lesbian couples were already grinding their hips together and we could hear the moaning of the Batcouple behind their easel. Even Molly and Brett were getting into it at the front of the room, as her head bobbed over his drumstick that was pointing straight up in the air.

"Looks like everybody's gotten a head start on us," I said, placing my hand on her chest. "Lie down on the table so I can properly fuck you."

Bree paused, as she pushed back against me gently.

"Don't you want to see your creation first? Take a look in the mirror at the design on painted on you."

I stepped in front of the glass and gasped when I saw Bree's work. The fake milk melons blended in perfectly with my own artificially elongated tits, giving the impression of multiple swelling breasts covering my chest. I glanced down and nodded at the way she'd woven the strings of cherries around my waist to look like a hanging skirt, then strategically placed strawberries around my thighs to disguise my pussy.

"Very impressive, young lady," I said. "I particularly like the little touch where you added a dab of chocolate-colored paint at the tip of the strawberry right over my clit. Very clever—and very sexy."

"Can I lick it off you before you do me?"

"By all means," I said. "I've been dreaming about you eating my pussy this whole week."

Bree stepped toward me and reached out to cup my breasts, then leaned down and took my left nipple into her mouth. I tilted my head down and looked at the bizarre sight of many fake tits on my chest and moaned.

"Yes, Bree," I painted. "Suck my tits. *All* of my tits."

She lifted her head and began licking the tips of my faux milk melons and purred.

"Mmm," she said, smacking her lips. "They taste wonderful. So sweet."

She licked each of my fake melons clean, then placed her head over my right breast and circled her tongue around my areolas as she rolled my erect nipple around in her mouth like a lollypop.

"You're such a good student," I sighed, recalling how I'd taught her to mix up her technique.

"I studied hard," she said, popping her mouth off my rigid nipple.

"I bet you did," I said, placing my hands around her hips and swinging her over to the edge of the painting table. "Now let me have a little fun with *your* sweet fruit."

I moved the paint materials to the side of the table, then lifted her up onto the edge and kneeled down in front of her. Spreading her legs wide, I drew my tongue up the side of her thighs then licked her dripping slit from the edge of her rosebud all the way up to her steaming clit.

"Fuck, Jade," Bree grunted. "That feels so good. I want to feel you inside me."

I looked up at her and smiled, then slipped two fingers inside her tunnel as I puckered my lips over her nub and sucked her into my mouth. As I began to thrust my fingers inside her, she grabbed the back of my head and began to rock her hips into my face. I could taste the sweet smell of sugar filling my mouth as the dark purple paint began to stream down my face.

"Yes, Jade," she said. "Fuck me with your fingers. I'm so close—"

I pulled my fingers out of Bree's cunny and glanced up at her with my stained face.

"Not yet, baby. I want to feel you pressing up against me when you come. Lean back a bit more."

Bree tilted her back down toward the table and rested her weight on her two elbows as she watched me position the big eggplant in front of her pussy. I slowly inserted the slender end in her opening, then I moved in closer to her and lifted my right leg onto the table beside her. I pressed the thick end of the tuber into my hole and pressed my hips forward as the fruit disappeared inside both of our holes. When our vulvas merged and we felt our clits touch, Bree threw her head back and squealed.

"Oh my God, Jade," she yelped. "That feels incredible. Fuck me with your big purple dildo."

I grunted in pleasure, as much from the incredible sensation of the squash sliding inside me as from Bree's dirty talk. I angled my hips up and began thrusting harder against her hips as we ground our clits against one another. Bree's eyes suddenly glazed over as I realized she was on the verge of coming from the tip of the eggplant rubbing against her G-spot.

"Fuck, Jade," she suddenly screamed. "I'm going to cum! Fuck me with your big cock. Oh God—I'm cummming!"

As I watched a deep flush roll over Bree's pale chest while she bucked wildly against my hips, I listened to the sound of moans and sighs filling the rest of the room. This was one workshop I'd never forget, I thought, as I pressed my mound against Bree's, squirting red and purple paint all over her belly.

R eady for more erotic chills and thrills? Enjoy the next volume in Jade's Erotic Adventures:

Some toys are a little more fun to play with than others...

Sneak peek:

Most of the women in our group were wearing jeans and were reluctant to drop their leggings as they pressed the vibe gently against the seam of their pants. But a few had come prepared with skirts and summer dresses, and I watched excitedly as they slipped the two-pronged device under their hems and began to moan in pleasure...

READ MORE..

VOLUME FIVE

THE MASSEUSE

1

———————

Ever since my playdate with Hannah at the rooftop spa in downtown Chicago, I felt a certain void in my love life. I'd enjoyed the various flings with my many lovers over the past few months, but there was always an expectation when the sex was over to move on to the next stage of intimacy. If either partner wasn't ready to invest further in the relationship, inevitably someone's feelings got hurt when one or the other walked away. Every now and then, it was nice to just have a simple, no-strings-attached, take-no-prisoners *hook-up*.

But it was more than that. I longed for the experience of being *feted*, of having my body worshipped by someone whose only focus was giving me the maximum amount of pleasure in the limited amount of time we were together. I wanted to return full-circle to my first experimental foray into the world of anonymous sex at the Fantasy Feast dinner party where I could lie back and let someone service my body. Even if I had to pay for it.

One lonely night when I needed to feel the touch of someone's else's hands on my body, I flipped open my laptop and typed in the search words *private masseuse*. I knew it had to be a female, not a man. Beyond my rapidly increasing proclivity toward having sex only with other women, the kind of massage I had in mind involved more than just the typical therapeutic rub-down. When things got hot and heavy, I needed my partner to keep his dick in his pants while focusing his attention only on pleasing me.

Which was something I'd found very few men capable of doing.

The first few results that came up on the screen provided a list of 'licensed massage therapists' who were available to make house calls in my area. But I knew this was code for the traditional, non-sexual type of massage. Besides, I wasn't sure I wanted my new paramour to know where I lived. Beyond the prying eyes of my nosy neighbors, I didn't want to experience another awkward moment when I had to kick another putative lover out of my house. I wanted to walk in, an *out*, freely on my own terms from this professional relationship.

I scrolled a little further down the page and hesitated when I saw a listing titled *White Orchid Massage–experience the pleasure of tantric massage.*

Okay, I thought. This sounds a little bit more like what I'm looking for. The word 'tantric' suggested a slightly *different* kind of massage treatment.

I clicked on the link and a description appeared beside a picture of a scantily clad masseuse massaging a woman's bare lower back:

Tantric massage is the art of caressing one's body where the boundaries disappear and the recipient learns to experience an elevated and prolonged form of pleasure and relaxation. Your energy flow is stimulated by our personal Goddesses while your senses are gradually awakened toward their maximum potential. Particular attention is focused on attending to the sensitive personal areas of a man's lingam or a woman's yoni. Book a session today to experience the ultimate expression of personal body worship.

Yes, I thought. *That's what I'm talking about: personal body worship. This is what I've been looking for. But who exactly are these goddesses, and what do they mean by a man's lingam and a woman's yoni?*

I clicked on the button below marked *Lingam Massage*, and some black and white illustrations of a woman's hands massaging a man's erect penis appeared with a text box to the side.

> *The Sanskrit word for the male sex organ is Lingam, which is loosely translated as the 'Wand of Light'. In tantra, the Lingam is honored as the vessel that channels a man's creative energy and pleasure. The goal of the one-hour lingam massage is to caress the entire sensitive area including the testicles, perineum, and the Sacred Spot (prostate), allowing the man to surrender to a new, enlightened form of pleasure. Orgasm is not necessarily the goal, but it can be a welcome and pleasant side effect.*

Orgasm isn't the goal? What the hell else do you expect the recipient to experience after one hour of massaging his dick, balls, and perineum?

But I liked the symbolism behind the words 'honoring' his sexual organ and enabling him to experience an 'enlightened form of pleasure'. Something told me that although orgasm wasn't the primary goal, most clients of this special form of massage therapy left with a very happy ending.

But it wasn't *male* pleasure and orgasm that I was interested in. I wanted these special massage goddesses to focus on administering a unique form of female-oriented pleasure. I clicked on the next button marked *Yoni Massage*, and some more erotic illustrations of a woman's hands massaging a woman's vulva appeared with another line of text below.

> *Yoni is the Sanskrit word for the vagina, which means the 'sacred temple' of a woman's body. During the yoni massage, the Goddess creates a unique space for the receiver to relax, from which she can enter a heightened state of arousal and ultimate pleasure. When orgasm does occur, it is often more expanded and more satisfying. While delivering a yoni massage, the giver should not expect anything in return, but simply allow the receiver to enjoy the experience and lose herself in the prolonged pleasure of being worshipped for the sexual person she is.*

Fuck yes, I panted out loud. That's exactly what I wanted.

Someone to focus her attention entirely on my pleasure, who'd tease and torment me until I experienced the ultimate form of satisfaction. But even though I knew it would be an entirely one-way form of erotic stimulation, I still needed to be able to connect in some way with my partner. What did these so-called Goddesses look like? I wouldn't be able to truly immerse myself in the experience if I didn't find her attractive.

My gaze shifted to the menu on the sidebar, where a map displayed red pins showing the location of White Orchid goddesses in major cities throughout the United States. I clicked on the pin centered over Chicago and a photo of a pretty African-American girl named Violet appeared with a link for more details. The page opened with a picture of a dark, slender woman about my age wearing a skimpy leotard that hugged every inch of her lithe figure. It showed her leaning over a massage table while caressing the upper thighs of another woman lying face down with a small towel barely covering her upturned ass.

But it was *Violet's* ass that drew my immediate attention. Slender and curvy with separate volleyball-sized globes, the downward seam of her tights divided them into perfectly shaped spheres that made it look like her butt had been carved out of marble. I felt my panties begin to dampen as I imagined watching her sylphlike figure flexing and bending while she laid her hands on my body. I read the brief bio beside her picture, then my attention was drawn to the top of the page where a drop-down menu outlined her list of services.

I clicked on the Yoni Massage button, where some erotic pictures of Georgia O'Keefe floral artwork framed the detailed description of her ninety-minute intimate massage sessions. Although the verbiage referred to cryptic terms such as 'somatic pelvic floor exercises' and 'sexual energy cultivation techniques', I had little doubt, just as with the thinly-veiled symbolism of the Georgia O'Keefe paintings, where exactly she intended to focus her attention.

The massage sessions were provided at her personal studio and offered in blocks of four, each lasting roughly ninety minutes, with home assignments and email check-ins between sessions. There was no appointment form or payment link–only an email address where I was encouraged to leave a detailed message with my personal details and booking requests. I immediately clicked on the link and began composing a carefully worded message:

Violet,

I'm interested in booking a session for your one-on-one personal yoni massage. I work from home, so I'm available pretty much any time to meet at your studio, but weekends are my preferred time to concentrate on personal enrichment.

Please let me know the next available slot you have to fit me in. I look forward to learning more about your tantric exercises and experiencing your enlightened form of body worship.

Sincerely,

Jade

After I clicked send, I immediately winced at my not-so-subtle choice of words asking for a 'slot' to fit me in. But as I continued scanning her website page further describing the yoni massage procedure accompanied with more illustrations of the masseuse probing her client's orifices in various sexy positions, I pulled down my panties and thrust my fingers inside my hole, mimicking the Goddess's techniques.

You can press your fingers into my slot any way you like, I panted, running my eyes over her tight figure while I hunched over my keyboard feeling my pleasure beginning to rise...

2

———————

By the time I finished coming down from my self-induced orgasm, I already had a new message notification in my in-box. I opened my mail and excitedly clicked on the message from GoddessViolet.

Jade,

Thank you for your inquiry regarding my services. I have an opening for yoni massage this Sunday at 2 p.m. if that works for you.

My fees are $600 for a four-massage package, with each massage offering a deeper and more intense stimulation of your sacred temple. I also offer a separate introductory massage for $200.

Please click on the PayPal link below to select and make advance payment for your preferred option. Once you complete the payment, I'll send another email with the address for my studio.

I look forward to our time together and feel blessed to share these transformative practices with you.

Love and blessings,

Violet

After reading her message, I sat back in my chair, contemplating my options. Six hundred bucks was a considerable sum, and although everything looked above-board on her website, I still couldn't be sure this wasn't some kind of scam. I clicked on the payment link and chose the two hundred dollar introductory option, then waited patiently for a reply with the additional details. It took a painfully long time for her to reply, but after she confirmed receipt of my payment and provided me with the location of her private studio, I breathed a sigh of relief.

For the next three days, I grew increasingly excited about my upcoming encounter, shaving my legs and armpits twice to make sure there'd be no unnecessary friction between any part of my skin and Violet's soft hands. Fortunately, my earlier laser hair treatment had already removed the last traces of any hairs from my mound and vulva. I must have come at least ten more times lying in front of my dressing room mirror imagining the sexy masseuse exploring every inch of my body.

By the time Sunday came around, my skin already felt like pins and needles in anticipation of Violet's tantric caresses. There was something about the idea of lying down and letting somebody bring me to the height of pleasure while she watched me writhe and moan in front of her that drove me crazy with desire. I'd always enjoyed having someone manually manipulate me to orgasm as much as oral or full-contact sex, knowing they could just sit back and savor my sexual response while concentrating all their energies on pleasing me.

When I drove to the address provided by Violet in her email, I was relieved to see it wasn't a cheap strip mall typical of those quick rub-and-tug operations. On the contrary, it was a beautiful luxury highrise with a commanding view of Lake Michigan only a few blocks away. If this was her primary source of income, I thought with a smile, she must run a pretty good book of business. I parked my car in the guest parking area then headed to the foyer where I buzzed the button for suite 2402.

"Hello?" a soft voice answered after a brief pause.

"It's Jade," I said. "I have a two p.m. appointment."

There was a loud buzz and I opened the unlocked entrance door then made my way to the elevator bank. I found it odd that she hadn't offered a more friendly greeting before buzzing me in, and during the long elevator ride to the twenty-fourth floor, I suddenly began to have second thoughts.

Just how safe is it to be walking into a stranger's highrise on the pretense of anonymous sex? I'd always wondered why most masseuses preferred to provide the service at their clients' homes rather than their own residence. Was this some kind of trap where someone just *pretending* to be Violet enticed me into his home only to hold me prisoner and have his way with me?

I was just about to tap out a warning message to my best friend Hannah on my phone when the elevator opened. The hallway was tastefully decorated with plush wool carpets, brightly illuminated wall sconces, and expensive brass door fixtures. I peered down the corridor in the direction of Violet's apartment near the end and put my phone back in my purse.

Fuck it, I said to myself, shaking the cobwebs out of my head. *If someone wanted to lure me into some kind of dangerous arrangement, they wouldn't do it in a place like this. Or give me their address, which I could easily share with my friends. She's probably doing this at her place as much to protect herself as me.*

When I reached her door, I paused to summon my courage, then tapped twice on the shiny lacquer surface.

Even the entrance to her 'studio' is upscale and enticing, I thought.

When the door swung open and I saw Violet peering out at me with a sweet smile, I breathed a sigh of relief. She was wearing a long silk kimono with a single white orchid nestled in the side of her upswept hair held back in a pretty bun. She was lighter-skinned than she appeared on the website, and with her smooth, caramel-colored complexion, large brown eyes and full sensuous lips, she reminded me of young Beyoncé.

"Good afternoon," she said standing to the side, motioning for me to enter her apartment.

When I walked through the door, she offered to take my coat then hung it in the adjacent closet. She led me to a large living room dominated by floor-to-ceiling windows displaying an unobstructed view of Lake Michigan, glistening like a sparkling jewel in the mid-afternoon sun. Her apartment was tastefully decorated in a minimal Japanese ethos, with a low-slung sectional sofa, large glass coffee table, and floral prints of George O'Keefe paintings on the wall. In the center of the room stood a long massage table covered in a white terrycloth towel.

My pussy fluttered at the sensual imagery of the setting and I peered at Violet with raised eyebrows.

"Wow," I said. "I've never had a massage in such a beautiful place. You have magnificent taste in your decor."

"Thank you," she said, motioning to a closed door a few feet behind her. "If you'd like to get changed, you can use my powder room. You'll find a cotton robe hanging on the back of the door."

"Thank you," I said, taking her cue to not waste any time and opening the door to the change room.

When I got inside, I closed it softly behind me, then leaned back against the partition while staring at myself in the oval mirror over the vanity.

Holy fuck! I mouthed the words silently, looking at myself in disbelief. Not only was Violet even more beautiful in person than she appeared on her website, her massage studio was something out of a fantasy dream. This wasn't some cheap massage parlor where you'd walk in for a quickie then hightail it out of there so as not to be seen. This was more like the luxury upscale spa Hannah and I'd gone to a few months earlier where we were feted and spoiled for much of the day. The difference was that in *this* place, I had both the masseuse *and* the exquisite surroundings all to myself for the next ninety minutes.

As I began disrobing and neatly folding my clothes on the tasteful sidestand to the left side of the sink, I began singing the melody to the Beyoncé song Irreplaceable.

To the left, to the left
To the left, to the left
Everything you own in the box to the left

In the closet that's my stuff, yes
If I bought it please don't touch...

I'd always thought the singer was one of the most beautiful women I'd ever seen. I must have watched the sexy video of that song a hundred times, fantasizing that it was me squatting over her sexy legs while she sat in front of her makeup mirror in a slinky negligee. And now I had the chance to relive my fantasy with a dead ringer who was about to touch me in the most intimate way.

After I removed all my clothes, I looked at myself in the mirror appraising my naked, freshly primped body. I still had a pretty sexy figure for a woman in her mid-thirties, with firm plump breasts sitting high on my chest, a narrow, toned waist, and long slender legs. I wondered how much attention the *front* of my body would get from Violet during this first encounter. I knew most masseuses only attended to the back of their clients' bodies while focusing on relaxing and removing the knots from their muscles, rather than stimulating the more erogenous areas of their figures.

No matter, I said to myself, slipping my arms through the sleeves of the waffle-patterned robe hanging on the back of the door and tying the belt loosely around my waist before swinging the door open.

Either way, I planned to give my sexy masseuse ample access to my 'sacred places', whether I was lying face down or face up.

3

When I emerged from the powder room, I was surprised to see that Violet had removed her robe and was preparing her tools on a side table next to the massage table. Instead of the long silk robe, she was now wearing a thin cotton tank top with matching white cotton tights. The tight fabric clung to every curvature of her body and when she swung around to greet me, I gasped audibly when I saw her full figure for the first time.

Her breasts were petite, but they had an exquisite elongated, scooped shape that made the front of her skimpy t-shirt tent and bulge with prominent sensuous darts poking out from her hardened nipples. Her thin cotton tights also left a minimal amount to the imagination, with the soft fabric flowing over her flat pelvis and sensuously curved hips to her shapely, well-toned legs. I could see the cleft from the slit of her pussy as the fabric clung to her like a second skin, daring me to soak up her body with my wide eyes. In a way, it was even *more* erotic to see her cloaked in the soft white covering barely concealing her dark areolas and sexy camel toe, beckoning for me to approach her closer.

"May I take your robe?" she said, holding out her Madonna-toned arms in front of her.

"Um–yes," I stammered, momentarily pulled out of my trance.

I turned around and she softly pulled the robe off my shoulders then placed it on a side table beside the sofa. I peered at the massage table inquisitively, then turned back around to face Violet.

"Do you want me to lie face up or down?" I said, unsure of the protocol with this new procedure.

"Let's go face down to start," she smiled, extending her arm toward the table.

I lifted my right knee and climbed onto the bench, extending my legs straight down behind me. There was no customary hole at the head of the table where I'd normally place my face to relax my neck muscles, so I turned my head to peer out over the wide expanse of sparkling blue water. As soon as I saw the soothing picture of the gently lapping waves and reflected sunshine, I immediately began to feel the sexual tension ebb away. Whether this was by design or incidental, I wasn't sure. But for a few brief moments, I forgot about the primary purpose for my visit and flitted my eyelids in sublime bliss. Even if I just had to lie here watching this spectacular scenery for an hour and a half, it would almost be worth the two hundred dollar price of admission.

But it didn't take long for my *other* senses to be awakened as Violet opened her scented bottles of massage oil and the smell of jasmine and chamomile filled my nostrils. I breathed the heavenly scent in as I expanded my lungs and my chest rose and fell gently on the padded table. I could hear the sound of oil dribbling into her hands as she turned one of the bottles upside-down, then rubbed them together slowly. My pussy quivered knowing that she would soon lay her moistened hands on my skin, and I extended my arms to my side, inviting her to begin touching me.

I was a little disappointed when she started at the foot of the table with my feet, but I smiled peering up at the large analog clock hanging on the near wall, knowing she had a full ninety minutes to explore the rest of my body. I relaxed the muscles tensing in my shoulders and buttocks, happy to bide my time while she worked her way up toward my waiting temple.

As she separated each of my toes between her slippery fingers and kneaded them softly and sensuously, I was tempted to talk to her to break the awkward silence. But I knew from previous massages that masseuses preferred to work in silence, encouraging their clients to relax and let all the external distractions melt away. The whole point of a massage was to concentrate on the soothing feeling of being caressed, and I had no intention of disrupting Violet's mojo at the outset of our erotic encounter.

But that didn't stop me from letting my mind wander to all manner of sexual imagery while she squeezed and kneaded my extremities. As she pulled her fingers slowly down each of my toes from the ball of my foot to the toenails, I imagined it was my *clit* she was pinching between her fingers while she stroked my hard shaft and teased the tip of my nub. Whenever she slipped her fingers between my toes, I channeled her inserting her slender digits between my dripping *labia*, feeling my wet tunnel gripping her tightly. And when she grabbed my feet and pressed her thumbs against my soles while she pulled my toes against her washboard-hard tummy, I imagined toe-fucking her pussy while she gripped me in the throes of passion.

By the time her fingers moved to my ankles and began working their way up the inside of my calves, I was already soaking wet while I unconsciously ground my mound into the moistening towel beneath me. I spread my legs apart, inviting Violet to move closer to my apex, but she seemed in no hurry to attend to my quivering pussy. Instead, she wrapped her fingers around the curvature of my calves, rubbing them softly and slowly with her warm, slippery hands. Unlike the firm and sometimes painful kneading of my muscles that most masseurs were accustomed to administering, her touch was always light and sensuous, focused instead on titillating and stimulating every square inch of my skin. Reflecting back on what I'd read on the White Orchid website, I knew that she had a plan for eventually reaching my 'sacred temple', with the goal of heightening my arousal to achieve the 'ultimate pleasure'.

I tried to relax my arms and the rest of my body while she worked her way further up the inside of my thighs, but I couldn't help curling my upturned fingers in a come-hither motion in the direction of my aching sex. But just as her thumbs began probing the edges of my tumescent lips, she suddenly shifted position and moved up to the *head* of the table, placing her moist hands on my shoulders and upper back. This time I could detect the scent of my own juices intermingled with the aromatic massage oil as her hands slid over my pliant skin, and I turned my head away from the direction of the lake to watch Violet more closely.

As she stood to the side of the long table to gain better access to my upper back, I stared at her crotch while she leaned and stroked my shoulders and neck softly. The fabric of the white cotton tights pulled and stretched as she swayed her body overtop of me, and I could feel my mouth beginning to water while I imagined sucking her sweet pussy into my mouth. She must have known what was on my mind while she did this, because she hesitated for the longest time pressing the bottom of her undergarments sensuously against the padded corner of the table while she moved her hands progressively further down my back.

I was disappointed when she shifted position once again, denying me ready viewing access to her lower body, but I smiled when I noticed a small wet spot forming in the seam of her pants below her vulva. This time, she moved her hips directly over the top of my head while she extended her arms further down the center of my back toward my flexing buttocks. She placed her thumbs together, sliding them sensuously down the valley in the center of my back, and I lifted my ass, trying to narrow the distance between her probing fingers and my puckering lips. Making my torment all the more intense, while she pressed her palms further down my back in a series of forward-and-back movements, she gently pushed her pubis against the back of my head.

Whether she was doing this for her own amusement or mine, I couldn't be sure. But it took every ounce of my willpower not to lift my head and clamp onto her pussy like a wild boar catching its prey after a long chase through the underbrush. By now I was panting

heavily, and she must have felt my breath on her upper thighs straddling either side of my head. As she neared the small of my back with
her probing thumbs, I tilted my hips as far as I could in her direction,
pointing the cleft of my ass directly up toward her face. The further
she probed down my body, the closer her torso leaned over the
surface of my back, until I could feel her pointy breasts and hard
nipples touching my skin.

I groaned quietly, begging her to press her fingers into my crack.
When she finally did, my cheeks quivered, anticipating her reaching
my aching sex. Instead, she wrapped her hands around the globes of
my ass and squeezed them firmly, tantalizing me with the tips of her
fingers as they touched the outside edges of my external labia. I
grunted more loudly and swiveled my butt in circles, signaling to her
that I was desperate for her to administer to my yoni as her website
had promised.

Recognizing my impatience, Violet released the pressure on my
buttocks and threaded her thumbs into my crevasse, rolling them
softly over my puckering rosebud. I groaned like a cat in heat when I
felt her touch my sensitive tissue, and I spread my legs further apart
to make it easier for her to slide her fingers over my crescent toward
my swollen lips and buzzing clit. As she leaned her torso more firmly
atop my back and pressed her mound harder against my moistening
head, she began angling her palms inward, caressing the outside of
my dripping labia with the tips of her fingers while she continued
stimulating my sphincter with her thumbs. The combined sensation
of her fingers probing my anus and the edges of my widening gash
simultaneously was driving me crazy with passion, but she still
hadn't touched me in the most sensitive area that would lead me
toward a much-needed orgasm.

When she finally began pressing her fingers further down my
crease toward my flaring slit and pinching my folds between her
index and middle finger, sliding them sensuously along the length of
my engorged labia, I hummed a sigh of pleasure knowing it wouldn't
be long before Violet finally brought me to sexual nirvana. But just as
she began pressing her digits into my pulsing hole, I heard a soft

chime and she withdrew her hands from my private areas as quickly as she had entered.

I twisted my head to peer up at her inquisitively, and she turned around to face the large clock on the wall while reaching over to the side table to dry off her dripping hands with a small towel. I looked up at the clock and was horrified to see the large hand pointing straight down, marking the completion of our session at three-thirty. Somehow, in all the heat of the slow buildup, I'd completely lost track of time.

"It appears that our time's up for today," Violet said nonchalantly. "I hope you enjoyed your introduction to tantric massage."

So that's her game, I thought, shaking my head in dismay. *She suckers me in with this so-called introductory session, driving me to the point of near-delirium then sends me packing just as I'm about to get off. Talk about a honey trap.*

I was pissed beyond belief, but the sight of Violet standing before me with the front of her cotton ensemble drenched in a combination of massage oil and my own sensual juices soon made me forget about her questionable business practice. The wetness had made her t-shirt nearly transparent, and I gawked like a newborn baby at her large brown medallions and pointed nipples pressing against the thin fabric. Even the front of her *tights* was soaking wet, pulled up between her flaring labia at the base of her mound. I wasn't sure if it was from her own juices released while she was grinding against my head or from the sweat pouring out of my hair as I got increasingly turned on, but it didn't matter. All I could think about was continuing her program of tantric massage and getting as close as I could to this beautiful goddess again as soon as possible. She had me hooked like a fish, and she knew it.

"How soon are you available for another session?" I asked meekly, sitting up on top of the giant wet spot I'd created in the middle of the massage table.

4

---

fter my equally titillating and frustrating initial massage session with Violet, I had to wait a whole week to see her again. In the intervening time, I vacillated between fuming over the disappointing ending she'd delivered and reliving her slow but intense buildup. Even though I didn't experience my usual climactic finish, I hadn't felt so turned on for so long in a very long time.

During my subsequent masturbation sessions, instead of rushing toward orgasm in the usual manner, I brought myself close to the edge repeatedly, resisting the temptation to fall over the precipice and quickly come down from my highs. There was something strangely liberating about being able to sustain such intense pleasure for as long as I wanted without always feeling the need for the final payoff. If this was what tantric sex was all about, I was rapidly becoming a passionate proponent of the mysterious practice.

By the time the following Sunday rolled around, my entire body was buzzing from my extended edging sessions, and I was eager to feel Violet's magic hands upon me once again. When I arrived at her studio and she opened the door, she was already wearing her sensuous white cotton undergarments, and we wasted no time getting started.

"Face up or face down?" I asked succinctly after shedding my street clothes in her powder room.

"Down," she said, equally matter-of-factly.

I climbed up on the padded massage table and extended my arms behind me, turning my head to peer out at the calming expanse of blue water extending out to the horizon. This time I was determined to relax and simply enjoy the voyage Violet took me on, realizing this process was far more about the journey than the destination.

She began once again at the foot of my body, but this time, instead of clasping both of my feet at the same time, she focused her attention only on my left foot, caressing the hard instep and my soft sole with gentle circular motions of her moistened hands. I could smell the gentle aroma of apple intermingled with the other scented oils, and my mouth began to water once again imagining myself lapping up her juices as she approached my erogenous zones. The combination of her firm kneading of my dorsal bone and the soft pressing of her digits into the pliant flesh of my sole reminded me of the sensation of a lover running her hands down over my pubis into the loose folds of my vulva. I purred like a kitten soaking up the exquisite slowness and eroticism of her touch.

As she shifted toward the top of my foot, instead of moving up the insides of my lower legs, this time she rolled her hands over the bump on the outside of my ankle like a pitcher softening up a base-ball before delivering it to the opposing batter. Except in this case, I was transfixed by her pre-delivery ritual, already losing focus on why I was hunched over the plate, watching her graceful movement in the reflection of the big picture window.

When she began running her hands up along the outside edge of my leg, I couldn't help flexing my calves and thighs in autonomic response to her sensuous touch. As she approached my downturned pelvis, she slipped her fingers under my hips, tracing the curved ridge along the top of my crest. Although her fingers never got closer than a few inches from my tingling mound and pussy, the feeling of her sliding her fingers over my hard bone was one of the most erotic sensations I'd ever experienced.

I tilted my body a few inches away from her to give her some more space, and she pushed me further onto my side, with the front of my body now facing her. I turned my face to peer in her direction and was happy to see her newly oil-stained bodysuit displaying her beautiful brown skin underneath.

As she began running her palms over the side indentation of my waist, I could feel the goose bumps on my skin beginning to rise while I watched her tits jiggling in her tight tank-top. Although the upper part of her ensemble wasn't as wet as the lower portion, I could see her large brown areolas and protruding peaks through the light-colored fabric, daring me not to ogle them like a star-struck fangirl.

When she placed her palms on my quivering tummy and began moving her hands toward my mashed-together breasts, my mouth opened unconsciously, desperately wanting to suck on her succulent teats. I could feel my own tips hardening the closer she got to my mounds, and when she encircled them with her palms, rolling the tips between her thumbs and forefingers, I gasped at how delicious it felt. I'd heard rumors how some women unconsciously reached orgasm from breast-feeding their babies, and now I understood how sensitive this part of the body could get when properly stimulated and caressed.

I groaned as Violet cupped my breasts, teasing me ever-so-gently with her warm, oily hands and soft fingertips. I probably could have come if she'd continued twisting and rolling my nubs for much longer, but just as before, she moved on just as I was nearing the turning point. I was sad to see her take her attention away from my engorged tits, but what she did next soon had me wishing she'd climb on top of me and have done with me.

Tilting my upper body further back, she pressed her palms firmly against my upper chest while she spread her fingers apart approaching my neck. As she encircled my narrow isthmus, I tilted my head up, and she squeezed my throat gently with the open palms of her hands. I'd never felt so vulnerable and sexually charged having someone else's hands on me, and I grunted like a wild animal lost in the clutches of a predator. While she was doing this, I could have sworn that her nipples pressed even further out against the flimsy fabric of her cotton t-shirt, and I detected a slight upward curl of her lips as she grasped me in the delicate embrace.

Was she getting just as turned on as I was from all this sexy imagery?

If so, I was more than happy for her to take whatever further advantage she desired of me, feeling my body's sexual energy rapidly rounding second base. But she obviously had no intention of suffocating me, and her hands continued their upward momentum as they rolled over my chin and jawline. When her apple-scented fingers moved next to my lips, I opened my mouth and she curled them into my cavity while I sucked on the tasty juices and kneaded her phalanges playfully with the tips of my teeth.

Two can play this game, I smiled, preventing her fingers from pulling out of me while I glared up at her with piercing eyes.

Instead of trying to remove her trapped fingers from my mouth, she curled her thumbs around the dripping edges of my lips, tracing a line around the raised edges, mimicking the caress of my outer labia. When I unconsciously groaned from the symbolism of her erotic touch, she pulled her fingers out from my loosened grip, then glided them up the side of my cheeks toward the bottom of my ears, curling them around their perimeter and pinching her fingers around the outside edges.

By now, I was moaning like a cat in heat and twisting my body in sexual abandon, eager for her to take me anyway she could. Her slow, teasing buildup was driving me crazy with desire, and I clasped the sides of her forearms, trying to pull her toward me. But she tensed the muscles in her strong arms as she resisted my attempt, running her oily fingers through my hair and over the back of my scalp. I didn't care for a millisecond that she was making a mess of my carefully coiffed hair while I looked up at her, begging her to fuck me.

Seeming to acknowledge my torment, she pulled her hands away from my face and moved them slowly across the side of my shoulder, tracing a line down the side of my arm with the lightest of touches, making my hairs stand up on end. When she reached my hand, she interlaced her fingers with mine, then lifted my arm, pressing it over my head. Then she clasped the underside of my upturned limb, threading her other hand with equal tenderness up the soft skin on the other side. When she reached my armpit, she paused for a moment, massaging the indented space firmly with her oily thumbs, now even further moistened from the saliva of my mouth.

"Oh God," I moaned, amazed at how her touching me in every place other than the most sensitive areas of my body could make me feel this electrified.

With my arm still held gently over the top of my head and lying pinned on my side, my breasts were pulled off-center and rolling atop one another, creating a new kind of sensation I hadn't felt before as my oiled flesh rubbed sensuously together. All the time I was moaning with every hair on my body standing on end, Violet watched me with her big doe eyes and glistening lips. I wanted desperately for her to lean over and suck my bullets into her mouth, bringing me to orgasm just like the breastfeeding mothers I'd heard about, but I knew that was too much to hope for at this still-early juncture.

She angled my arm gently back down onto my side, placing it softly on the table in front of me, then traced a line all the way down the hourglass-shaped side of my back, up and over the curvature of my ass and down the back of my upper thigh, pausing to caress the tender space behind the back of my knee. Then she pronated her hand and pulled my knee slowly up toward my hips, forcing my legs into a bent-knee scissor position.

I was now lying on my side on the massage table, drenched in massage oil, with my legs splayed into a side-split position, with the glistening gash of my billowy cunt freely displayed for her viewing pleasure. I could feel my juices pouring out of me while her gaze turned toward my slit, dripping over my engorged lips and down the front of my lower thigh. I felt incredibly sexy and exposed in this compromising position, and if she'd so much as *blown* anywhere in the direction of my flaring snatch, I'm sure I would have come in a nanosecond.

Realizing I was now about as aroused as I was ever going to be, Violet slowly rolled her palm over the arc of my upturned hip and turned her hand sideways, curving the side of it softly between the crack of my ass. The feeling of her oily hand slicing my cleft like a soft bread knife was another sensation I'd never felt before, and I tilted my pelvis toward her, desperately trying to bring her hand closer to my aching clit.

Clearly trying to extend my agony as long as possible, she waved the side of her hand gently up and down the length of my crease, stimulating my anus and the lower reaches of my opening with a slow, measured touch. Growing increasingly impatient, I glanced up at the wall and noticed that it was three-fifteen. There was only fifteen minutes left for Violet to bring me to the peak of pleasure. I was all for the idea of extending this intense feeling as long as possible, but sometimes a girl just needed to get off.

Noticing me peering up at the clock, Violet opened her hand and pressed her fingers further down toward my slit. When she reached my opening, I was elated when she curled them inside me, pressing her three middle fingers deep inside my tunnel. I groaned in excitement, angling my hips to extend them as far inside me as possible. For a few brief moments, I was content to simply hump her fingers embedded inside me, but the angle of her hand reaching over from the side made it difficult for her to stimulate my G-spot in the usual manner.

I twisted my hips in a circular motion trying to angle her hand in the direction of my most sensitive part and we she realized what I was attempting to do, she began flexing her index finger forward and back, finally caressing the magic spot on the inside of my pussy. I groaned in delight at the pleasant sensation, but something was still missing. As much as I was enjoying the feeling of her fingering my hole and teasing my G-spot, I still needed some direct contact with my clit.

I tilted my hips further upward, sliding her pinky up the outside edge of my labia and when I felt it make contact with my tingling gland, I groaned deeply, finally beginning to feel the familiar pangs of my orgasm approaching. Seeking to add more pleasure to my rapidly building excitement, Violet simultaneously extended her thumb toward my tight pucker as she circled her pinky over my swollen bulb.

Fuck yes, I thought, growling like a wildcat. Finally, she's hitting all the right buttons. I could feel my orgasm rapidly approaching, and I gripped the sides of the massage table while I stared at Violet's sexy tits pressing against the soft fabric of her t-shirt, preparing for the inevitable release. But just before I passed the moment of no return, the dreaded chime sounded again, and Violet paused with her hand deeply embedded in my tunnel. For a brief moment, I thought she was going to continue to finish me off, and I groaned when she began to pull her hand out of me.

What the fuck? I thought, panting wildly. *This isn't tantric massage— it's tantric torture! How can she do this to me, knowing how much I needed the ultimate release her website had clearly alluded to?* As she slowly began to clean up, I couldn't help asking the obvious question.

"That was wonderful," I said, sitting up reluctantly. "But when are you going to take me to that magical place of enlightenment your website promised?"

"Remember, the purpose of tantric massage isn't just about reaching sexual climax," she said, wiping the oil nonchalantly from her hands. "It's an opportunity for you to connect with your inner feelings and extend the pleasurable sensations to their maximum degree."

"But your website suggested that when orgasm is achieved this way, it is often more expanded and intense than usual. Isn't that one of the sensations you help your clients achieve at some point in this process?"

"Yes," she said. "But remember, you still have two more sessions in your scheduled package. Most of the pleasure is experienced during the slow and extended build-up."

"Okay," I said. "But I don't know if I'm going to be able to hold out much longer. What can I look forward to during my next session?"

"At stage three, the process will become more interactive, with closer contact between the two of us, adding an extra level of stimulation and excitement. I think you'll find the next stage in your journey takes you to an entirely new level of fulfilment."

I wasn't entirely sure what she meant by more *interactive*, but if it involved more body contact with her magnificent figure, I knew that would be more than enough to allow me to achieve my ultimate goal.

"You're a very demanding coach," I smiled. "I'm looking forward to improving my batting average the next time around."

"Next time we'll see if we can deliver some *home runs*," she nodded, adding to my athletic analogy.

Ready for more erotic chills and thrills? Download the exciting first story in Victoria Rush's new erotic fantasy series, *The Enchanted Forest*:

Sometimes it's not just the grass that's greener on the other side...

Sneak peek:

As she began to bob her head up and down on the erotic fungus, imagining what it would feel like to suck a real man's cock, she felt her pussy throbbing once again. Unable to resist the growing temptation, she turned around and positioned her dripping slit over the tip of one of the toadstools and slowly lowered herself over it until it filled her cavity. Unlike the erotic flowers, which felt more like a woman's face against her cunny, this exotic plant left little doubt about its intentions. Warm, firm, and spongy, she sighed as she rocked up and down on the turgid toadstool, feeling it probing her deepest depths...

READ MORE

MORE FROM VICTORIA RUSH:

Choose your next toe-curling fantasy from over thirty-five spicy stories in Jade's Erotic Adventures. Browse the full collection here:

Click to scan your favorites...

FOLLOW VICTORIA RUSH:

Want to keep informed of my latest erotic book releases? Sign up for my newsletter and receive a FREE bonus book:

Spying on the neighbors just got a lot more interesting...

9 781990 118807